Absolutely Riveting

PRAISE FOR WILLIAM BERNHARDT

"*Exposed* has everything I love in a thriller: intricate plot twists, an ensemble of brilliant heroines, and jaw-dropping drama both in and out of the courtroom. William Bernhardt knows how to make the law come alive."

— TESS GERRITSEN, NYT-BESTSELLING
AUTHOR OF THE RIZZOLI & ISLES THRILLERS

"*Splitsville* is a winner—well-written, with fully developed characters and a narrative thrust that keeps you turning the pages."

— GARY BRAVER, BESTSELLING AUTHOR OF
TUNNEL VISION

"Bernhardt is the undisputed master of the courtroom thriller."

— *LIBRARY JOURNAL*

"William Bernhardt is a born stylist, and his writing through the years has aged like a fine wine...."

— STEVE BERRY, BESTSELLING AUTHOR OF *THE
KAISER'S WEB*

"Once started, it is hard to let [*The Last Chance Lawyer*] go, since the characters are inviting, engaging, and complicated....You will enjoy it."

— *CHICAGO DAILY LAW BULLETIN*

"[*Court of Killers*] is a wonderful second book in the Daniel Pike series...[A] top-notch, suspenseful crime thriller with excellent character development..."

"I could not put *Trial by Blood* down. The plot is riveting—with a surprise after the ending, when I thought it was all over....This book is special."

"*Judge and Jury is* a fast-paced, well-crafted story that challenges each major character to adapt to escalating attacks that threaten the very existence of their unique law firm."

"*Final Verdict* is a must read with a brilliant main character and surprises and twists that keep you turning pages. One of the best novels I've read in a while."

SHAMELESS

SHAMELESS

WILLIAM BERNHARDT

BABYLON BOOKS

For my WriterCon family
"A good writer possesses not only his own spirit but also the spirit of his friends."

"There is a virtue in shamelessness."

— DAVID BROOKS

PART I

THE MIRROR CRACK'D FROM SIDE TO SIDE

1

Sandy gazed into the mirror on the wall. His image stared back at him, accusing, glaring, challenging him to explain how he'd made such a mess of his life. Was that him or his evil twin, a doppelganger he could no longer control? His life seemed defined by doubles—double life, double-crosses. But, he tried to convince himself, if he just doubled down on this operation—double time—he might survive. One more day.

Maybe he should change his name to Gemini. Given his current situation—double trouble? double jeopardy?—he should change his name to Tantalus. No torture could exceed the pain he experienced now. Except perhaps what lay ahead if this sting failed to deliver its venom.

His heart hammered as if he were dangling off the edge of a cliff. Prometheus, then? Sisyphus? He was hanging by a single finger and if he screwed this up, he could face his final plummet. He had to get the job done and he needed her help to do it. But she was not cooperating. If he couldn't get her in that chair, he would have to resort to...whatever was necessary. Otherwise, he was dead. Charon. Hades. Or worse than dead. Given who he had breathing down his neck, worse than dead was an all-too-real possibility. He'd studied mythology extensively during his school days because he loved it—not because he expected his life to become a reflection of it. Another hero missing his highest and best potential, felled by hubris.

He took a deep breath and wrapped his arms around her, hoping she wouldn't notice that his hands were trembling. "You really turn me on, baby." He nibbled her neck.

She hovered over the stove. "I'm busy."

"C'mon. You know you want to."

She reacted with a simultaneous eye roll and pursed lip. "I don't know that at all." She had two pots on the stovetop, one cooking the spaghetti, the other warming the marinara. "I told you, I'm busy."

"Dinner can wait."

"It really can't. The sauce will burn."

"Turn off the heat."

She slapped her hands down on the kitchen counter. "Cool your jets, okay? I'm in the middle of something."

"It can wait." He pulled her tight against him. His hands started roaming.

She blew dark hair out of her eyes. She still held a wooden spatula, which made it hard to deflect his advances. "Have you not heard a word I've said?"

"My brain isn't working, honey. Another part has taken control."

"You need to improve your listening skills."

"Your body is talking. And I hear it loud and clear."

"Are you for real? Do you hear words of consent? Because there haven't been any." She whirled around and shoved him back. "What is it with you lately, anyway? You never get enough."

He grinned. "That's 'cause my sweet-assed babe is such a hottie."

"Is that supposed to flatter me? Because it doesn't."

This was not going the way he wanted. The way he needed. He didn't have the option of playing the sensitive male who put her desires first. And he didn't have the option of waiting. She might get tired. She might go out on a job. She might decide she needed to conserve her energy. "Seems like you don't mind it too much once we get started."

She shook her head, eyes closed. "What women do to stroke male egos." She waved the spatula at him. "Just let me finish dinner. Then…maybe."

He grabbed her hand. "I need it now, baby. I can't hang around here forever."

"I get it. Wham, bam, thank you, ma'am, and you're out on the street. Maybe visiting the next woman on your list."

"It isn't like that. I want you."

She turned back to the stove. "Fine. Have at it. You can thrust while I cook."

"It's gotta be over there. In the chair."

"Why? I can multitask."

"It's best in the chair. You sitting in my lap, totally in control. Hot as hell."

"I'm plenty hot cooking, too," she said, slicing the mushrooms.

"I do love watching that perfect butt of yours wiggle." He placed his hands on her hips. "You have the tiniest waist. Compact little body. Not an ounce of fat on you. Fantastic package. Especially from behind."

"Especially from behind? Like, you prefer it when you can't see my face?"

Why was this going so wrong? He was saying and doing everything that had worked in the past. But when he really needed it, nothing seemed to please this cut-rate Helen of Troy.

He caught another glance of himself in the mirror. Five foot ten, bearded, barely a wrinkle. Still young. He should be building, not crumbling. He should have a stable life with a home and a business with actual clients. He was well past thirty and what did he have to show for it? No fortune, no friends, just a random assortment of losers sporting the mythological nicknames he gave them. And all his sins closing in on him.

How did this happen? How did everything go so wrong?

And what would be the inevitable climax? Would there be a *deus ex machina*? Or a final fall from grace?

"You're not listening to me," she said, her shrill voice recalling him from his reverie. "You're using me."

"Doesn't everyone?"

"I'm sick of it. Totally, completely sick of it."

He stepped forward, pinning her against the stove. "Stop resisting."

"No, for once, you listen to me. You—"

He clapped his hands over his ears. "I don't have the time or inclination."

She stepped around him, freeing herself. "Stop shutting me out. You need to treat me like a human being, not your personal puppet."

"I don't want to hear this!"

"You're gonna hear it, like it or not. You—"

"Shut up! Shut. *Up!*" Without even thinking about it, he thrust his elbows back—and hit something solid. Followed by a sickening crunching sound.

He spun around. She clutched her nose with both hands. Blood streamed from her nostrils, trickling through her fingers.

She stared at him, unblinking. Stunned.

"Oh my God. Oh my God." He reached out, horrified. "Honey, I didn't mean—I—I—"

She pushed her hands between them, backing away. Her nose, still bleeding, looked as if it had been flattened.

"Baby, I'm so sorry. I didn't mean to hurt you. Let me help."

She tried to speak, blood slicking her mouth and chin. "Stay...away from me." She reached for the phone in her pocket. "I'm calling the police."

"Don't do that." He took a tentative step forward. "You can't do that."

"Watch me." Her eyes seemed to have trouble focusing. She fumbled with her phone, unable to unlock the screen.

"Honey? Are you okay?"

Her knees buckled. She reached toward the nearest wall for support, but instead hit a shelf loaded with his souvenir beer cans. All at once, the cans came crashing down. She frantically flailed, trying unsuccessfully to grab something for support. She lost her balance and tumbled backward. The back of her head hit the wall.

She cried out in pain. Her eyelids fluttered.

Did she have a concussion? He wasn't sure. He didn't think he'd hit her that hard, but she seemed barely conscious. "Sweetie?" Damn, damn, damn. He didn't need this. And he definitely could not afford to be hauled off by the police.

She recovered, at least a little. She brought her phone back to eye level. "Be...quiet." She punched the screen and this time managed to get to the phone app.

He'd tried to be patient, but this was her fault. First she wouldn't cooperate. Then she wanted to turn an accident into a prison sentence. With his record, even a minor arrest could take him off the streets for the rest of his life.

"Look, just rest for a moment, okay? I'll get something to stop the bleeding. Sit in the recliner."

She managed to stumble to her feet but still wobbled, lurching with each step. She made it to the chair, but as soon as she was situated, dialed 911.

"What is the nature of your emergency?"

"*I told you not to do that!*" he bellowed. He jerked her up by her hair, ripping strands out by the roots. Once she was more or less upright, he punched her hard in the stomach. She buckled over like she'd been hit by a speeding car. The phone clattered to the floor. She raised her hands, trying to fend off the next blow.

"*Why wouldn't you listen to me?*"

His mind raced. What now? She'd become a liability. But if not her, who? It would take so long to set everything up again. And time was one thing he did not have much of...

To his surprise, she started limping toward the kitchen. He didn't know what to do, but he couldn't let her escape. He grabbed her again by the hair, yanking back hard. He swung her around and she slammed into the wall face first. Her nose bled even more. She staggered like a top at the end of its spin, wobbling out of control.

She'd been beaten before. He knew that. She could take a punch. But maybe not like this. He was bigger than her and much stronger. He could do anything he wanted.

He never wanted this! But he could feel his options draining away...

Double trouble. double jeopardy, double exposure.

Double whammy.

You can't leave it like this, he told himself. You have to finish the job.

She clutched her stomach. Had he broken her rib? She started crawling toward the door, so he kicked her. Hard. He felt the crunch. Something bad was happening in there...

He squatted down to her level. Her eyes seemed glazed as if she were barely there.

He gripped her tightly, one hand around her neck. She tried to squirm but didn't have the strength. He pinned her down on her back. He leaned in, putting his full weight on her throat, pinching off the airway. She raised her hands, trying to push him away. He ended that with another punch to the gut.

He closed his eyes and squeezed. In just a few moments, it would be over...

Or so he thought. He was completely unprepared when her fist hammered between the legs.

The blow electrified him. His eyes ballooned. His groin burned and sharp daggers of pain raced up and down his body.

Before he fully understood what had happened, she'd squirmed out of his grasp.

Had she been faking? Misleading him? Making him overconfident?

If she got outside, into the hallway, someone might hear.

He pushed to his feet just in time to feel her fingernails scrape his face.

He screamed. His hand went to his cheek. Blood bubbled to the surface. He wiped it away but still felt the stickiness between his fingers.

Damn. This girl could fight.

"Son of a bitch!" she gasped. "Did you think you were going to knock me out, then have your way with me? Then kill me? You've got another think coming."

She wasn't going for the door. She was going for the kitchen knives. The wood block beside the oven held five big ones. She grabbed the largest and pointed it at him.

Serrated blade. Slightly bent, but that wouldn't make it any less effective.

She crouched like a tiger, a fierce expression on her blood-streaked face. "You're not the first man to lay a hand on me." There was an unmistakable growl in her voice. "But you're gonna be the last."

2

K enzi peered at the man on the witness stand. She didn't delude herself into thinking her steely gaze would make him come clean...but then again, it never hurt to try.

Kenzi typically practiced in family court, where witnesses tended to be nervous and unaccustomed to being grilled by lawyers. But today she was in civil court representing the plaintiff in a suit alleging breach of contract, medical malpractice, and intentional infliction of emotional distress. The judge was hearing a pretrial discovery motion, and the man in the witness chair was Emil Anderson, CEO of the Washington State Center for Reproductive Wellbeing which, despite its altruistic name, was a large and prosperous for-profit health-care corporation.

"Do you know the plaintiff?" Kenzi asked.

Anderson sat up straight, a bit stiff. He kept blinking, as if something were in his eye, or a contact lens was about to slip. She knew from the company's annual report that he was over forty, but he looked at least a decade younger. "I do. Julia and her husband came to my office seeking help conceiving a child."

"Why did she come to you?"

"Their prior efforts had been unsuccessful. They wanted to try in-vitro fertilization."

"Could you please explain to the court what that is? Just in case there's some uncertainty about it."

Anderson pivoted around to face Judge Dugoni. The judge's facial expression suggested he already knew everything there was to know, but experience had taught Kenzi that it never hurt to make sure. Dugoni was a relatively new appointee and probably had been assigned a slew of unwanted administrative duties. Sometimes even the most experienced judges didn't have time to do as much prep as they would like.

"Of course," Anderson replied. "In-vitro fertilization is a complex, lengthy process in which an egg is extracted from a woman, fertilized in the clinic, then implanted in the woman's uterus."

"Does this always result in a pregnancy?"

"Not always. We have an eighty-percent success rate. Julia had to undergo extensive hormone treatments so she could produce multiple eggs."

"But she did get pregnant, right?" Julia Battersby was Kenzi's client, the fair-haired woman sitting at the plaintiff's table beside her husband with a pained expression on her face. Every time Kenzi looked at her, she wanted to cry. Pregnancy was supposed to be a blessed event. For Julia, it had been nothing but misery.

"She did. And she delivered a child. Just as she dreamed of doing."

"You're aware that there were...subsequent problems?"

"That's why we're here. But we very much dispute the plaintiff's claims." Anderson inhaled deeply, a signal that he was about to become expansive. "Pregnancy is a stressful time when many new hormones rage through a woman's body. Sometimes the woman's behavior is not entirely rational, whether you're talking about something as simple as late-night cravings or something more serious like postpartum depression. I believe Julia is experiencing what is called dissociation. A feeling that she lacks a connection to her newborn."

"You realize it's been over six months since the baby was born."

"I do. These conditions do not clear up overnight."

Or ever, in the present case. "We're here today because you've resisted our request for records pertaining to other embryos you implanted at or about the same time as my client's procedure. Why won't you produce the documents?"

"I can't." Anderson spread his hands wide. "We owe a duty of confidentiality to our clients. That's part of the written contract we sign. I have no problem producing documents pertaining to your client's case, but we absolutely cannot produce records relating to others. These are delicate, sensitive, private matters. Records are sealed and restricted for a good reason. No one wants strangers poking into their private matters. And we're bound by HIPPA regulations."

"Wouldn't you agree that my client has a good reason for asking?"

"I do not. I mean no disrespect...but Julia doesn't need our private records. She needs counseling. Therapy."

"Even though she believes the baby you gave her is not her own?"

"As I said before. Dissociation."

Kenzi frowned. She wasn't going to get anywhere with Mr. Spock. He resisted all attempts to inject human emotion into the matter. Better to put someone on the stand who would acknowledge that bringing babies into the world was an emotional experience, not a cold business transaction.

She tugged at the bottom of her Alexander McCourt gabardine double-breasted jacket. She'd accessorized with a rose-red scarf and matching hair pin to add a splash of color. She was barely five-feet-five and sometimes felt she had to be loud to be noticed.

Would Judge Dugoni see the case the way she did? She ran her hands through her side shave, flipping the top hair to the left. Probably best not to overthink this. She had a plan. Stick with it.

She sidled beside her client and whispered, "Ready to take the stand?"

Julia looked if she would prefer almost anything else in the world, but she nodded. She was in her early thirties, slender, obviously distraught. Her husband, Carl, had one arm around her. He was almost as fair-haired and fair-skinned as she was. They could easily have passed for a Nordic couple. "I'll do whatever it takes."

"Great." Kenzi ended her direct examination. No cross from the opposition. The judge directed her to call her next witness.

"Julia Battersby. I believe she will be our last witness."

Judge Dugoni nodded. He obviously approved of the suggestion that this hearing would be over soon.

Julia took the stand and Kenzi walked her through her story. At trial, she would go into this in far more detail. But for a discovery motion, an expedited treatment was sufficient. There was no jury to sway.

Although it never hurt to remind the judge that there were human beings trapped in this legal conundrum...

"About nine months after the implantation of the embryo, you gave birth, correct?"

"I did."

"Any complications?"

"Nothing significant. The baby was born naturally."

"Boy or girl?"

"Girl. We named her Ellie."

Kenzi took a step closer. "Why are we here? What was the problem?"

"The problem was..." Julia hesitated, licking her lips. "My husband and I were...shocked. I remember seeing him step away from the birthing table. I expected him to rush forward, anxious to hold his child in his arms. But that wasn't what happened."

"What did he see?"

"He saw the baby's jet-black hair, for starters. Far darker than his. Or mine. Or anyone in our family."

"But those things happen, right? DNA is complex and—"

"It was more than just hair color. Ellie's skin tone doesn't resemble ours. I remember hearing Carl gasp, 'She's Asian.' He doesn't have a bigoted bone in his body, but he wasn't expecting this. The baby looked nothing like either of us. Carl has a daughter by a previous marriage. And Ellie looked nothing like her."

"How did this make you feel?"

"Objection." Brent Ellery, opposing counsel, rose. He was a graying man in his mid-fifties who'd made a career of defending doctors and hospitals. "This is a factual inquiry. The plaintiff's emotions are not relevant."

Kenzi responded. "I totally disagree. It's not possible to talk about something as sensitive as children and childbirth without touching on emotions. We're not robots. And frankly, the defendant knows this. These fertility clinics would not be so profitable but for human emotions."

Judge Dugoni nodded. "I'm going to allow it."

Julia answered the question. "It made me feel terrible. Like somehow, even after all the extraordinary measures we took to become pregnant, I'd still wasn't a real mommy. We've raised Ellie and I love her—but I couldn't shake the feeling that something was wrong. And it was my fault."

"Did that worry you?"

"Of course it did. Carl was convinced the clinic made some kind of mistake. But if Ellie wasn't my child...whose child was she?" Julia's voice choked. "If I had someone else's child...who had mine?"

"What did you do?"

"At first, nothing. I didn't know what to do. There was no question of babies being switched in the nursery. I gave birth to her. I was fully awake and aware during the delivery. I contacted the clinic, but they insisted that no error had been made and babies don't always come out looking like clones of their parents. That's an exact quote. Clones. I asked for records pertaining to other births at the same time and they refused." She wiped her eyes. "This was supposed to be the happiest moment of my life. But it turned into an enduring misery."

"What did you do next?"

"Some time passed. I don't know what I was thinking. Maybe I hoped that if I just rode it out, things would change. But of course, that didn't happen. We couldn't afford a laboratory DNA analysis, so I bought one of those test kits you can get online."

"And?"

"The lab report was hard to follow. It said the results were 'strange.' But one thing was absolutely clear. Carl and I were not Ellie's biological parents."

"Your honor, I'd like to offer the DNA report as Exhibit Six." Kenzi distributed a document to the judge and opposing counsel. She returned her attention to Julia. "I'm sure the defendant will claim those online tests are not one hundred percent accurate."

"Maybe not. But to Carl and me, this was confirmation of what we already believed. This child was not ours. So I contacted a lawyer. You." She made a small smile. "I knew about you from your Twitter livestreams. I thought you'd be sympathetic to a woman in an impossible situation. And I was right."

"That's why we filed this action. And in the meantime?"

"We've been raising Ellie, trying to be the best parents we can possibly be. But I can't stop wondering where my child is. Carl and I are not rich. We spent almost everything we had to get this baby. We can't afford to do it again." She leaned forward, her eyes pleading. "I want to know what happened to my child!"

"Of course you do," Kenzi said quietly. "And you believe the fertility clinic has the answers?"

"They obviously switched up the embryos somewhere in the process. Small wonder they're stonewalling us. They don't want word of this titanic screw-up to get out. But I have the right to know what happened. Let us see the records. There can only have been a few babies born during the same period. DNA tests could easily determine which one belongs to Carl and me."

Kenzi turned to Judge Dugoni. "That's all we're asking, your honor. Please grant our discovery motion. Make this clinic produce the relevant records so we can learn the truth."

"To which we object," Ellery said, a weary tone to his voice. "We've submitted our brief. This is simple postpartum depression and dissociation. If every mother who doesn't feel a connection to her child has the right to invade the clinic's records, our promises of confidentiality are meaningless. Imagine if a mother came along and wanted to use this excuse to invade attorney-client privilege. I suspect the court would not be sympathetic."

Judge Dugoni stared into the distance, batting his lips with a finger. "You're probably right about that."

Kenzi jumped in. "But that's not what this motion is, your honor. This isn't even a case of doctor-patient privilege. This is a wealthy health-care corporation burying records that could shed light on a litany of civil offenses. While there might be some impact on other non-litigants, we can mitigate that by restricting the circulation of the documents. Holding hearings in chambers. Sealing transcripts."

The judge nodded. He pondered another moment, then spoke. "I have daughters myself. I was in the room when they were born. I can't even imagine what it would be like to have...to have an experience like this one. Sometimes I think these modern, new-fangled scientific approaches are not as helpful as they seem." He looked down and shuffled his papers. "That said, this hearing isn't a referendum on fertilization. It's about whether you have the right to inspect records relating to other parents employing the services of the fertility clinic. Parents who are not involved in this suit. Who don't want to be involved in this suit."

"Your honor, I'm not going to ask you to judge this case in advance of trial. I can't predict what the records will tell us. But I think you can see how much Julia and her husband have suffered. Please—give me the tools I need to get to the bottom of this situation. Allow us to learn the truth. That's all my client wants." She stepped toward the bench. "Children are the cornerstone of family. Let these people know who their children are."

3

Kenzi walked back to her office from the courthouse. She hadn't live-streamed yet today. She knew her many followers were keenly interested in this bizarre fertility clinic mix-up, which had been covered extensively by *The Seattle Times*.

She hadn't expected the judge to rule from the bench, but he appeared to have been moved by Julia's testimony and, she hoped, Kenzi's argument. The ruling was straight-forward. There would be no distribution of the requested documents beyond the parties and their counsel. No unnecessary photocopies. She would have to visit the defendant's office and mark the specific documents she wanted copied. But the documents would be produced, and that would be the first step toward getting what Julia wanted—the truth.

Chalk another one up for Team Kenzi. And since she got a positive result, she decided to reward herself with a stop at her favorite taqueria. But first, the livestream.

She explained the result. Then she delivered the sermon.

"Do you hear what I'm saying, ladies? It's only natural to want children. Even career girls like me know that children trump everything. Where would I be without my Hailee? I know I'm supposed to be her anchor, but the truth is—she's mine. If you're having problems conceiving, consider adoption. There are many wonderful kids out there who need a loving parent. But if you decide to pursue extraordinary measures to conceive a child who is biologically yours—don't go to the first clinic you find with a flashy webpage. Do your research. Some clinics have extensive protocols in place to prevent errors. And some do not. Consult your doctor or other experts in the field. Go to the library and do the research. It's worth the trouble. Trust me."

———

ZELDA PLACED the open end of the glass against the thin wall and pressed her left ear—the good one—against the other end.

She could hear the conversation in the apartment next door with a startling degree of clarity. She pulled her pink bathrobe around herself and brushed her beauty-shop hair from her face. Who needed fancy spy gear? Sometimes the simplest approaches were best.

"What's the problem, baby? You know you want it."

"I know you want it. I'd rather see what's on Netflix."

"C'mon, honey. A man's got needs."

"Is this because you love me, or because you're a sex addict?"

"It's all about you, baby. I love your luscious little butt. You're the only girl for me."

"I've heard that before," the woman said, but it must have worked, because a few seconds later, the dialogue was replaced by groaning and gasping. Zelda was sure she heard some zippers peeling.

"Ah! Ah! Ahhhh!'

"Yeah, baby? You like that?"

"*Don't touch me there!*"

The sudden screech took Zelda by surprise. She jerked away from the wall. The glass fell to the floor and shattered.

The noise on the other side of the wall subsided.

Well, hell. Here she was, enjoying the nice little soap opera next door and something had to go and spoil it. Zelda tiptoed to her storage closet for a broom and dustpan to clean up the mess.

That woman next door should know better. Zelda had caught a

glimpse of her in the hallway and she looked attractive, educated, well-dressed. Too smart to be running around with a loser like this, one who seemed to have a different woman in his apartment every other day. This man was not husband material. Although a woman could forgive a lot for a man who knew what he was doing when the lights were out.

She stood close to the wall, just beside the gold foliate mirror she'd found a few weeks before at a flea market. Even before her ear touched the glass, she could hear the moaning. They were back at it.

She hoped that woman next door was careful. That man was trouble with a capital T. And that woman might be trading an eight-second orgasm for a problem she'd bear the rest of her life. However long or short that might be.

———

KENZI NOTICED the workers were still laying carpet in the reception area of the law firm. Not that there was anything wrong with the old carpet. But even though her brother Gabriel was technically the managing partner, her father, Alejandro Rivera, still made all the major decisions. He wanted his firm—the largest and most successful Hispanic-controlled firm in Seattle—to look prosperous. So out with that crummy four-year-old carpet. In with the new Charney-blue velvet pile. Here in Splitsville, it was nothing but the best for the soles of your shoes.

The lawyers in town called Rivera & Perez "Splitsville" because it specialized in divorce, but more and more they seemed to be diversifying and Kenzi led the charge. She'd handled several criminal cases lately, including two murder trials, and now she was handling a highly publicized civil suit against a prosperous fertility clinic. She thought this was a positive development. She'd become less enchanted with the firm fanning the flames of unhappy marriages, augmenting the pain for billable hours. She always pushed for early settlement. But her father preferred that the firm be the leader in one specialty field—divorce—rather than a dabbler in many, and knew that short cases rarely led to large fees.

She approached the desk of Sharon, her assistant and research expert. Sharon was super-smart and one of the few people on Earth she totally trusted. Sharon was about Kenzi's age but had the curmudgeonly attitude you'd expect from someone twice as old. Kenzi didn't care. They'd formed a professional and personal bond that couldn't be replaced. "I assume you've heard the good news?"

Sharon looked up from her work. "I did listen to the KenziKlan stream, of course."

"You were messing around on the internet during work hours?"

"I consider that part of the job. Since, you know, my boss is the one streaming."

There was an edge to Sharon's voice and something going on behind her eyes. Kenzi wasn't sure what it was, but over the years, she'd become better than most at reading people. She'd worked as a counselor for several years before law school. She believed that gave her some insight into the way people thought. "Everything okay?"

"Why wouldn't it be?" Sharon replied, in a way that was completely unconvincing. "Everything okay with you?"

"So far."

"Julia must be ecstatic."

"More like guardedly optimistic. Now that the clinic has been ordered to produce documents, they will likely produce mounds of documents, hoping we won't find the smoking gun in the haystack."

"Mixed metaphor. But I get it. You're going to be in their conference room scrolling through dull documents for days. Those documents can be exported from the EMS easily enough. They're required to keep records in the export format mandated by HIPPA. But they'll make it hard for you to find what you want."

"Yeah. About that." Kenzi raised a finger. "I was thinking this sounds more like a job for my ace research partner."

Sharon looked horrified. "Kenzi. No."

"Research is your specialty."

"This isn't research. This is document production. The most boring job in the legal world. Don't do this to me."

"I'm afraid I might miss something. I've never been a big reader. All those hard long medical words. The job calls for someone more studious and intellectual."

"Kenzi..."

"And besides, I'm going to be busy with another case."

"Which one?"

"I don't know. But something will come up."

"Kenzi!"

She scurried away, only to run smack dab into her sister. "Emma! What brings you up from the basement?" Because she did not handle divorce work, Emma officed on the lowest floor the firm occupied. Kenzi thought it was an awful place, but Emma seemed to prefer it. Emma was challenged in the social-skills department and much more at home with books and computers than with people.

Emma was decked out in her usual black Goth look, highlighted by straight-cut bangs. "I came to see how you were holding up."

"Holding up? Is there some reason..." She glanced back at Sharon. This must relate to whatever Sharon was not telling her.

"You're my big sister. Aren't siblings supposed to...be concerned about one another?"

"That is in the sibling handbook, I think."

"I don't know how you pulled off that win in court today," Emma said, changing the subject. "I thought Dugoni would shut you down before you finished making the request."

"I appealed to the family man in him. But that doesn't—"

"And family is supposed to rally 'round one another in times of crisis, right?"

Okay, now she was seriously worried. "What's the crisis?"

Emma's brow creased. "I know family strife isn't your favorite thing."

"She did a wonderful job with my family last Christmas," Sharon said. "They're still talking about how wonderful you were, Kenzi."

"Yeah, yeah, yeah. Cut to the chase, you two."

Emma turned to Sharon, her eyebrows knitting together. "You didn't show her the paper?"

Sharon cleared her throat. "I was getting around to it."

"Paper? What's in the paper?"

"Of course, we've known for some time," Sharon said. "Since the hackers broke the list. But we kept it to ourselves."

"You kept secrets from me?"

"It wasn't a secret. You were too busy with the Moreno case to keep up with the news. And I didn't want to bother you when you were in the midst of something so much more important."

"What the hell is it you two goons aren't telling me? Something about me? You?"

Emma shook her head. "Father."

Kenzi pulled a face. "The distinguished Alejandro Rivera, Esquire, one of the leaders of the Seattle legal community? He's in trouble?"

"Like you wouldn't believe."

Sharon spread the paper out on her desk. Kenzi took one look at the headline—and gasped.

4

Kenzi stared down, her eyes transfixed. "*Papi*? Taylor Petrie?"

Emma avoided eye contact. "I saw his name on the first list that leaked. But you were busy and no one else seemed to notice, so I didn't say anything."

She looked at Sharon. "And you knew about this too?"

Sharon gazed skyward. "Maybe..."

"But—Taylor Petrie is that awful dating app people use when they're—they're—"

"Yeah." Emma shuffled her feet. "That."

Kenzi drew in breath as if to fortify herself. "When they want to cheat on their spouses. Have an affair."

"We really didn't need you to say it out loud."

"But—But—" Kenzi felt as if she were lost in a daze. "*Papi*? Our *Papi*?"

"So it would seem."

"He's only been married to Candice for—what?" Candice was the woman her father married after he divorced her mother. "A year or two?"

"It's been six, but who's counting?"

"As far as I could tell, they were getting along. Did you have a hint of any problems?"

Emma shrugged. "He wanted a much younger trophy wife. He got one. But they didn't seem like they had much in common. I never got the Romeo and Juliet vibe."

Sharon agreed. "More like Prince Charles and Diana. Candice hasn't been by the office to see him in years."

"Why would she? This is a law firm. It's boring."

"At first, she dropped in a couple of times a week to have lunch with him. But no longer."

"He's probably busy with..."

"Yeah. Exactly."

Kenzi threw back her shoulders. "I'm not going to sit around wondering. I'm going to get some answers. I'm marching into his office right now."

Emma grabbed her arm. "That might not be such a good idea."

"Actually, it is." Sharon pushed a pink message slip across her desk. "He asked for you."

———

HERA CHECKED her iPhone for the fifth time that day and probably the hundredth time this week. No text. Not even a voicemail message. Nothing.

Okay, now she was officially worried.

She couldn't kid herself. She'd been worried all along, since the first moment her precious Athena disappeared. Hera cared about all her girls, and she made a point of not playing favorites. But whether she let it show or not, deep down, she had favorites, like everyone else. And Athena was one of hers. Tiny little thing, but Hera loved every square inch of her.

She glanced at herself in the mirror by the front door. Was it just possible she'd been doing this too long? Wasn't giving her girls the guidance they needed? She felt like a mother to them, and a mother needed to occasionally tell her daughters when it was time to take a long look in the mirror...

What happened? And even more disturbing—was this her fault?

The bell above the front door chimed. Selene waltzed inside. She wore a short tight skirt, dark red blouse highlighted by black lace and fishnet hose. "All done."

Hera nodded. "Went well?"

"Like always. The boys love me."

"You have a pleasing personality."

"That's one way of putting it." Selene glanced at the phone in her hand. "No word from Athena?"

"Nothing at all."

"I'm sorry." Hera knew Selene was one of the smartest women who worked for her. If time came to retire, she'd imagined Selene might take over. Not that she would ever retire. But it was nice to think about. "I saw her going out with some guy. I wish I'd said something. Or done something."

"You had no way of knowing."

"Yeah. Except maybe I did."

"What do you mean?"

"I heard what they were saying. She said something about fixing dinner for him. And he got this repulsive leer on his face and said, 'The only thing I want to eat is not in your kitchen.'"

"Gross."

"I know. Gave me chills."

"Okay, he's a creep. Some of them are. Doesn't explain why she disappeared."

"No. But something else might."

"Like what?"

"While he was on his way out, his jacket flipped open a bit. And I couldn't help noticing."

"Yes?"

"He was packing a gun. Appendix holster. Ready whenever he wanted it."

———

KENZI ALMOST TIPTOED as she entered her father's plush corner office. If the rest of the firm décor would be described as expensive, his office would be described as palatial. The walls were mahogany, the area rugs were handsewn and custom-made. His small conference table held a rotating collection of sculptures by Hispanic artists, some of whom he actively patronized.

Alejandro Rivera sat behind his desk in an atypically relaxed pose, feet on the edge, head tilted back, eyes fixed on the ceiling.

Kenzi and Emma were almost seated before he seemed to notice them.

His head tilted slightly. "Both of you?"

Emma tended to not evince much emotion, but the worry line between her brows was plainly visible. "I can come back later, if—"

"No. Stay. Might as well get all the misery over at once." He sighed. "You can see why I wouldn't be anxious to have this conversation. Much less with my daughters."

Kenzi wasn't sure what tone to strike. Humor? Sympathy? Sadness? "Best to rip the Band-Aid off all at once, *Papi*."

"I suppose." He swung his feet—encased in black Italian crocodile-skin loafers—off the desk. "I suppose you've seen the *Legal Journal?*"

"We...have."

"I've always known I had enemies in the Bar. Hard to avoid that when you've been as successful as I have. Biggest divorce firm in the city. Only Hispanic State Bar President. A vacation home on Puget Sound."

Is that how he was viewing this? As retaliation?

"I suppose it was just a matter of time." He spoke as if delivering a monologue, never making eye contact with either daughter. "I saw my name on the list when hackers first busted the Taylor Petrie website. But there were thousands of names and I managed to escape notice. At first." He chuckled a little. "Guess I'm not as famous as I think I am, outside the legal community. Inside..." He waved a vague hand toward the newspaper spread open on his desk. "Inside the legal community, I'm more noteworthy. Shouldn't be surprised that they put me on the front page."

The only surprising thing, Kenzi thought, was that the legal community still had a publication printed on paper. She assumed the entire staff was over seventy.

She couldn't help but notice that, although he was griping about the press, he wasn't addressing the main issue. "*Papi*, you know better than I do what legal actions we can take if you're being wrongfully maligned."

He licked his lips. "We won't be doing that."

Which was his indirect way of addressing the elephant in the room. "Okay. Got it."

He spread his hands across the desk. "You're going to find out eventually, so let me just tell you. Yes, I had an account on Taylor Petrie. I did go out with two women I met there. One of them worked for an escort service. I met several more women through that outfit. Including one I saw several times. The one I ultimately ended up in an ongoing relationship with."

An escort service? This story got worse and worse with each chapter. "May I ask what this woman's name might be?"

She hadn't expected this question to be the source of embarrassment, but his face colored. "Venus."

Seriously? "Is that her real name?"

"I have no idea." He pressed his fingers against his forehead. "You can see the difficulty. Why publicity is so unwanted."

"You're the headline today, *Papi*. Tomorrow it will be someone else. This will pass."

"We'll see. This isn't just about Taylor Petrie. If they find out about Venus, it will get worse."

"I think the best thing you can do is lay low for a while. Don't make any statements or public appearances. Stay mum. If there's nothing new to feed the story, it will go away. A few months and it will be forgotten."

"I doubt that."

"I don't. You're too important to the Seattle legal world. You know every judge on the bench personally."

"They'll stop taking my calls."

"Half of them wouldn't be where they are today but for you. They won't forget that."

Emma jumped in. "Maybe this would be a good time for a vacation. Hole up in that place in Tuscany you love so much. I bet Candice would enjoy a change of scenery, too."

He sat up, his feet thudding heavily on the rug. "There's a problem with that."

"The resort's already booked?" Kenzi guessed.

"No. Candice has filed for divorce."

Oh. "That's how she feels today. But after a few days she'll remember how much she loves you and how much you've done for her."

"Doubt it. She's moved out."

Damn, damn, damn.

"She got wind of the story even before it hit the paper. Moved into an apartment some time ago."

Kenzi fell backward into her chair.

"She wants a ton of money. She's playing on all the bad publicity. Trying to turn it into a gravy train."

Truth to tell, Kenzi had never liked Candice, the trophy wife who was only a few years older than she was. "Have you talked to her? Maybe...explained things? Apologized even?"

"She's ghosting me. Doesn't reply to my texts or calls."

The woman was serious. "If there's anything we can do...you know you only have to ask."

"I need to assemble a legal team."

Kenzi and Emma looked at one another. "*Papi*...we can't be your lawyers. We're related to you. Closely."

"You think I don't know that? I've already contacted someone. No, I had something else in mind, Kenzi. I was hoping you could help me with...the management of the firm."

Sometimes, like now, Kenzi wished she had her sister's ability to remain stone-faced amidst startling developments. But she didn't. Her eyes widened and her lips parted. What did he mean? It seemed like only yesterday he passed the managing-partner reins to her younger brother Gabriel, possibly the least qualified person to hold that job in the entire firm. He'd explained that it would be a much-needed boost for Gabe, a confidence builder, and all but admitted that he chose

Gabe over her because he was male. Like they lived in feudal England or something. And now she was the one he turned to for help?

She didn't want to come off thirsty, but surely she couldn't be faulted for wanting to hear more. "And...you think I should be the one to do this?"

"There's no one I trust more than you. And your sister."

"I assume Gabriel will continue...doing what he does."

"Don't play passive-aggressive games. We both know how inept he is. I'd hoped that he'd rise to the challenge when I put him in charge. But so far, that hasn't happened. And if I'm going to be out of the picture for a while, I want someone tougher in charge."

"You can't demote Gabe. He'd be crushed."

"I don't care about titles. I just need someone to do the work."

She drew in her breath. "I won't replace Gabe. But I would be willing to...collaborate. If it's okay with him."

"It will be. Thank you. And now, if you don't mind—"

As far as she was concerned, this conversation was not over. "Who's going to be your divorce lawyer?"

"I would've thought that was obvious."

It wasn't. And when Kenzi heard the name, she got the biggest surprise she'd had yet.

5

"Crozier? Lou Crozier?" Kenzi wondered if her ears were working properly. "You must be kidding!"

"Why? He's one of the best lawyers in town. I'd be willing to say he's the best divorce lawyer in town who's not currently employed by my law firm."

"But he's like...your archnemesis."

"My competitor. Not my enemy. Candice is my enemy. And the enemy of my enemy is my friend."

"His firm is the only divorce shop in town that comes close to ours in terms of profits or prestige."

"Because he's good. I don't know why you're acting as if this is so astonishing. You've been on the other side of cases Lou's handled. You know how effective he is."

"But—but—" She turned to Emma but saw no help coming from that quarter. "He's a nutcase!"

"I assume this is a reference to his political beliefs."

"His crackpot ultra-right political beliefs."

"There is nothing wrong with being conservative. You should be more tolerant."

"He was at the Capitol building on January sixth. Cheering for the insurrectionists. He—"

Her father cut her off. "Kenzi, Lou can believe in the man in the moon for all I care. The only issue is whether he's a good lawyer. And he is. I need someone who will push hard for an early settlement."

"Which is exactly why Crozier's a poor choice. Never once have I been able to settle a case with him until he'd milked his client with motions and discovery. That is not what you need."

"Indeed it is not." He leaned forward and, for the first time since this conversation began, smiled. "And that is why, my darling daughter, I would like you to be at the settlement conference."

"Crozier will never go for that."

"In fact, it was his idea."

"But—you're my father. I can't—represent—"

"I don't want you there as my lawyer. Or Candice's. I want you to be the mediator."

———

ICARUS POUNDED on the door to the Rain City Escort Agency. No one answered. He pounded harder and eventually started shouting.

It made no difference. No one opened the door.

"Hera! Stop hiding. I know you're in there!"

He felt like an idiot, standing on the street screaming. He'd been up since midnight writing code, staring at a screen for so long it made his head hurt. He felt certain someone was on the premises, but they were pretending he didn't exist.

"Hera!" He pounded on the door so hard he thought it might crack. And just when he considered giving up, he heard footsteps inside.

He waited, poised and ready...

The door opened just a crack. A chain kept the door tethered. An Asian face appeared in the gap. "Go 'way."

It wasn't Hera. It was one of her girls. If he remembered correctly, she was called Selene. "Where's Hera?"

"Busy. Much too busy for the likes of you."

"She needs to make time."

"She has no time to make. Scram. You're trespassing."

"I'm not leaving until we talk. It's...about business."

Selene arched a painted eyebrow. "Which business?"

"Your business."

"Look, if you want to do some business with me, I got some time."

"I would never do that."

"No. You'd only pimp out your sister and steal the profits."

He rushed the door, which accomplished nothing. The chain held fast. "You don't know anything about it."

Selene wrapped her chemise around herself. "I think I do."

"I'm not leaving till I see Hera."

"Then I hope you brought your toothbrush."

She started to close the door, but he managed to wedge his foot into the opening.

"Icarus, don't make me call the police."

"You won't. You don't want them looking around. You—"

A new figure loomed in the opening. Hera appeared all at once, like a ninja. She was half-a-head taller than Selene and much wider. She filled the gap and then some. "Five seconds, Icarus. Then I'm setting your shoe on fire and closing the door."

"I want to know what happened."

"So do I."

"I have a right to know."

"So do I."

"She was my sister."

Hera hesitated, obviously perplexed. "I thought we were talking about Athena."

"I don't care about Athena. I care about my sister. Venus."

"I'm supposed to believe you care about her now? You need to take a long look in the mirror. You only come around when you want something."

"That's not true!"

"I take care of her. You take care of yourself." She kicked his foot out of the gap and slammed the door shut.

"I'm not leaving till we talk, Hera.

"Hope you brought an umbrella. It's gonna rain tonight. Downpour, they're saying."

"I don't care about—"

"We had another gang shooting last night. This is turning into a rough neighborhood."

"Wait a minute. Don't—"

"Disappear, Icarus. And never darken my doorstep again. If you know what's good for you."

———

Kenzi loved Sherman's Ferry. This upscale brewpub not far from her office was originally a private club, but over time, it was so embraced by local lawyers that they discontinued the dues and invited everyone inside. The Seattle legal community was large but lawyers tended to know one another, particularly those who shared the same specialty. Over the years, Kenzi had found Sherman's offered a better chance of meeting legal colleagues than the state bar convention.

Sharon came with her and brought her new paramour Kate Corrigan, a homicide detective. Kate was as white as Sharon was Black, plus tall, blonde, and tough in a physical way that sometimes scared Kenzi a bit. Presumably gave Sharon chills too, but in a different way. In all the years she'd known Sharon, she'd never seen her more taken with anyone she dated, male or female.

Of course, since Sharon brought a date, she was forced to wonder why she was sitting without one. When was the last time she'd been on a real date? Two years? Three? She couldn't blame the fact that she was raising a child anymore. Hailee constantly pushed her to get out. She couldn't blame her job. It did keep her busy, but she managed her own schedule. She could make time for what she deemed important.

Had she become so accustomed to being alone that she didn't feel the loneliness anymore? Was she afraid? Had she forgotten how to do it? She wasn't sure. But she couldn't help wondering if it was time to open the door that had been closed so long. There could be worse things than snuggling up to another warm body...

Like the two people at her table were currently snuggling up to each other.

"Still working that murder case?" Kenzi asked Kate. "The woman in the park? The kitchen knife?"

"Unfortunately, yes." She didn't need great powers of understanding to see that this troubled Kate. "Even after all these weeks, we don't have a clue what happened. We can't even identify the victim. All we can tell is that there was a major struggle. And she lost. If I don't get some answers soon, the chief is going to replace me."

Sharon laid a hand on her arm. "You need a new case. You've been on this one too long."

"I'll take a new case when I solve this one. In the meantime, I don't want distractions. Or the taint of failure."

"You drive yourself too hard. You need to relax more."

Kate arched an eyebrow. "Did you have something in particular in mind?"

Kenzi fanned herself. "Oh my. Am I imagining it, or is it getting hot in here?"

Sharon grinned. "Not as hot as it's gonna get tonight."

Kate tugged at her arm. "I think you're making your boss uncomfortable. Maybe we should change the subject." She turned to Kenzi. "Sharon tells me you're about to add 'mediator' to your resume."

"So it seems."

"How does that work? I mean, this is kinda strange even by your standards. You're not exactly a stranger to these litigants. Since you had Christmas dinner with both of them."

"It's what my father wants. And so far, Candice is ok with it too. I do have a rep for promoting speedy and equitable settlements. Divorce is hard enough on everyone involved. There's no reason to drag it out." She signaled the waiter for another vodka martini. "I'm just relieved my father didn't ask me to represent him. Even if the court permitted it, that would've been unbearable."

Sharon agreed. "Bullet dodged."

"Talk about awkward. 'So, Daddy, did you and Candice have a healthy sex life?' Ugh. No way."

"The settlement conference could get uncomfortable."

"Bickering I can handle. Talking about Daddy's sex life—ick."

"Speaking of ick." Sharon pointed. "Crozier Alert."

Kenzi twisted around. There he was, her least favorite lawyer. And now, her daddy's divorce lawyer. "Does he live here? Seems like we see him every time we come."

"I thought one of the reasons you liked Sherman's was the great networking."

"I draw the line at Crozier." Unfortunately, he spotted her before she could turn back around, and like every unwanted guest since the dawn of time, he made a beeline directly for her.

"Kenzi!" He approached with both arms outstretched. His bass voice boomed above the din of the bar. He had a salt-and-pepper combover that looked as if it had been glued into place. "How nice. I don't think I've seen you since we wrapped up the Moreno case."

Kenzi steeled herself. "Apparently we're about to work on another case together."

"I know." He pressed his hands together, as if in prayer. "And let me say how sorry I am about this divorce. Your father and Candice seemed so happy. Terrible that it has to end like this."

Did her father and Candice ever seem happy? Kenzi wasn't sure. But her perspective may have been skewed by the fact that she didn't like the woman. And on some days, she wasn't totally crazy about her father. "It's the way of the world."

"So true. Sad but true. I have nothing but the highest respect for your father. He's a great man. A titan."

Really? On more than one occasion, Crozier had tried to hire her away from the family firm. This sounded more like a eulogy than a compliment. "Thank you for saying so."

"I know your father and I have been competitors in the past, but that's only increased my respect. I know how hard it is to build a firm the way he's done. And although this divorce is a tragedy, I'm honored that he chose me to be his representative."

Chose you to be his pit bull. "I'm hoping we can wrap this up as quickly as possible."

"I think that's what everyone wants. Which is why I'm so glad you've agreed to mediate. You may be the one person who can get this job done. Contrary to what others may think, I believe your connection to both parties may help."

"I hope you're right."

"Your father has suffered enough with this...public shaming. He doesn't need any more problems."

Kenzi nodded politely. "The adversarial system can be—"

"I mean, look what they did to Kyle Rittenhouse."

"Now...what?"

"The media trashed him for a year. Then they locked him up, destroyed his life. And how did it end? Complete exoneration. He's an American hero. A martyr."

Kenzi bit her lip. Don't engage, she told herself.

"Now they're going after everyone who dissented on January sixth, everyone who challenged an obviously fixed election with legitimate political discourse. It's like we've forgotten what the courts were designed to do—provide a civil, peaceful way to resolve disputes and hold people accountable for their actions."

She eye-checked Sharon, who was fuming. Time to change the subject. "Have you heard who's representing Candice?"

"No. I don't really care, as long as it isn't Wreck-It-Rhonda. Can't tolerate that woman."

Not surprising. Rhonda Stanley constantly outflanked him.

"You know," Crozier said, "my offer still stands."

"Your...offer?"

"Come work for me. As soon as this divorce is over. I'm glad to see your father is finally acknowledging that you exist, but he doesn't appreciate you. Not the way he should. He manipulates you. Uses you when he needs you, then forgets about you."

"Actually..." She glanced at Sharon, but she was kissing Kate. Probably something Kate initiated to keep Sharon from erupting. "...that may be about to change."

"Is he going to dump Gabriel and make you the managing partner?"

"Well...no."

"I will. Just a few years after you join. Once you've got the lay of the land. I'll retire and give it all to you."

She recalled a previous convo when Crozier told her about a bizarre prophecy he'd received. "Because you're going to be appointed to the Supreme Court?"

"As God is my witness. I had a vision. It will happen, mark my words."

"You're very generous, Lou. But I have to decline."

"Because you want to stay stuck in the mire? Never achieving your true potential?"

No. Because working for you would be a betrayal of everything I believe. "I have to follow my own vision."

"Sorry to hear that. But the offer remains on the table. Any time you care to accept it. You can bring your entire team." He gave her a parting wave, then disappeared.

She turned and faced Sharon. "What do you think? Want to join Crozier's firm?"

"Want to be seduced by the dark side of the force? Never."

"He'd probably give you a fat raise."

"It would take more than that."

"Like what? Benefits?"

"More like, chains. And a whip. Which I suspect he would rather enjoy."

"Again, ick. Why is this conversation so disturbing? I thought we came here to have fun."

Sharon smiled. "Fun is for other people. Lawyers revel in the ick."

6

Kenzi managed to cut herself off after three martinis, so she was not staggering when she got back to her apartment. Which was good. Hailee was surely still awake and likely would want to give her crocheting lessons, or listen to Dean Martin music, or...whatever retro hobby she was pursuing at the moment.

Hailee sat in the center of their living room wearing a crocheted shawl and a beret. Her eyes were closed. She often did that when she listened to music, which she preferred on vinyl, because the sound was "more authentic." Given that she listened to Rat Pack crooners, the vinyl seemed appropriate.

She sat in her wheelchair, as she usually did, especially this time of night. Hailee had ME—myalgic encephalomyelitis. Despite her effervescent personality and boundless enthusiasm, she became physically tired much more quickly than others. She could walk unaided, but not for long. Her condition seemed stable, but there was always a possibility that it would worsen. Some people with ME eventually were unable to move or to take care of themselves. That was the looming specter casting a shadow over both their lives.

Kenzi spoke quietly so as not to startle her. "Is it Dean Martin night?"

Hailee's eyes opened. "Mom. Seriously? It's Sammy Davis, Jr. He's so dope."

"I always get those two confused."

"Their voices are not remotely similar."

"But the songs. The arrangements..."

"Also not remotely similar. Sammy is a high-energy belter. Dean is a relaxed warbler."

"Do you ever listen to anyone...more recent? Like Adele? Or Billie Eilish?"

Hailee rolled her eyes. "Sometimes I wonder who the teenager in this house is. I know you're busy, Mom, but you need to expand your musical interests beyond what's playing on FM radio this week."

"No doubt." She pulled up a chair. "Honey, we need to talk about something."

"Granddad's divorce?"

As usual, her daughter was way ahead of her. "You've heard?"

"How could I not? It's all over the internet."

"I suppose you must be shocked."

"Nah." She wheeled herself around. "Are you hungry? Should you eat something? How much did you have to drink?"

Remind me who the parent here is? "I'm fine. Honey, you don't have to avoid unpleasant subjects. It's best if we talk—"

"Mom, I've known Granddad was on the Taylor Petrie list since it first leaked. It was only a matter of time till the press got wind of it."

"And...you understand what it means?"

"That my granddad wanted to have sex with someone other than Candice? Yeah. Got it in one." She sham-shuddered. "Cringe."

Kenzi felt her face coloring. "I know that must be disappointing..."

"Oh, whatevs. Honestly, can you blame him? Candice is kind of... not on his level."

"That's no excuse."

"You don't like that woman any more than I do."

While true, it wasn't the point. "There's no excuse for cheating."

Hailee gave her a little side-eye. "Except we don't know that he was cheating, do we? Only that he was thinking about it."

"Well..."

"Did he tell you anything? Did he confess?"

She considered. He mentioned an escort service and Venus, but he never mentioned sex. "No. He didn't."

"There you go. And while we're at it, how do we know Candice wasn't cheating? She's much younger than he is. And I never thought she loved him."

Kenzi had doubts on that score herself, but she kept them to herself.

"I think she was in a tough place and Granddad gave her the financial support she needed. But love? When did you see any indication of that? For her, this was a marriage of convenience." Hailee paused. "Now Granddad—he thought she was hot stuff. And yet, he still ended up on Taylor Petrie. Exposed by an anonymous hacker."

During the Moreno case, Kenzi learned who the hacker was. But she'd kept the info to herself. "If you want to talk about it, I'm here."

"Thanks, Mom. But I really don't. There must've been some serious unhappiness in that relationship."

True. But at least they had one. Unlike her. "You know, we should do something this weekend. Get out of the apartment. Spend some time together."

"What did you have in mind?"

"I don't know." She tried to think teenager. "There's a new Marvel movie opening."

"What is this, the eighty-seventh one?"

"Something like that."

"I probably wouldn't enjoy it. Since I haven't seen the previous eighty-six."

"Or we could eat someplace you would like. Maybe...Olive Garden?"

"Have we ever eaten at Olive Garden?"

"I hear it's popular."

"If we're going to eat, let's go someplace authentic. There are some local-table eateries near the seaport."

That was her daughter. "You pick. Plan it out. We'll do the weekend together. Mother-daughter time."

"But Mom...don't you need to prepare?"

"To mediate a settlement conference? I could do that in my sleep."

The crease subdividing Hailee's forehead told her there must be more. "What about the disciplinary hearing?"

"The...what?"

Hailee grabbed her laptop and opened a webpage so her mother could see. "Granddad has more to worry about than the divorce. The Disciplinary Committee of the Bar Association is coming after him. There's a hearing to show cause why he shouldn't be suspended. Or lose his law license." She looked up. "What happens to Rivera & Perez if the senior Rivera can't practice law anymore?"

———

SANDY DUCKED around the corner just in time to avoid the bullet barreling toward his head.

Double time. Double fast. Double danger...

He heard the high-pitched whine and felt the impact as the bullet hit a brick wall. Small fragments dusted his face. He clenched his eyes shut.

That's how close he'd come to being dead.

"You can't get away from us!"

He shouted back. "I just need more time."

"You've had plenty of time. We warned you. We're dead serious."

Pun intended? "It's not that easy. I've had...difficulties."

"No more excuses."

Another bullet rang out. If he hadn't made it to the corner, he'd be dead. He could hear footfalls on the pavement behind him.

If he wanted to survive, he needed to move.

So pathetic. After all he'd done. Everything he'd been forced to do. Athena. Venus. The new chick. Circe 2.0. What had it gotten him? All he'd done was buy time. And not nearly enough...

He crossed the street as quickly as possible, careful to avoid creating a consistent line of sight between himself and the man holding the pistol. He'd pawned his gun, a decision he now deeply regretted. What a fool he was. Coalemus incarnate. Certainly not

Cassandra. He couldn't see one second into the future. And right now, that was probably a blessing.

He ducked down an alley and raced to the other side of the block. Not for one minute did he imagine he was safe. He ran into a bar, waved at the bartender, then bolted out the back door. No one even looked up.

He'd done this before.

He knew his pursuer was close behind. His pulse raced. Sweat dripped from every pore. He'd pushed his luck too far. Now they wanted him dead.

Surely he could make this better. There must be some way, some hope. If he could just get the money. Or if he just had something they needed...

Damn this miserable world! He was supposed to be someone by this point in his life. Someone important. Someone respected. Not running and hiding and unable to please people who were dangerous when displeased. He'd been to college, majored in Classics. What went wrong?

He crossed the street and made for another alley. He thought it would be more secluded, harder to spot. But it left him less room to maneuver. If the gunman appeared, what could he do about it? He didn't even see a good dumpster to hide behind.

As if on cue, another bullet rang out, whistling as it ricocheted from one surface to another. He dove face first, scraping his chin on the pavement. But he was still alive. He scrambled to his feet and ran, even faster than before.

He tried to think clearly, difficult as that might be when your heart pounded and your pulse raced at the speed of sound. He was just three blocks from the apartment. She might be waiting for him. If he could get there, he could get his next job done. That might buy him some time.

Or not. He could pay down the interest, but never the principal. He needed a big score. Something to erase the problem for all time.

Later. Right now, he needed to stay alive. He knocked over some trash cans, making a tremendous clatter. Nice move, Sandy. Might as well raise a flag that said, *I'm over here*!

He blamed all his problems on women. He'd be better off without them. It wasn't so long ago when that dumb vicious skank almost killed him. For what? Because he accidentally broke her nose? And now this—

He froze.

And found himself staring into the barrel of a gun.

"End of the road, Sandy."

The man stood at the other end of the alley. How had that thug gotten ahead of him?

"You ran a merry chase. But it's over. You're going to pay up with the only thing you have left. Your life."

7

K enzi pulled the laptop closer. "They want to revoke his license to practice law? Why?"

"Conduct unbecoming. Bringing the profession into disrepute."

"That's ridiculous. He's one of the leaders of the legal community."

"Was." Hailee pointed to a paragraph in the news item. "Apparently there's a provision in the Code that allows the Bar to expunge members who engage in illegal, immoral, or unbecoming conduct. And that's the excuse they're going to use to get rid of him."

Kenzi knew this was all too possible. She'd seen it done. Sometimes it seemed like these disciplinary committees spent more time going after lawyers with personal problems than they did policing lawyers who practiced unethically. She supposed that was easier. True ethics violations were hard to prove. But it was easy to go after someone whose imperfections had been splashed all over the front page.

Kenzi stared at the article, but her mind was elsewhere. "If *Papi* loses his license, it would destroy the firm. Not to mention him."

"You can't represent your own father, Mom."

"In a court case. This is different."

"There are other lawyers in town."

"I'm always happier when I have my hands on the reins."

"Because you're a control freak."

"No, because—" She stopped. Come to think of it, maybe she was a control freak. At any rate, this would have to be dealt with before it completely spiraled out of control.

"We have another concern, Mom. Even worse than this one."

Wonderful. "And that would be?"

Hailee pulled her phone from her pocket. "Twitter."

Of course. Her self-appointed social media manager would be concerned about fallout in the Twitterverse. "You think this is going to hurt our KenziKlan numbers?"

"It might. No one likes adultery, unless the person in question can present themselves as some kind of major martyr. I don't think that's going to work for Granddad. I would recommend that you get this divorce over with as soon as possible."

"That is always the goal of a settlement conference."

"Then get rid of the disciplinary hearing. Is there some way you can...plead it out?"

She wasn't sure. Divorce too often turned into a competition to see who could say the most awful things about their spouse. It was not hard to imagine Candice mentioning something—or inventing something—that would cement the Bar Association's case. "Hailee...about our weekend plans..."

"It's all gucci, Mom. You need to work."

"No. We're still going to spend time together and eat at that... plant-food place." She drew in her breath. "But maybe not all weekend."

Hailee grabbed her arm. "That sounds terrific."

"And then I need to get back to work."

"Don't you mean 'we'?"

"Uh...what?"

"Because I'm your trusted partner. You let me help with your cases in the past."

"Honey. This is about your grandfather."

"All the more reason I should be involved. It's a family matter. I'm a big girl. I can handle it."

She hardly thought fourteen qualified as "big girl." But she admired the fighting spirit. Not to mention that family loyalty. "Okay. You're on board. But start tomorrow. You need to get some sleep." She knew Hailee didn't like being babied. But she did tire easily. And an active day presented special challenges.

"You should sleep, too, Mom."

She had a point. She wrapped her arm around her daughter. "Thanks for taking care of me."

Hailee grinned. "It's a tough job. But someone's got to do it."

———

SANDY STARED BACK at the man facing him in the alley. He couldn't outrace a bullet. Better to scrutinize the man's eyes. That was where he was going to learn if he had any hope of remaining alive.

Double dealing. Double danger.

"I can pay it off," Sandy said, trying not to sound desperate. "I just need a little more time."

"Time's up, chump. The word is given. Execution orders have issued."

"That does not make good business sense. You shoot me, Kingsley gets nothing."

"I'm not risking—"

"There's no risk. Don't let me go. Follow me. I'll put the cash in your hand."

"I'd still have to kill you."

"But wouldn't you be more of a hero if you came home with the cash? Instead of a penniless corpse?"

He watched the eyes. He could see the thug was thinking.

"I dunno, Sandy. The boss is pretty pissed."

"Nothing makes him happier than money."

"I suppose. Wish I could consult my pals." Sandy heard a shuffling noise. He could tell the gunsel heard it too. "Wait a minute. I think they caught up to us."

"True. Fred's right behind you."

"Excellent. Hey—"

And the instant the man turned his head to peer over his shoulder, Sandy grabbed a lid from the nearest trash can and hurled it. The man fired, which led to a tremendous clanging sound. Sandy ducked.

He didn't know where the bullet went, but it hadn't gone into his heart and that was all that mattered. He rushed forward, knocking the man to the ground. The gun flew out of his hand. Sandy kicked him hard, right between the legs.

And took off running again.

He was almost there. He wasn't sure she was. But she had to be. She had to be.

He'd gotten lucky this time. But he couldn't count on that lasting forever.

Double down, double jeopardy, double or nothing...

Right now, he thought, panting, his throat dry and his heart racing, maybe he should be pushing his luck. Before his luck ran out completely.

Only his brains and quick thinking had kept him alive this long. And luck. Tyche on the half shell. Fortuna at Rainbow's End. But he couldn't afford to take any more chances.

Either he got these bastards off his tail...

Or these bastards put him in a coffin.

———

ICARUS ALMOST THREW his cellphone out the window. Temper, temper, he told himself. Yes, this was frustrating. Venus was always supremely frustrating. But phones were expensive. Use some sense. Even if your sister seems completely brainless, that didn't mean you have to act like an idiot.

He'd given up imagining Hera was ever going to help him. If he wanted to fix this, he would have to do it himself.

Was that even possible? Or like his namesake, had he been young and brash and flown too near the sun? Soon to pay the final price...

The only person who could save himself—was himself. And he wasn't at all sure he could do it.

Desperate men resorted to desperate measures...

ZELDA PULLED the curtains from the front window, just enough that she could see out. Not enough that he could see in.

Yes. Him again. Which woman would it be this time, she wondered?

Must be nice. Right now, only her television kept her company, and there was nothing sexy about that. Though she had indulged a fantasy or two involving that handsome Drew Carey. In her daydream, she won the showcase round and he swept her into his arms and told her she was the most priceless item on the stage...

But that only remained amusing so long. If that man came upstairs, she'd know about it. Whether they were fighting or screwing, they put some spice in her life. Like those internet videos. A little spice in a life that, in its seventh decade, seemed to have grown stale. Frigid, even.

She crossed her fingers. Maybe this would be her lucky day.

HERA SENT SELENE TO CHECK VENUS' apartment. She found no one and no clues. Venus had disappeared from the face of the earth.

And that worried her. How could it not, after what happened with Athena? She loved Venus, troubled though she was. Maybe because she was so troubled. Hera tended to take in strays. With Venus, you were talking about a stray who had strayed. Repeatedly. Which made her love the girl all the more.

Call in, she thought, as if somehow subvocalizing the idea might make it happen. Which it didn't.

Was it time to give up? Call the cops? Order a tombstone? She didn't know. Venus might just be having an extended encounter with a new client. But what if she were in danger? She couldn't love that girl more if she were...

Venus liked to meditate. She liked to pray. Was it possible she'd holed up in some monastery or retreat or...

No. Venus couldn't afford it. At the end of the day, it was always about money, wasn't it?

She opened the drawer beside her bed. The silver pistol glistened in the light.

She wasn't there yet. But a real possibility was looming...

She glanced at the increasingly unfamiliar face in the mirror. Was that who she was? Was that what she'd become?

She didn't want to go there. Not yet. Not ever.

But if she needed to, she would. For Venus' sake. And her own.

8

Kenzi checked her phone. It was after eight on a Sunday night. The weekend was almost shot and she hadn't accomplished half what she'd hoped.

And she was stuck on the telephone. With a forensic scientist. Which as far as she was concerned, was the ninth circle of hell.

"Are you absolutely sure?"

"To a high degree of medical certainty."

"That's not good enough."

"That's as good as it gets."

Kenzi ran her fingers through her side shave. Scientists. There was a reason she usually let Sharon handle this sort of thing. "If I make a motion, I have to be able to tell the judge the truth is not in question. And I need a more reliable source than some cheap online test."

Dr. Greggson was a DNA expert, one of the few around town who wasn't connected to the Washington State Center for Reproductive Wellbeing, the clinic her client was suing. "You need to understand that even though people sometimes act as if DNA evidence is a magic bullet, it isn't. DNA scans must be read. Interpreted. There's always room for error. Although in this case, I have to say, there's less room for error than in any case I recall in my entire career."

"Then you don't believe Julia's daughter is Julia's daughter."

"Convoluted phrasing, but I take your meaning. The baby girl your client has been raising is almost certainly not biologically hers, even though she gave birth to the kid."

"You're saying the fertility clinic made an error."

"Certainly looks that way. And sadly, mistakes of this nature are not unprecedented. There have been two such cases in California alone."

"What happened?"

"The clinic switched the embryos. Implanted them in the wrong mothers."

"Then—Julia's daughter is out there somewhere, but—" Kenzi felt a sudden clutching in her chest. "Some other clinic customer is raising Julia's baby?"

"Just as Julia is raising theirs. Didn't you get the clinic's records?"

"A room full of them."

"The answer is somewhere in there. Find out who else was having an embryo implanted at or around the time your client did. Favor Asian parents, because DNA suggests at least a partial Asian heritage. Then ask the court to issue subpoenas to likely suspects. Get DNA exemplars."

To learn the truth, she would have to invade the private lives of nice people who might not even suspect there was a problem. Then ask them for DNA from their baby. Because, by the way, your baby may not be your baby.

This had to be the worst assignment on earth. But it had to be done. She would have to staff up. Reassign or hire people to sift through the documents. Even then, it could take weeks to find what they needed. If it existed. "I think I understand."

"Let me know if you need a DNA expert down the line."

She would. But right now, she didn't need a scientist. She needed someone with the magical ability to extract a needle from a haystack.

———

SANDY WAS SICK OF WAITING. The weekend was almost over and he still hadn't found Venus. The hideous revelation he'd received made that imperative. He'd thought having thugs gunning for him was the worst thing that could possibly happen. Till he learned Venus was about to spring something worse.

How had she found out? Was it that stupid selfish irrresponsible brother? They called him Icarus for a reason. Why didn't he crawl into his laptop and leave everyone else alone? It was infuriating. He had skills, but refused to use them, instead letting his sister support him.

If Venus spilled what she knew, he'd be in even worse trouble than he was already. If she went public, he wouldn't be the only one embarrassed. The only difference was, when he had a problem, he scrambled for a solution.

When Kingsley had a problem, he killed someone. Like Atreus with his brother. And then some.

Where had she gone?

Maybe, just maybe, now that it was dark, he could risk going out. He knew Venus didn't like to launch the work week without being...as she liked to say...*amazed*.

He shook his head. What passed for humor these days...

Double the pleasure, double the fun...

He felt his phone buzz. He'd been so self-absorbed he'd missed a call.

He pulled his phone out and glanced at the Caller ID.

She had something she wanted to tell him.

He listened to the voicemail message. And gasped.

After a few minutes, his respiration calmed, his heart rate returned to something approaching normal, and he was able to think semi-clearly.

How could everything go so wrong so fast? If he wasn't hanged one way, he'd be hanged another. Why did this always happen to him? Why was the only luck he had always bad luck?

He stared at the door. And the mirror. When he peered into it, he saw worlds upon worlds upon worlds. Including the hideous one yet-to-come.

Unless he prevented it.

He grabbed his coat and, for the first time in many hours, ventured into the darkness.

KENZI GLANCED AT HER CELLPHONE. The day had been exhausting. She was ready to sleep.

But she'd agreed to meet Candice's lawyer, Iris Jacoby, who wanted to "iron out a few roadblocks" before the settlement conference tomorrow morning. Which sounded good in principle. But the conversation seemed much more like an attempt to unduly influence the mediator than a stab at streamlining the process. Which showed a lot of gumption, given that the other party was Kenzi's father.

They'd met at a restaurant near Kenzi's apartment. So far, the only thing she liked about Candice's lawyer was the fact that she normally practiced in Los Angeles—so Kenzi probably wouldn't see her ever again.

Iris was ten or fifteen years older than Kenzi. She admired Iris' fashion sense, though not her obviously dyed platinum hair. The raspy voice strongly suggested that giving up smoking was still on her bucket list. Kenzi wondered if this woman would have concerns about her acting as mediator. But at the moment, that seemed to be the least of her worries.

"Look, Kenzi, there's a reason they call me the Divorce Lawyer to the Stars. It's what I do. And why do those high-dollar clients trust me? Because I know what I'm doing."

"I'm sure you do, Iris. And tomorrow morning, you'll have the opportunity to—"

"Did I tell you about my case with..." And then Iris dropped the name of a marginally famous rapper. "He didn't get it. He kept screaming at me. I told him not to kill the messenger, but he wasn't listening. He said, 'I paid for her insane lifestyle the whole time we was together. Why do I gotta keep making payments now? It ain't fair!' I just smiled and said, 'You married her, sweetcakes.'"

Iris did have a certain flair, but as far as Kenzi could tell, the advice she gave her clients was no different from what any other competent divorce attorney would offer. "I'm hoping we can resolve this case—"

"Or there was the actress married to this big-time movie-producer guy. The divorce was already going to make her independently wealthy, but she seemed outraged when I explained that it would not be possible for her to continue flying on the movie studio's private jet. I gave her my best lowered-eyebrow look. 'Honey,' I said, 'you may be rich, but you are no longer Mrs. Producer.'"

"If we could talk about this case—"

"My point being, Kenzi, that I know my way around the block. I don't see how your stepmother could possibly be more difficult, or this case could be more complex, than some of the stuff I've handled in the past."

She hoped Iris was right. "If we can wrap this up tomorrow, it will benefit everyone."

"How much would that be worth to your father?"

"I—excuse me?"

"Give me a number, Kenzi. You're basically asking for a favor. Rapid resolution. Which we can probably make happen. But you have to make it worth our while."

———

VENUS PULLED the hood over her head and held it in place as she entered the park. The wind blew strong and steady, and it felt as if rain might start at any moment. But that wasn't the reason for the hood.

She had to make sure she wasn't seen. Wasn't recognized. This was the first time she'd been out in days. She wanted to make sure it wasn't her last.

It would've been smarter to stay hidden. But she couldn't bear it any longer, all alone, apart, separated from everyone she knew. The one she loved. Wasn't this rich? She'd gone so long with an endless parade of men, never once feeling anything for any of them. But when love finally entered her life, she couldn't risk going out.

She wished she could take her stupid words back. But that wasn't the way the world worked, was it? She was just trying to carve a little something out for herself. Build a future that went beyond next week. That would never happen with Hera. The woman had a good heart. But the money wasn't there. Especially not with Icarus keeping most of her earnings for himself.

That was her brother, the one with mad skills that could support them comfortably till the end of time. But since he refused to do it, she had to continue scraping out an existence, one man at a time...

Was it wrong to want something better, something for herself, something that might last? Using what she knew to her advantage?

This maze had always been a retreat for her, a place she could visit to get her head together. She needed that more than ever now. She needed a path to the future.

She reached the center of the maze, wind howling, storm brewing. She knew she couldn't stay long. Nonetheless, she knelt, closed her eyes, and let her negative thoughts float into the ether. Show me the path. Show me the way home.

She heard something stirring behind her, even above the wind.

She turned, and to her surprise, found herself staring into a mirror held by the last person she wanted to see here.

"Do you know what you've done? Do you have any idea?"

Sadly, she did. "I'm just trying to get ahead. To get away. I want a place of my own where—"

"Look at yourself in the mirror, Venus. Take a good long gaze."

She tried, but the mirror trembled as the wind whipped it back and forth.

"Your soul is damaged, and that damage is spreading like a disease. Soon we'll all be infected."

Venus couldn't bear to listen. Because she knew some of it was true. "I'm just trying to survive."

"That's what we all want. But I don't have a chance unless you disappear."

"You're acting crazy—"

"Maybe I am. But you made me this way. I need peace. I need rest."

"We all do."

"You're about to find yours."

Her eyes widened as she saw the mirror rise, then come crashing down. "No! Please! *Nooo!*"

The impact made her eyes go black. She heard a thunderous noise in her head and the tinkling of glass around her shoulders. The pain was searing. She fell to the ground.

Then she felt nothing at all.
She didn't even have time to scream.

9

Kenzi stared at the self-anointed Divorce Lawyer to the Stars, not quite sure she'd heard the woman correctly. "Are you asking for some kind of side action?"

"Of course not. This is for Candice."

"Let's not mess around with petty gamesmanship. Let's try in earnest to resolve—"

"What you want is to sew Candice's lips shut."

Kenzi didn't think she could take much more of this. "That is not at all what I'm saying."

"Of course it is. Your daddy has had a deluge of bad press. Now he's got the bar on his back."

"If you want to make some kind of deal, you should talk to my father's lawyer."

"Fine. But I want to suggest something to the mediator. You know what I consider my primary job here?"

"Extracting large sums of money?"

"No. Though most clients do like that. My job is to find a way to tell my clients' stories. To make sure they're heard. Give them a voice. Often that's what they want most, even if they don't realize it. Once I assure them the world is listening, everything else becomes much simpler."

"We're not going to have a lot of time to—"

"Make time, Kenzi. It's in everyone's best interest. I'll dial Candice down. Drain the hate away. But let her feel heard. I suggest you give each client a half hour to tell their story. Then we'll split the parties up. You can shuttle offers back and forth."

Kenzi was getting a bad feeling about this. "You'll support that? Try to help the settlement. Not thwart it?"

"Why would I ever do that?"

"I dunno. Money?"

"If you think that, you don't know anything about me. I always push for settlement. I have more clients than I can handle. And I bill $950 an hour, so I don't need to drag cases out. I find my clients are happy to pay my fee and always feel they've gotten value for their money. They might feel differently if a case went on for years. I don't let that happen."

"I hope that's true."

"Scout's honor. Hey—you don't have to take my word for it. Have you read my book?"

"You...wrote a book?"

"Yup. Published it myself. It's the bestselling divorce primer on Amazon. I make almost as much from that as I do from my practice."

"Impressive."

"For that matter, I give the same advice on my podcast."

A podcast, too. Now she was starting to feel insecure. Was a podcast better than a livestream?

"Divorce is always painful. I think our job is to anesthetize the pain. Not augment it."

"Then we should get along just fine. I'll see you in the morning."

"One more thing."

"Yes?"

She pointed a lacquered fingernail. "Don't try to upstage me. I've heard you think you're quite the fashionista. But one thing that comes from representing the stars—in time, you become the star. I've got a closet full of Fendi and Hermes provided to me free of charge, so long as I take pics of myself wearing the stuff and post them regularly. I guess you could say I'm an influencer. Certainly Fendi and Hermes think so. I don't want to change their minds. So wear something dowdy tomorrow."

"Excuse me?"

"We can do this the easy way, or we can do it the hard way. You decide."

"I can't believe—"

"I've had all kinds of clients. I've put up with all kinds of inappropriate conduct. I've even lost a few cases." She paused. "But I will not be upstaged. A girl has to draw the line somewhere."

———

FROM HER THIRD-FLOOR WINDOW, Zelda saw everything. Or so it seemed. Her laptop wasn't whispering to her anymore, so in her boredom, she pulled back the shades and gazed toward the park.

It was hard to see clearly. There were no streetlamps or other sources of illumination nearby. The moon was barely a sliver. But her eyes were still good and when she focused, she could be quite observant.

She saw that familiar face enter the park, the maze. And not long after, she saw the petite woman stagger out, her face and hands darkened by what appeared to be blood. She looked lost, confused.

The woman was rubbing her hands like Lady Macbeth. Saying something, or at least mouthing the words. She turned one way, then another. Took a long time before she pulled it together. Then she left the park, speeding like a bullet.

And they called Zelda a busybody. This time, people would be interested in what this busybody had to say.

She picked up her phone and dialed the police.

10

Kenzi chose the largest conference room the firm had, but it wasn't big enough. At least not for her comfort. She and her stepmother were going to be in the same room for an extended period of time in an extremely tense situation.

At least she was in the middle, not taking sides, not playing favorites, simply acting as a facilitator. But the scowl on Candice's face suggested that she saw this as one more manipulation by her husband, marshalling his vast forces against her. Why did Candice agree to it?

Candice was a small woman, a few inches shorter than Kenzi, but trim and shapely. She obviously went to the gym on a regular basis. Kenzi didn't like to inventory women, but she couldn't help but notice that Candice had possibly the best butt she'd ever seen in her life. And of course she wore a top-notch designer outfit, perfectly accessorized.

She had never much cared for Candice, but to be fair, she had barely spent any time with her. Judging by appearances, the lack of love was mutual. When her stepmother entered the conference room, her demeanor was frosty. She seemed detached, or shaken, as if she barely knew what she was doing.

"Kenzi," Candice said.

"Thank you for coming, Candice. I'm sorry about the circumstances."

"I hear you're keeping busy."

"True." Was there a subtext here? "Lawyers never sleep."

"Oh, some do. But not you. Your father says you're handling criminal cases now."

She laughed, too loud and hollow. "I bet he was griping about that."

"Actually, he said you were one of the most effective trial lawyers he'd ever seen."

"He's probably glad all that law school tuition paid off." If she recalled correctly, there had been talk way back when about Candice going to law school. But that never happened. Come to think of it, there had also been some talk about children. But that never transpired either.

She couldn't think of anything intelligent to say, so she defaulted to her reliable standby. "I love your shoes."

"Coming from you, that's quite a compliment."

Apparently the small talk had gone on long enough. Candice took a seat.

The main problem, of course, was that she still blamed Candice for the dissolution of her parents' marriage and all the hardship that followed. Fair or not, in the back of her mind, Candice would always be the other woman. The one who tore the Rivera family apart. Even if it wasn't true.

The conference table was long enough that she could put Candice and Iris on one side, her father and Crozier on the other, and herself on the far end. That way she could see everyone. But didn't have to be too close to anyone.

Candice still seemed distracted, like her body was there but her brain was somewhere else. Maybe that was her technique for dealing with stress. Calgon, take me away...

Crozier spoke. "Do you have a plan, Kenzi? A roadmap you want us to follow?"

"Iris has requested that each party be allowed, either on their own or through counsel, to make an opening statement setting out their positions and goals. I think that's a fine idea that might well speed us along to our ultimate destination." Never hurt to flatter counsel when you wanted something from them. "I do think half an hour seems extreme, though. We don't want to be here all day. I was thinking maybe...ten minutes."

Iris snorted. "Baby doll, I can't say hello in ten minutes."

Especially when you're billing $950 an hour? "Please try. If both sides request more time, I'll take that under consideration."

"How gracious of you."

The attitude was no surprise. As promised, Iris had dressed to the nines. She wore a sleeveless Fendi blouse that she insisted was years old, though it looked rather fresh to Kenzi. Her slacks were much tighter than most women would be comfortable wearing to work—but they did look good on her. Kenzi didn't object to looking sexy now and again—except maybe not at the office. Get too chic and people stop taking you seriously. Might not be fair, but the legal world was still largely run by men and sometimes you just had to be realistic about it.

Kenzi hadn't dressed down, but she had kept it basic. She told the KenziKlan she was slumming.

Once Iris began speaking, Kenzi understood what the woman had meant before about the importance of telling your client's story. Even though Iris had been on the case barely forty-eight hours, she had Candice's tale of woe down pat and told it in the way that would be most sympathetic. Even though there was no judge to be swayed, this did serve purposes. First and foremost, it pleased her client. Second, it might put some fear in her opponent, inspiring him to settle to avoid pubic embarrassment. And it allowed Iris to try out some themes, see how they played, see how the opposition responded. Never hurt to give your drama a trial run.

"Just to be clear," Iris said, "I want an early settlement as much as anyone. Candice wants to settle. Divorce is painful enough. Once people start fighting in court, tempers rise, people make poor choices, and everyone loses. I don't want that." She inhaled deeply, rasping. "But I'm not about to give away the farm. My client has serious griev-ances. She must be compensated for the cruelty she's endured at the hands of her husband."

"Wait a minute," Crozier said. "Let's not start a bunch of libelous—"

"I believe this is my turn to speak," Iris insisted.

"I don't care whose turn it is. If you start telling lies, I'm going to jump in. I won't let you run riot and dominate the conference."

"I don't know what you're talking about."

"I'm talking about your standard strategy," Crozier replied.

"As if you would know. Have I seen you in LA repping any superstars?" She fanned her face. "No, that was me."

"I know how to read." Crozier reached into his briefcase and pulled out a paperback book. *Getting Past It: A Profitable Primer for Divorce*. Iris' book.

Kenzi had to suppress her smile if she was going to maintain any claim to impartiality. It seemed Crozier had done his research. And some Amazon shopping.

"I now read from chapter four," Crozier said. 'Remember that the settlement conference can be a great opportunity for you to make your case so well it never gets to a judge, because you've struck terror in the hearts of the opposition. But that won't happen if you let the mediator run the show. You must run the show. Run that conference well enough and you'll be remembering it fondly from your beach house in Cabo.'"

Crozier closed the book and gave Iris a firm gaze. "You are not going to steal this conference. I know Kenzi well enough to believe she will not permit it. And in the unlikely event that she doesn't stand up to you, we're walking out. You can make a grandstand play and it might amuse your client, but it will guarantee we don't settle today."

Crozier and Iris looked like two schoolkids facing off on the playground, daring the other to blink.

No one blinked.

"Okay," Kenzi said, "let's get back on track. Iris, please continue your opening statement. And I will ask the lawyers not to interrupt one another unless it's absolutely necessary."

"Which it never is," Iris murmured. "This is a settlement conference, not a death penalty case." She glanced at her notes and resumed her train of thought. "My client did her best to make this marriage work, but sometimes everything is not enough. Especially when your partner isn't trying at all. When he's bored and inattentive. When he never wants to do anything with his spouse. When he actively discourages her from having any life of her own. When he's seeing other women and trolling the internet for affairs."

She glanced up. "Sorry to be blunt, Kenzi, but your father is a serial adulterer. I think we all know this."

Her father looked uncomfortable but remained poker-faced. Crozier started to interrupt again.

Iris raised her hand. "Hold your horses, Crozier. You can make your impassioned denials when it's your turn. But let's get real for a moment. Adultery apps. Escort services. Face it—he's a sex addict."

Kenzi bit down on her lower lip.

"Yes, Candice had food to eat and a roof over her head. But her husband didn't keep the bed warm at night. He betrayed her, literally from the moment this marriage began. He and this latest bimbo, Venus, have been spotted out on the town. Candice's friends have snapped pics of them at restaurants, plays. Candice told him to end it and he refused, so she left. You can't expect her to remain tethered to a man who can't keep his zipper zipped."

Her father's voice was low, almost sub-guttural, but still perfectly audible to everyone in the room. "Candice hasn't been a model of propriety. And she hasn't fulfilled her...marital obligations."

Iris sighed. "And now the mudslinging begins. The lying. Disgusting." She blew her bangs out of her eyes.

"Excuse me for interrupting," Crozier said, "but I can't let these huge lies stand. The truth is, the petitioner was the first to stray. While I won't deny that my client has had outside relationships, that only began after the marriage was irreparably shattered by her salacious conduct."

Candice's eyes lit, but she remained silent.

"Plus," Crozier continued, "she has been a poor steward of her husband's fortune, squandering thousands on clothes she didn't wear and antiques she didn't need. She has already milked her husband to such an extent that his hard-earned fortune has been seriously diminished. She's benefitted enough from this marital mistake. She's not entitled to more."

Candice spoke. "I never spent more than the puny allowance he allowed me. He kept me on a leash. A tight one. He wanted his arm candy. But he treated me like his dog."

"Okay, I think we've gotten off track here." Kenzi spread her arms across the table. "These were supposed to be opening statements. Not arguments." She tried not to become frustrated. They didn't sound as if they were anywhere close to settling. But sometimes people needed to blow off steam. Once they did, they were more likely to resolve their differences. "You've got a few more minutes, Iris. And then you get your ten, Lou. And then we're going to roll up our sleeves and get to work. There's no reason why we can't wrap this up today. I'm determined to see that happen."

No one argued with her. Good. Maybe now that they were past those initial outbursts, the deliberations would proceed smoothly.

After all, things couldn't possibly get any worse...

———

DETECTIVE KATE CORRIGAN stared at the bloodied corpse sprawled on the ground in the middle of the maze. She hadn't heard from the medical examiner yet, but the jagged glass around the victim's throat provided more than a few clues about what happened. It might have been mercifully quick. But not painless. Blood was everywhere.

She spoke to the nearest uniform. "Hair and fiber done?"

"Just about, ma'am."

Lieutenant Bale was relatively new and perpetually polite, so she held her tongue. She hated "ma'am." But she also knew "detective" was a mouthful. "Did they find anything?"

"They don't normally share their thoughts. But I only observed one Eureka moment."

"And that was...?"

"Something about a green fiber."

"Ooh. Exciting." She was being sarcastic, but she knew that entire cases could be made or crushed by forensic evidence that at first seemed trivial. Sometimes, in a murder case, that's all you have. People don't typically commit murder with a lot of witnesses around.

Circumstantial evidence becomes paramount. "What is this place, anyway?"

"It's a labyrinth. A meditation maze."

"And you know that because…"

"I attend that church across the street. We're the ones who installed this in the park."

"And what exactly is it you do in a meditation maze? Get lost in your thoughts?" She started to chuckle—then realized she was laughing alone. "That was a joke, Bale."

"I know, ma'am. Very clever."

"Right." She gazed across the expanse. The corpse appeared to be in the dead center—oh, there she was being clever again—of the maze. She detected a single winding path that started at what must be the entrance and wound around, forming concentric circles till it reached the center. "I used to love mazes when I was a kid. But what exactly is the point of this?"

"Restores balance. Encourages creativity. Helps people find peace. Quiet. Prayer, if you believe in that sort of thing."

"I take it you do."

"I wouldn't go to church if I didn't."

"Of course not."

"People make stops along the path, pause, turn their thoughts inward. Then move to the next station. I do find a few moments of self-reflection can be good for the soul."

"Wasn't so good for this woman."

"No, ma'am. Obviously not. Wasn't there another murder near here not long ago?"

"Yes. Also a woman. Still unidentified. Corpse found on the other end of the park."

"Dangerous place to bring your kids to play."

"So it seems." Kate gazed at the skyline. Other than the church and the park, there wasn't too much out this way. She did see an apartment building nearby. Probably where the eyewitness lived. Looked like it had seen better days, but still probably wasn't cheap. Give it another few years and the yuppies would seize it, remodel it, and triple the rent. Seemed like everyone wanted to live in Seattle these days. Until they found out how much they would have to pay for the privilege of being rained on half the year.

Her eyes returned to the corpse. She couldn't touch anything yet, but that didn't stop her from looking. "Bale, am I right in thinking that's a big mirror around the poor woman's neck?"

"That's how it looks to me. Not that I've...you know. Made a close inspection."

Couldn't blame him for that. "Murder by mirror?"

"So it appears."

"Is that even possible?"

Bale shrugged. "The mirror shattered around her head. Jagged glass shards cut into her neck. If they severed the carotid, she could be dead in five or ten seconds."

Kate felt a shiver race up her body. She was supposed to be inured to this sort of thing. Murder didn't creep her out anymore. Except this one did. It was still morning, but she was ready to be done for the day. At home with Sharon, with a big bowl of popcorn and some stupid Netflix movie.

"Maybe her name is Alice," Bale suggested.

That snapped her out of the reverie. "Now...what?"

"The victim. Maybe her name is Alice."

"Because..."

He titled his head toward the corpse. "Alice Through the Looking-Glass."

Ugh. And he thought her joke was unfunny. "I hope you're not correct." But then again, why *would* anyone kill with a mirror? Which they would've had to bring to this park. A gun would be much simpler. Or a knife, if they didn't want the racket. But a mirror?

"Excuse me."

Kate looked up. An older woman stood just outside the maze. She was maybe seventy or so. Her hair was in curlers, something Kate hadn't seen in decades, except in bad movies. And was she wearing a bathrobe? A pink fuzzy bathrobe?

"Excuse me looking the way I do. I didn't want to miss you. You're a police officer, aren't you?"

Kate took a step toward her. "I am. How can I help you?"

"My name is Zelda. Like Fitzgerald's wife. Or that video game."

Kate had no idea what she was talking about. "Last name?"

"Lehman. I live in the apartment building nearby. On the third floor. My window faces the park."

"I understand. What did you want to talk to me about?"

"I saw this happen. I called it in." She tossed her head to the side. "Well, I didn't see the murder. But I saw a woman stagger out of here covered in blood."

"Right. I have your description."

"I've seen that woman before. And after a good night's sleep, it all came back to me." Zelda offered a big smile, obviously proud of herself. "I know her name."

————

DESPITE THE ROCKY START, Kenzi was pleased with how well the settlement conference progressed. Candice seemed upset that she wasn't going to get a huge piece of the family fortune, but most of her husband's assets, including his stock in the law firm, were held in a trust created decades ago by his father, the original founder of the firm. Even Iris agreed that a trust and its assets were not marital assets —especially when the trust pre-dated the marriage. For that matter, he'd bought and paid for their home before they met and his was the only name on the deed, so that wasn't a marital asset, either. He'd paid her living expenses and she hadn't worked. She was entitled to some compensation for the income and growth her husband had seen during the marriage, which would not be insignificant. But if she had visions of joining Mackenzie Scott on the list of billionaire philanthropists— that wasn't going to happen.

How on earth, she wondered, had her father, not only a lawyer but a divorce lawyer, failed to get a prenup? It seemed the obvious thing to do, especially with a second wife. Did it slip his mind? Was he too much of a romantic?

Iris slid a piece of paper across the table. "I've talked with my client, sweetie, and we've made a few amendments to your recommendations. Alejandro bought that new china for her. Even if it wasn't formally a gift, it basically was a gift, and gifts are not marital property. Also, we want a housing allowance for the first year. Give her a chance to get established."

Kenzi glanced at her father. He offered the tiniest nod, which she took to mean, fine. Let her have it. Let's get this over with.

"And if we can agree on that and a few other items, Kenzi...I think we have a deal."

Kenzi felt as if her heart had skipped a beat. It was still morning, and they might actually reach a settlement?

"This is a testament to you, Kenzi," Iris commented. "Your prep is paying off. You've been nothing but fair. On the whole, your recommendations have been sound ones."

"Agreed," Crozier said. "When can we sign the papers and deliver the check?"

That made it even more amazing. This was one for the record books.

All at once, she started feeling good about herself. She had done good work, hadn't she? She was helping her father get through a tough time. She was taking a role in the firm's management. This could be the start of a whole new era. This could be when she crossed the Rubicon and—

Her thoughts were interrupted by a pounding on the door.

Her eyes swept across the room. She could see everyone else was as surprised as she was.

"*Police*. Open the door."

The police? This was a raid? Of a settlement conference?

"If you do not open the door, we are authorized to use force."

What? Kenzi didn't know what to say. Dealing with the police was not a typical mediator function.

The booming voice returned. "Have it your way—"

"No, wait." Kenzi sprang to her feet and opened the door. She didn't recognize the two men at the forefront, but she spotted Kate in the background, and Sharon standing a few steps behind her. "I don't know what you think is happening in here. We're just having a litigation meeting. In a divorce case. Which—"

"Is Candice Rivera present?"

"Yes, but—"

The officer pulled a folded piece of paper from his pocket. "We have a warrant for her arrest."

"Candice?" A thousand thoughts raced through Kenzi's head. Could this be one of Crozier's dirty tricks? "On what charge?"

"Murder in the first degree." He pulled handcuffs out of his pocket. "Please step aside."

11

Kenzi let the officer in, but she did not stop talking. "Who's been murdered?"

He brushed past her. "I'm not here to have a conversation."

"Candice has been in this conference room for the past two hours. With multiple witnesses. When did this alleged murder occur?"

"I'm not the district attorney." He took Candice by the arm and not-so-gently pulled her to her feet.

Candice looked as if she were confronting a ghost. Her face was pale. Her hands shook. "Iris? What's happening? Do I have to go with them?"

Iris waved a hand in the air. "I don't do criminal."

Kenzi rolled her eyes. Useless.

"I don't want to go to jail! Someone *do* something. Can they—can they get away with this?"

Iris shrugged. "Seems wrong to me. But I don't practice around here. Maybe gonzo law flies in Seattle."

Neither her father nor Crozier spoke. They both seemed stunned. The officer shoved Candice toward the door.

"Ok, I do practice around here," Kenzi said. "And this seems completely unnecessary. Candice is represented by counsel. You should've called and given her a chance to surrender voluntarily."

"Sorry. Got my orders."

Behind him, she saw Kate holding a spread hand beside her head with the three middle fingers folded—the universal signal for "Call me." She nodded.

"Please." Candice looked scared and desperate. "Iris? Allie? Someone?"

Kenzi could feel her frustration. Here she was in a room full of lawyers, including one she was married to. And yet cops were hauling her away and no one was doing a thing to prevent it.

"*Please!*" Candice cried as the officer dragged her through the door. "Someone! Iris!"

Iris spread her hands in a don't-look-at-me gesture.

Kenzi gritted her teeth. "I can't stop this, but I'll come visit you, Candice. Soon as they let you have visitors."

To her side, her father gave her a stony glare. Crozier's expression was not much friendlier. Tough. She wasn't letting Candice face this alone.

"In the meantime, I'll try to figure out what this is all about. There must be some mistake."

"Thank you." All at once, tears burst from Candice's eyes.

The officers turned away and Kate followed them. Kenzi needed to get somewhere she could make a call. She knew Kate would give her the straight scoop. Something about this entire situation smelled. Even if she didn't like Candice, she had a hard time believing Candice was capable of murder.

She heard her father clear his voice. "If I may remind you, Kenzi, we agreed that it would be best for the firm if you discontinued... dabbling in criminal matters."

"You don't care what happens to her? You'll just let her rot in jail?"

"I'll call Shel Harrington. He probably doesn't know what's going on." Harrington was the local district attorney.

"This wouldn't be happening unless the DA knew about it. And authorized it."

Her father drew in his breath. "I'll find someone who can handle this." He glanced at Crozier. "Least I can do."

Yeah. The very least. "You do whatever you want. I promised I'd look into this and visit her in jail. And I keep my promises."

———

SANDY WANTED to tear his hair out, but he knew that wouldn't solve the problem. And his hair seemed to be disappearing at an alarming rate on its own. Double time. Double or nothing. No need to help it along.

But he had to do something. His world was disintegrating. People were stalking him. He had no way to make the money he needed. At least, not unless he developed some new...clients. And how could he do that when he was afraid to go outside?

He had eliminated one problem. But that had not improved his situation. He may have made it worse.

This whole mess was spiraling out of control and he faced a gruesome potential payback. Double indemnity. And then some.

Maybe he should call Hera. She might know something useful. She might even be able to help him get his business back on track. If she was so inclined. She knew lots of ladies. But the cops probably had her place watched...

A phone call. Then a meeting. Someplace safe. Someplace neutral.

She wouldn't want to do it. She wouldn't want anything to do with him. He would have to educate her about a few realities. He could do that. He could be Moros, god of impending doom.

Hera didn't want cops dropping by any more than he did. She was probably burning all records that might link her to Venus. Or might appear to give her a motive...

She could light the fires. But he knew how to fan the flames. Right back in her face.

———

KENZI ENTERED the jailhouse as soon as possible. She knew Candice had been booked, searched, questioned, and forced to wear those hideous orange coveralls and flip-flops. Someone at the front desk informed her that Candice had refused to answer any questions unless she had a lawyer present. At least she'd learned that much from being married to a lawyer. Or maybe she learned it from watching television, who knew?

When asked, Kenzi informed the front-desk clerk that she was a lawyer representing Candice, which was a stretch, since they'd never even discussed the matter. But he wasn't going to let her in because she was a concerned stepdaughter.

Kenzi wanted to learn as much about this mess as possible. But the main thing she wanted to do was make sure Candice knew she was not alone.

To her surprise, the meeting was conducted by teleconference. She knew that during the lockdown, many jails and prisons started using Zoom to avoid potentially virus-spreading contacts. She could see the advantages, but she didn't like it. Zoom conferences had their place, but they were no substitute for being in front of someone, in the same room, face to face.

Only a few hours had passed, but Kenzi did not have to be a mind reader to realize something had changed. She could see it in Candice's eyes.

Candice was tired. And uncomfortable. And scared. Terrified, even. Who wouldn't be?

Kenzi wanted to ask many questions, but before she had a chance, Candice jump-started the conversation. "Have you figured out what this is all about?"

"Somewhat. I mean, it's still sketchy. But I have some idea. The victim's name is Vanessa Collins. Apparently went by Venus. I'm assuming..."

"And you're correct." Candice shook her head. "I'm sorry. This is so awkward. She's the woman your father has been seeing. They've been spotted together on numerous occasions. He decided he'd rather be with this...escort floozy...than be with his wife."

"This woman was wrecking your marriage. Which of course..."

"Gives me a motive to murder her. Don't I know it."

"But..." She hoped Candice would say it on her own. Without prodding.

"Why would I do that? I don't blame the woman."

"You didn't..."

"No. I didn't murder her."

"The police are convinced that you did."

"I'm the obvious suspect."

"True. And police love nothing more than an obvious suspect. They have an eyewitness who can place you at the scene of the crime. A park not far from downtown. With a meditation maze. Near an Episcopal church. True?"

"How would I know what some rando witness said?" She sighed. "But I know the place."

"The police say you killed Venus, then tried to get a big divorce settlement."

"Seems like overkill. Surely one or the other would be sufficient revenge."

This was not the attitude a wrongly accused woman needed to take. At least not in public. "You knew about Venus?"

"I knew. I found her name in your father's phone contact list. I know his password. That's how I found out he was having affairs."

"Affairs? Plural?"

"You heard me."

"At the settlement conference, he said you were cheating also."

"Trying to steal the moral high ground."

"The eyewitness' name is Zelda Lehman. She has an apartment near the maze. With a window facing the park."

"Don't think I've heard of her before."

"She says she spotted you from her apartment window. According to her, you emerged from the maze...covered with blood."

"How did she know who I was?"

"She'd seen your photo in the paper. In connection with my father being on the Taylor Petrie site."

"Lady must have a fine memory. And a lot of spare time on her hands."

"But why would she say she saw blood if—"

"Probably only occurred to her after she learned someone was dead. Her imagination ran wild."

"Maybe..." She stopped herself. She wasn't here to judge. At this point, she wasn't sure why she was here. Candice appeared to be doing fine, given the circumstances. She certainly wasn't crumbling into a helpless heap. "And you don't know anything about the murder?"

"Of course not. Are they investigating your father? It seems like he had more motive than I do."

Okay, now the woman was making her mad. "My father is not a murderer."

"That would explain this rush to judgment, wouldn't it? He's friends with Shel Harrington. Maybe he got his friend to charge his wife, which gets him off the hook and puts me behind bars. Saves him the expense of a divorce settlement."

"That is preposterous."

"Maybe. But it makes more sense than accusing me."

It was time for her to get out of here. She wasn't helping, and Candice wasn't telling her everything she knew, just fragmented pieces, as little as possible. "My time is almost up. Is there anything I can get you? Anything you need? You're likely to be here awhile."

"You don't think I'll get bail?"

"Bail is not common for first-degree murder charges, but it's not impossible. You have no priors, right? Since this was allegedly an act of passion, you're not likely to repeat the crime. You're not a flight risk. And you can make bail—with your husband's help."

"Good. Get me out."

"My father would have to put up—"

"He'll put on a show of being supportive. Even if this was all his idea."

"Anything else you need?"

"Yeah. A lawyer."

"My father is calling—"

Candice laughed out loud. "You think I'm going to let him pick my lawyer? He'll pick the most incompetent person he knows."

"You're being unfair."

Candice smiled, such a broad smile it was almost frightening. "Poor sweet Kenzi. He's screwed you over more than almost anyone. And yet you're still the loyal little daughter, desperate for Daddy's approval."

"I am not at all—"

"I want you to be my lawyer."

Kenzi froze. "You...*what?*"

"You heard me. I don't trust your father. But I trust you."

Her head seemed full of fog. "We barely know each other."

"You're a fighter. You understand the problems women have in this world. You've handled criminal cases before. Despite your father being dead set against it. This is your golden opportunity to do it again— with a case he won't want you handling. It's perfect."

"I don't think it's appropriate to represent my own stepmother."

"Why? You were willing to mediate the divorce settlement."

"That's not at all the same thing."

"We're not blood relatives. As you said, we barely know each other. You can be objective."

Sounded like a lot of trouble to her. And a big mistake.

"Best of all"—Candice leaned into the screen—"this will give you a chance to show who's really in charge of your firm. Allie is on the way out, Gabe is worthless. You're the future. This is where you make that clear to everyone. You're running the show, and what your father wants or doesn't want is irrelevant." She paused. "Plus, you'll be helping a woman who desperately needs help. That's supposed to be your credo, isn't it?" Another strategic pause. "I think the KenziKlan would be disappointed if you didn't represent me."

"That's a big ask." The scary part was, Candice was starting to make sense. "I'll give it some thought."

"At least enter an appearance. Get a bail hearing set."

"I can do that." After all, the jailhouse authorities already thought she was representing Candice. "There's one major problem, though."

"And that is?"

Long pause. "I don't really like you, Candice. Just being honest here. I don't think you like me either."

"Who cares? There's always conflict between the new wife and the daughter of a previous marriage. So what? You're a fantastic attorney with a killer work ethic. Scrappy fighter. Smart as they come. If anyone can win my case, it will be you. What else matters?"

Candice leaned in so close her head must've pressed against the camera. "Please, Kenzi. I *need* you." For the first time, Kenzi saw vulnerability in those eyes. Desperation. "Don't let your father come between us. I'm a woman in need. And I'm begging you to help me."

12

Kenzi huddled around the small table in her private office with Sharon and Emma. For this meeting, doors were closed. She didn't want to be paranoid, but this case had far too much to do with the people in this building, especially her father.

Emma was being tight-lipped and typically unexpressive. Sharon kept covering her mouth and shaking her head as if she were seeing a joke invisible to everyone else.

"I got to hand it to you, Kenzi," Sharon said. "You have a knack for getting in the middle of situations no one else could even imagine."

"A stepmother is not a blood relative. I'm not violating any rules. And soon, she won't even be my stepmother."

"I wasn't talking about rules. I was talking about common sense."

"Look, she needs help. That's what we do, isn't it? Help women who need it?"

"In the first place, sweetie, she can afford any lawyer in town."

"Except she can't. She hasn't worked for years and has little money of her own."

"Your father isn't going to let her be assigned to a public defender. But if you take the case, you'll get all kinds of flak."

"But not because she's my stepmother. Because I'm a divorce lawyer."

Emma leaned in. "At this point, Kenzi, I think it's time to stop pretending you're just a divorce lawyer. That's not all you do and it hasn't been for a long time. I'm not even sure it's what you do best anymore."

"You don't think I'm out of my depth?"

"I prefer to think you're plumbing new depths. You had a great following as a matrimonial law expert. But divorce is not that complicated and divorce lawyers are everywhere. A lawyer capable of handling first-degree murder charges? Much harder to find. I think you're carving a new niche that could make you a legal superstar." She paused. "I mean, more than you already are."

"I have thirty-three thousand followers on Twitter."

"Keep handling murder cases that get this kind of publicity? You could hit the six-digit numbers. Even seven."

That would certainly please Hailee. And it wouldn't bother her, either. In time, maybe she could stop being a lawyer and become a full-time influencer. Stay at home and make money recommending perfume and lip-glow balm...

"Could we get back to the case?" Sharon asked. "Because this is going to be a lot of work. Tons of research. And I know all too well who usually gets stuck with the research."

Emma seemed taken aback. "I've done plenty of research."

"You do the glamour jobs. The infiltrations. I do the boring grunt work. I've been buried in documents from that fertility clinic, and I haven't seen your pretty little butt helping." She turned. "Kenzi, how can you be sure Candice didn't do it? She did have a motive. Betrayed wife seeks vengeance."

"You think she stalked Venus in a park and practically decapitated her with a mirror? I don't think that's her style."

"That's no one's style," Emma replied. "Unless they have serious mental illness. And this killer clearly did." She paused. "Don't I recall hearing you complain last Christmas that Candice was insane?"

"Because she didn't like stuffing."

"That's not the only time."

"I was using the term in the everyday sense. Not the clinical sense."

Emma shifted gears. "What does Daddy say about this?"

"Nothing so far. But I think I can anticipate an unpleasant future conversation. Which is why I want you two to get to work. There are a million questions I need answered. Who was this Venus? Where did she come from? What was she doing in that park? Spend money. Hire staff if necessary. Let's dig in so deep the boss can't pull us out."

Sharon removed a folder from her tote. "Maybe we should hire a PI. I know some good ones."

"That crossed my mind as well. But let's see what you can learn first. At the very least, that will help you give the investigator more direction."

"Someone needs to talk to this eyewitness. Zelda Lehman. You want me to take that?"

"Would you mind? I need to prep for the bail hearing. After I make some calls on the Battersby case."

"Do you think you have a chance of getting Candice out on bail?"

"Probably not. But she wants me to try. Who could blame her?"

"Okay. I got Zelda. And I've already asked Kate to get me into the scene of the crime. Before everything has been removed."

"Fantastic. Everything going okay there?"

"Like you wouldn't believe. Kate is so patient. And a great cook. And also great at—"

Emma pushed out her hands. "We don't need to hear everything. A simple thumbs up is sufficient."

"Okay. Both thumbs up. Way up. Isn't it time for you to start dating someone, Emma?"

"Why would I want someone in my home making noise and cooking weird foods and watching anime when I want to read?"

That was a strangely specific response.

Sharon piped up. "I did get one bit of info from Kate. They believe that—" She turned her head. "I'm sorry. I just can't say 'Venus' without cracking up. That's so awful. The poor woman is dead."

Emma shook her head. "I know how you feel. How did our highly educated and erudite father end up with someone named Venus?"

"Who works for an escort service."

Emma covered her eyes. "Now we're really tumbling down the rabbit hole."

"Are we talking actual escorts or...sex workers?" Kenzi asked.

"I have no idea," Sharon said. "But I think someone ought to check it out."

"Add it to your list."

"No way. Emma can tackle that one."

Emma uncovered her eyes. "Me? I don't even like thinking about sex. Much less discussing it. Especially when my father is involved."

"I can't do everything. This one is yours."

Emma's head collapsed on the table. "If it turns out Venus was a prostitute, doesn't that give Candice even more reason to be angry? More reason to..."

"Hold her up to the mirror?"

"Stop. More reason to kill her."

"Maybe," Kenzi replied. "But if so, we need to know about it. Preferably before trial."

"Fine, fine."

Kenzi felt a vibration in her pocket. She pulled out her phone. "Yup. Bound to happen."

Sharon grimaced. "Judge?"

"Worse. Daddy."

———

HERA LIT a candle and inhaled the fragrant lavender scent. Seven women stood on the other side of the candle in a rough semicircle, eyes closed, softly humming.

"We remember you, Venus. We will never forget you. And we will never stop loving you. May you rest in peace."

Hera picked up the candle and passed it to Selene, who then passed it to the others. She hoped this didn't look like some weird cult of Satan worshippers or something. She wanted it to seem sincere and reverent. She loved Venus. She wanted to honor her memory. They had lost too many girls in too short a time. This tiny ceremony wasn't much. But at least they were doing something. Literally keeping the flame burning.

The truth was, even as much time as they spent together, she did not know that much about Venus. Was she religious? Did she go to church? If so, Hera never heard anything about it. What were her hobbies? What did she do in her spare time? How could she spend so much time with someone and care so much about them without learning more? All she really knew was that Venus had a brother, and that waste of space had disappeared. One day he's banging down her door and later, when he's needed, he vanishes. No one had appeared to identify or claim the body. Hera had to do all that. Hera paid off the funeral home and, once the medical examiner was finished hacking away at her, paid for her interment.

Venus deserved more. Better.

The police had grilled Hera extensively, obviously frustrated by how little she had to share. The cops had a theory about what happened to her, but it wasn't the only possibility. Hera could think of another that seemed much more likely...

But what she was going to do about it? This could be the solution to her financial woes.

Or it could make her the next target.

"Honey," Selene said. "The wax is dripping."

She snapped out of it. The candle had come full circle, and the wax was dripping down the side. In another moment or so it would burn her hand.

She wiped the side with a cloth, then placed it back in the iron candle holder. "I think it would be nice if some of us shared our memories of Venus. No pressure. Just whatever comes to mind. Happy thoughts. Sweet. Funny. Tell us what she meant to you."

Selene started. "I will never forget this one time, I wasn't feeling great but I had a client coming over and she agreed to take him for me. She didn't even have the right clothes for the occasion, but she didn't let that stop her..."

Good job. Selene understood. Something like this, so unexpected, so violent, reminded them how fragile they were. Selene was trying to make this memorial a success. A brief respite till they climbed back into the trenches. Fancy gowns, fake diamonds, fine dining. But at the end of the day, it was work. Work few of them enjoyed.

What happened to you, Venus? Why did you disappear? Why did you go out into the darkness?

She could have told that lovely girl the darkness would swallow her.

And she couldn't stop worrying about who the darkness would devour next.

———

"*Papi?*"

He sat up straight. He'd been slumped over his desk. His hair was mussed. He looked distraught. As well he might be. Bad enough to have a marriage fall apart. He surely didn't expect to see his wife hauled off in handcuffs.

Kenzi took the seat on the opposite side of his desk. "What's up?"

"I hear through the grapevine that you're representing Candice."

"You don't have to rely on a grapevine. My office is four doors down from yours."

He waved a tired hand. "You know how people like to gossip."

"I do." She drew in her breath. "I know you're going to say I should stay out of this, but—"

"I'm not."

She stopped. "You're not?"

He shook his head. "She's still my wife. I don't want her locked up. But that's what people are saying, isn't it? Someone is spreading the rumor that I asked Shel Harrington to arrest her so I wouldn't have to pay her anything in the divorce."

"But that isn't true."

"Of course it isn't true. I don't want anyone bearing our family name in prison. I'm glad you're on the case."

"And you won't mind me handling a murder even though I'm a divorce lawyer?"

He made a snorting noise. "That ship has sailed. Just get Candice out of jail."

"I will." She inched closer. "You know this means we're going to have to ask...questions. Probably uncomfortable questions. About you and Venus. And Candice."

"The police are coming over this afternoon to do precisely that. You can be next in line."

"Okay."

"But Kenzi...it might be best if you sent someone else on your team to interview me."

"Emma?"

"Maybe someone who isn't my daughter?"

"Sharon."

"Fine. Good. I like her."

"I'll add it to her list."

"I think some of what will have to be discussed might make you uncomfortable." He shifted his weight around. "You know, despite these...horrible circumstances...Venus was not a bad person. She brought me a lot of comfort during difficult times. I want to find some justice for her. But not by locking Candice away."

He seemed sincere. And filled with regret. All at once, she felt like she was the parent comforting a wayward child. "I'll take care of this, *Papi*."

"I know you will." He smiled, a broken, crooked smile. "You've always been the one I can count on. No matter what."

13

The courtroom was hardly packed, but given that this was only an arraignment, Kenzi thought the turnout was impressive. Did this many people really need to hear Candice say she was not guilty? Did they truly care whether she received bail? It was hard to imagine. But for many, television had turned courtrooms into theater. And bail was becoming increasingly controversial. In some jurisdictions, courts were skeptical of money-based bail, which obviously disfavored the poor.

Two officers brought Candice into the courtroom after affording her time to dress and groom. She appeared to be holding up well. To be fair, she hadn't been behind bars that long, but then again, given the pampered life she'd led, this was a major lifestyle adjustment.

At the moment, Candice's primary joy appeared to be that she was reunited with her cellphone. She was staring at the screen assiduously, tapping at the speed of light.

While they waited for the judge to arrive, Kenzi took a seat beside her. "Catching up on your tweets?"

"Just reading. I wondered if people were talking about this case."

Kenzi already knew the answer to that question. "And?"

"They are. They hate me. They assume I'm guilty."

"Ignore it. All they know is what the prosecution has leaked."

"Some of these comments are vile. They're basically death threats."

Murder trials often caught internet attention—but it wasn't as if Candice had been accused of murdering a beloved public figure. She was accused of murdering her husband's so-called escort. If anything, Kenzi would expect some people to be sympathetic. "We'll turn that around when we present our case."

"If I live that long. Can't we do anything? Sue? Force Facebook and Twitter to take down these lies?"

"I guess you haven't heard of Section 230?"

"What's that?"

"Shorthand for a federal law that gives social media platforms immunity from liability for anything their users post. You're not the first to dislike it. Supposed to promote freedom of speech."

"People have a constitutional right to call me"—she glanced back at her phone—"a rich-bitch bimbo from hell?"

"Sadly, yes." Time to change the subject. "How are you holding up? I know how unpleasant jail can be."

"I'm fine. Nice to be back in some clothes that fit." Kenzi had chosen her outfit, a gray dress that looked attractive but not flashy. Given the judge assigned to the case, she thought that was the best way to go. She'd dressed a bit more conservatively than usual herself. "Any chance you brought food?"

"Sorry, no. Not digging the jailhouse menu?"

"It's all carbs. I think most of it came from industrial-size tin cans."

"Sounds terrible."

"And being locked up is so boring you end up eating everything in sight just to have something to do."

"No television?"

"An hour a day."

"Books?"

"Yes, but you don't get to choose. They bring you one. I got a history of flooding in Pennsylvania."

"Sounds riveting. Visitors?"

"Not allowed yet. But I don't know who would come." She sighed.

"Sitting around in a closet-sized cell with an open toilet is enough to make anyone..."

"Stir crazy?"

Candice looked at her. "I was going to say, murderous and insane. But I thought better of it."

Kenzi noticed that the prosecution table was staffed by the district attorney himself. What was the deal? She knew Harrington had a huge staff. Did he not have more pressing matters to handle? Did he want to be on television? An election year loomed on the horizon.

She nodded in Harrington's direction. He motioned for her to come over. They met halfway between the tables.

Harrington was in his late forties, gray at the temples of his perfectly coiffed hair. His suit appeared tailored, an expensive pinstripe. "Is it too soon to discuss a plea?"

"Much."

"You know...you're not going to pull a rabbit out of your hat this time. We have your stepmother dead to rights."

"Heard that before, haven't I?"

He smiled. He was so smooth, so handsome, it required effort to dislike him. But she made the effort. "I understand why you're doing this. Your father is in a delicate position. I told him years ago that marrying that woman was a mistake, but he didn't listen. The heart wants what it wants, I suppose. We have an eyewitness. You know how rare that is, an eyewitness in a murder case? You need to start thinking about your endgame. I won't be vindictive. We can devise a result that benefits everyone. I'll consider it a favor to your father. She has to do time, but it doesn't have to be forever. I can arrange for her to be incarcerated in the most comfortable facility imaginable." He winked. "She can afford it."

Kenzi tried to smile but found those stubborn lips just wouldn't turn up. "When you're ready to make an offer, I'll pass it along. When will you be sending me copies of the relevant evidence? Including exculpatory evidence."

"In due time."

"Meaning, as late as possible?"

He chuckled, then turned back to his table. "My goodness, Kenzi, you are starting to learn how this game is played."

————

ICARUS AWOKE IN AN ALLEY. His throat was dry. His head pounded. He tasted blood.

He didn't know where he was.

It took several minutes, but he finally managed to sit up and take a personal inventory. His clothes were torn. His arm was bruised. He felt sick. And something...something was nagging at his memory. But what was it?

He couldn't remember. Flashes. Bits and pieces. But nothing coherent.

What had happened to him?

He noticed his sleeve was still rolled up. He'd slipped. He'd sworn he'd never touch meth again. But forever is a very long time.

Where was his laptop? He was useless without his laptop...

Slowly but surely, he raised himself to his feet, leaning against the brick wall for support. He was lucky he hadn't been picked up. One more offense for him and he was certain to do time. Probably a long sentence.

Might be the best thing for him.

But how could he help Venus if he was behind bars?

He had to help her. He had to.

Everything that had happened to her—everything—was his fault. He was the one who first introduced her to drugs. He was the one who first introduced her to Hera. And then her life began to disintegrate. And his.

There was still time. There was always time. If he could just keep his head screwed on straight long enough...

He continued leaning against the wall but slowly led himself out of the alley. One step at a time. Eventually, his strength returned. He could do this, he told himself. He could stay clean. He could do what needed to be done. Even if he didn't give Kingsley what he wanted.

Maybe it was time to put others first. And Venus first of all. He could make this right again.

And just about the time he'd convinced himself this day marked a new beginning, he saw the newspaper on the stand at the corner of Charles Street. With its blazing headline. About a murder...

His eyes slowly scanned the page.

And then he screamed.

———

KENZI KNEW Judge Underhill was in his early sixties, but he looked younger. Friends had warned her that appearances could be deceiving. He might look hip, but he was as old school as they came. He always favored the prosecution because, after all, if those defendants weren't guilty, they wouldn't have been charged in the first place, right? Rumor had it he was down on minorities and women in the courtroom, not that he could say that out loud these days. Not great news, since she was not only representing a female but very female and Hispanic herself.

Underhill called the case, read the indictment, and asked the defendant for a plea.

"Not guilty," Candice said, in an impressively firm voice. "To all charges."

"Your plea will be so entered. Are there any other matters that should be taken up at this time?"

Kenzi inched forward. "Yes, your honor. I've submitted a written motion. We respectfully request that the defendant be released on bail pending trial."

"We obviously oppose," Harrington tossed off, as if this matter were barely worth discussing.

"Not obvious to me." Kenzi was careful to look at the judge, though she was responding to Harrington. Counsel were not supposed to address one another during hearings. Only the court. "My client has no prior offenses. Not even a traffic ticket. She's a respected member of the community."

"The charge is first-degree murder," Harrington said, exasperated.

"The court doesn't let murderers run free. Imagine what people would think."

Meaning, imagine what the press will say. "I might remind everyone that my client has not been convicted, so referring to her as a murderer is grossly inappropriate."

"Accused murderer," Harrington said, with a small bow.

"And furthermore, while uncommon, there is precedent in this jurisdiction for allowing those accused of serious felonies to make bail when, as here, they have no priors and pose no threat to society. Surely even the district attorney doesn't believe releasing my client would put the community in danger."

"I can't rule out the possibility."

"The prosecution theory, your honor, which we completely deny, is that the murder was an act of passion against a woman allegedly conducting an adulterous affair with her husband. The likelihood of this happening again is zero."

"Unless she gets angry about something else. Plus, this woman can pay for a plane ticket. She could be in Argentina tomorrow morning."

"She's willing to wear a monitoring anklet," Kenzi responded. "I think that's unnecessary, but she will do it if the court deems it necessary."

"I don't even know if she can make bail of this magnitude," Harrington added. "She and her husband are currently in the middle of a divorce. I don't know why he would pony up for the woman who killed his—" He stopped himself. "For the woman who allegedly killed his lover."

Judge Underhill leaned back. "If the defendant can't make bail—substantial bail—this motion is a waste of time."

He was distracted by an audible stir in the courtroom. Kenzi twisted around.

Her father was in the gallery, on his feet, clearing his throat, his hand raised. "Your honor, I'm Alejandro Rivera. The defendant's husband." Probably an unnecessary introduction. She suspected her father and Underhill had known each other for years. "May I be heard?"

Harrington protested. "Your honor, it's not appropriate to take testimony at—"

Judge Underhill waved him down. "This is an arraignment, not an evidentiary hearing. Let's hear what the man has to say."

"Thank you, your honor." Although Kenzi knew her father could be a great orator when he wanted to be, today he spoke in a quiet, almost hushed voice. Hesitant. A little pleading, even. "Your honor, some of what the district attorney said is true. We are in the middle of a divorce, though I've instructed counsel to hold that in abeyance until this criminal matter is resolved. But I want to assure the court that I can and will meet any bail that is set for the defendant." He paused. "We are none of us perfect. But she's still my wife."

The judge nodded. "Thank you, sir. The court is well aware of who you are and will afford you all due respect in this matter." He redirected his gaze to the litigants. "While bail is disfavored in major felony cases, it is not unprecedented. In this instance, the court notes that the defendant has, until now, been an upstanding member of the community and poses no immediate threat. The court believes the flight risk is small. Therefore, the court sees no reason to charge the taxpayer for the significant expense of incarcerating the defendant until trial."

A small buzz from the gallery, but a large cry of outrage from the prosecution table. "Your honor!" Harrington shouted. Was he playing for the reporters? "This is a first-degree murder charge!"

"Yes. The court thanks you for reminding it of what everyone already knows. Bail is hereby granted. My clerk has the terms." He raised his gavel and pointed. "I'm releasing the defendant on your recognizance, Mr. Rivera. You are responsible, not only for obtaining the bail bond, but also for her conduct. It will be your responsibility to make sure she appears in court as directed."

"I understand," her father said. "Thank you, your honor."

The judge nodded. "I hope we can all move past this as quickly as possible. I will instruct my clerk to set the case down for the earliest possible trial setting. If the parties tell me they need more time, I'll listen. But I think it would be best for everyone involved if this didn't drag out any longer than necessary. Objections?"

Kenzi kept her mouth shut and was glad to see Harrington did the same. She knew she had a lot of work to do, but she worked best under pressure. She preferred to have a deadline.

"Very well. Court is now in recess." Underhill pounded his gavel again and disappeared.

Kenzi turned and faced her father. He'd need to run to the bank and execute the proper guarantees so the bond would issue. But before he left, she wanted to catch his eye.

He didn't move his lips, but his eyes seemed to be asking a question. Okay?

Kenzi replied the same way. Okay, *Papi*. Thank you.

14

During the years she'd worked with Kenzi, Sharon had repeatedly heard lawyers yammering about conflicts of interest. The ethical codes governing what attorneys and judges could and could not do were so complex that at times it made her head spin. But even though she wasn't a lawyer, for the first time, as she approached the meditation labyrinth in Conrad Park, she wondered if there was a conflict of interest rule that applied to legal assistants.

This was not the first time she'd visited the scene of a crime. But it was the first time she'd done so since she started dating one of Seattle's top homicide detectives. Did other people know? Would the young lieutenant standing guard smirk as she passed by? Could she be accused of using her connections to gain a workplace advantage? I mean, these days, you couldn't be too careful.

At any rate, she decided to play it cool, confident, and professional. As the lieutenant waved her past the crime-scene tape, she kept a detached expression on her face. Regardless of what was going on at home, she would conduct herself in a manner becoming to—

"That blouse really makes your eyes pop. Super sexy."

Her head whipped around. "Uhh...what?"

She saw Kate—Lieutenant Corrigan—gazing at her. "Have I mentioned that you have the most gorgeous brown eyes I've ever seen?"

She felt her face heating up. "Aren't you on duty?"

Kate winked. "Doesn't mean I can't appreciate a thing of beauty."

Sharon looked both ways at once. Could anyone hear this? No, of course not. Kate might be a flirt, but she was a smart flirt. She knew how to choose her time and place.

Sharon cleared her throat, trying to act normal. She didn't feel normal. She felt like she wished they were both back at her place...

She fanned her face. Get a grip, girl! You aren't seventeen. Stop acting like a silly schoolgirl. "Anything of interest here?"

Kate led the way. "I would say almost everything here is of interest. Assuming you're interested in bizarre, sick, demented murders."

"And who isn't?" Actually, she wasn't. But she knew that if she learned something useful, it would be worth the visit. Kenzi was already worried about what the DA claimed was a "mountain of evidence" piling up against Candice.

Kate led her to the center of the maze where the corpse had been found. All paths led to this central location. She was relieved to see the body had already been removed.

"I heard she was killed with a mirror. Can that be true?"

"Indeed it can." Kate pointed to a broken mirror resting on a plastic sheet. "Don't get near it. That's Exhibit Number 1. It's a large ornamental mirror. The kind of thing rich people hang in their foyer."

"Where did it come from?"

"Wish we knew. The killer smashed it over the victim's head."

"And that was enough to kill her?"

"The impact itself might've caused a concussion, leaving her unable to defend herself. But what killed her was the glass."

The frame was broken but intact. Almost all the glass was gone. What remained were jagged edges.

She winced. "The killer cut her throat?"

"Big time. It's an old mirror, with heavy leaded glass. Looks like the killer bashed her, then swung the mirror back and forth, using it like a saw to cut her throat."

Sharon felt her stomach drop. "Oh...geez. That must've hurt."

"For a brief time. Severed the carotid artery. She would've bled out —really, spurted out—quickly. She was probably unconscious in fifteen seconds. Or sooner."

"That is so bizarre. Someone will turn this into a murder podcast and make a mint."

Kate smirked. "Only a matter of time, right?"

"Why would the killer use a mirror when there are so many simpler ways?"

"That's the million-dollar question," Kate replied. "And I suspect, when we know the answer to that one, we'll know everything."

"Are you saying you're not convinced Candice did it?"

"I work for the police department. And we have significant evidence pointing her way. But." She paused. "Harrington thought he had to move fast. He knew this would get a lot of press. He wants to run for mayor. He has to seem like he's at the top of his game. I prefer to collect all the evidence before I start making accusations. As far as I'm concerned, we've barely begun to figure out what happened."

"But now, instead of trying to find out what happened, the police are trying to find ways to bolster the prosecution's case."

"Sadly true." Kate looked at Sharon squarely. "But I don't care about that. All I care about is finding out what sick bastard committed this crime. I'm not about to let a killer go free or help convict someone who's innocent. Even if it doesn't please my boss. I don't have to live with him. I have to live with myself."

Sharon turned toward her. "And with me. I hope."

———

ICARUS POUNDED on Hera's door. "Open up. We need to talk."

He heard a thin reedy voice on the other side. "Like all of a sudden you care so much?"

"I've always cared. I can't believe you'd say that."

"That's why you disappeared like a—" Silence.

To his surprise, the door opened. But just a crack. A chain lock held it firmly in place. He could see Hera's round face peering through the gap. "When I needed you—when Venus needed you—you were nowhere to be found."

"I had...a problem. I just found out."

"And now you're no use to anybody. You're a dangerous person. I can't let you near my girls."

"I'm not—I'm not—" He swallowed. "I'm off the junk."

"For how long? Ten minutes? That explains your calm demeanor."

"Have you read the papers?"

"We already held our service. Remembered your sister in our own way."

"But have you read how she was killed? There's going to be an investigation."

A few seconds passed before Hera replied. "Looks to me like the cops have already decided who did it."

"And you believe that?"

Her eyes averted. "Doesn't matter what I believe."

"If they start poking around..."

"Yeah."

Icarus jutted his chin. "They may turn up secrets certain people don't want revealed."

"Is this some kind of threat?"

"I'm just being realistic. All the rocks will get turned over."

"Yours too, I imagine."

"But I have nothing to lose. Especially now that Venus is dead." He paused, his teeth clenched.

Several moments passed. And eventually, he heard a clicking sound. The door opened a bit wider.

"You can come in. But no screaming. Don't scare anybody. Don't try to make it with any of my girls."

"I wouldn't—"

"And don't try to hit them up for money. I want you gone in ten minutes. If not sooner. I don't know if you've noticed, but I don't like you very much. And I don't trust you."

"But we have a lot in common."

Hera looked infuriated. "What are you talking about?"

"I'm talking about certain people that neither one of us ever wants to see again." He stared at her, and finally, the anger fell from his eyes. "And we both miss my sister. I don't want what happened to her to happen to anyone else. Including me."

———

SHARON LISTENED to Kate attentively and tried to act as if she understood. "They've already done a Marquis reagent test on scrapings from the mirror."

"Ohhh. Good..."

"It's a simple spot test that can give investigators some direction. Just a mix of formaldehyde and sulfuric acid. Color change identifies alkaloids and other related compounds."

"And that showed...?"

"Opioids. Can't be sure which. Wide range of possibilities. These days, sky's the limit."

"But if you found that on the mirror..."

"It's entirely possible that the murderer was acting under the influence of...something."

Sharon made a mental note. Kenzi would want to hear about this.

Kate pointed skyward. "See that fancy apartment building? That's where our eyewitness lives. On the third floor."

"Zelda?"

"That's her name."

"She was across the street and then some. And it was a dark night."

"I will admit it's not the best situation. But Zelda says she'd seen Candice before."

"And she just happened to be looking out her window?"

Kate allowed a small grin. "I get the impression Zelda does a lot of that. She's retired, widowed, and may not have the busiest life. So she keeps tabs on the people around her."

"Including anyone who comes to Conrad Park."

"So it seems. There's something else I wanted you to see." Kate put on some plastic gloves, then removed a green scarf from a plastic evidence bag. "This belonged to your client."

"And you found it at the crime scene?"

"No. We found it in her clothes closet."

"I'm not grasping the significance."

"We found a green fiber on the corpse. I brought the scarf out here to see if it matched."

Sharon pulled a face. "You can't possibly trace one thin fiber—"

"We can. Granted the forensic team is still running tests. But they've told me confidentially that by the time of trial they expect to be able to testify that the fiber came from Candice's scarf. Which conclusively puts her at the scene of the crime."

"That still doesn't prove—"

Kate raised a hand and lifted a finger with each word. "Motive. Opportunity. Eyewitness. Forensic evidence. And that's not all we found at her place."

"Don't tease. Tell."

"A big empty space on a wall in the apartment where she's been staying. Where a mirror might've been."

"Or anything else."

"We'll see. Let me tell you what I think. Confidentially. Because I care about you and know you care about Kenzi. Sure, the DA moved too fast, but this time, I think Kenzi has latched onto a loser. Candice is going down for the count. I know how wrapped up you get in these cases. I don't want you to be hurt."

Looking into those eyes, Sharon knew Kate was being absolutely honest. She genuinely cared. Which was new. And refreshing. "I can take care of myself. I'm a big girl."

"I know." Kate reached out and gently touched Sharon's hand. "But you're my big girl. And I'm going to take care of you. Whether you like it or not."

15

Kenzi placed her cellphone on the kitchen table and plopped down into a chair. What a day. Murder and mismatched babies did not go well together. They were making progress on the Battersby case. That family had been so wronged by the fertility clinic it bordered on the inhuman. Bad enough to screw everything up so dramatically. Worse to be obstinate when someone tried to learn what happened to their own offspring. She expected this sort of thing from corporate America. Circle the wagons, admit nothing. But she expected better from a company that was in the business of helping people build families. That put them in a position of intimacy and trust that made this stonewalling reprehensible.

She couldn't afford to be pulled in two different directions. She needed to prioritize. She started a list and tapped it into the Notes app on her phone.

Wait. There was something else she was going to do. Something she forgot when the phone call came. What was it again?

She slapped her hand down. Dinner! She was going to start dinner.

She leapt to her feet, turned—

And saw Hailee walking toward her with a tray. Covered with food.

"Hailee! I was supposed to fix dinner. We were going to spend some time together and...and..."

Hailee nodded. "And we still will. Sit down."

She should be the one saying this. Hailee was out of her wheelchair and, since she was cooking, that had been the case for some time. That simultaneously made her proud—and worried. She knew her daughter was a fighter. She hadn't given in and always pushed herself to do more. But she didn't want Hailee to endanger her health. Certainly not because her mother was obsessing over legal cases.

"Burgers and fries?"

"Comfort food," Hailee said, taking the seat beside her. "Don't worry. They're Impossible burgers."

Telling *her* not to worry? Hailee was the voluntary vegetarian. She'd come to it kicking and screaming. "And...chili fries?"

"Yup. Just beans and Impossible crumbles. Cut the fries with the mandoline. Cooked them in the air fryer so they won't be greasy."

She tried one. Delicious. "This is wonderful. But I feel guilty. I was—"

"Busy," Hailee said, cutting her off. "Sounds like you made a break-through in the Battersby case."

"It's clear the fertility clinic screwed up. We need to track down the parents who got my client's embryo. We've narrowed it down to a few possibilities."

"What if you find the other parents and they won't cooperate?"

"I can probably get a court order." She scooped up some fries. "But I'll try to set up a meeting first. See if we can work it all out peaceably. They must be as anxious as we are to learn the truth about these children."

"You'd think." Hailee took a bite out of her burger. "Mom...you'd tell me if I was adopted, wouldn't you?"

She gave Hailee a long look. "You are not adopted. Trust me. I was in the delivery room."

"But you'd tell me if I were, right?"

"Right. But the whole idea is ridiculous. You weren't switched at birth and there was no in vitro insemination, plus you look just like—"

And then she froze. Because they both knew what she was about to say.

You look just like your father. Who you haven't seen in years.

She wanted to bash herself over the head. Stupid, stupid, stupid...

Her eyes felt watery, but she fought it back. Tears would not help anything.

She stretched her hand across the table. "You've got my eyes."

"I know I do," Hailee said quietly. "And your brains. Thank goodness."

———

SANDY FELT panic rising in his throat. He couldn't escape the feeling that he was a dead man walking.

Sure, he'd escaped the goons so far, but he couldn't hole up forever. And he couldn't make money the usual way if he couldn't hit the usual haunts.

He was trapped like a fly in a spider's web. And the spider was awake. Even if it didn't know exactly where he was. It was only a matter of time. Like a '50s film noir. Like Oedipus trying to escape his fate. Unsuccessfully.

Double fisted. Double feature.

What had he ever done to deserve this? If he had a double, a twin, would he be just as unlucky? Was it impossible to escape a disastrous destiny?

He couldn't hit the singles bars, not with all those Canadian goons on the prowl. He couldn't risk a stroll to the seaport for streetwalkers.

Could he induce someone to come to his apartment? Without meeting them? Even that was risky. But he had to do something. If he could just make the next payment, maybe Kingsley would call off the goons...

Maybe.

His head twitched. Did he hear something? He was almost certain someone was outside the door. And not knocking.

His whole body tensed. Was this it then? Was it over?

He waited. No knock. No doorbell.

He heard a swishing sound. More like a whisper than a word.

Gun with a silencer? Would they shoot him through the door?

He heard soft footsteps moving away.

After enough time passed, he opened the door.

An envelope lay on the floor.

He stared at it for a ridiculously long time.

It wasn't sealed. One folded sheet of paper inside. Two sentences written in undistinguished block letters.

I KNOW WHAT YOU DID. GIVE ME A GOOD REASON NOT TO TELL.

———

KENZI FINISHED HER BURGER. She didn't need such a big meal. She needed to stay lean and mean. But she couldn't help herself. It was delicious.

How had a mother almost completely incompetent in the kitchen ended up with a daughter so talented?

But then, this daughter wanted to go to medical school, and her mother couldn't put on a Band-Aid without messing it up.

The child exceeds the parent. And she couldn't be happier.

Hailee stared at her across the kitchen table. She was obviously anxious to talk about something. "I've been looking into the victim."

"Venus?"

"That's the one. She has a brother."

"How do you know?"

"Found the birth records online. Real name is Edward but according to some posts I read—he goes by Icarus."

"Someone in this circle is big on Greek mythology."

"And Roman. Venus is the Roman goddess of love."

"Is there another sister named from Norse mythology? Maybe Brunhilda?"

Hailee giggled.

"Where is this Icarus? What does he do?"

"He's got a record. Drugs. Two convictions. Nothing too bad yet, but if it happens again, he'll do some serious time."

"If he's been arrested, he must've given the authorities an address."

"And I ought to be able to get that online." Hailee opened her laptop and pounded the keys. "Get this. Even though he's never been to college, apparently Icarus has incredible hacking and coding skills. Used to work for some Canadian firm till about a year ago."

"What happened?"

"Not sure. But he's considered a superstar. In, you know, illegal hacking circles."

"Have you learned anything about my client? Your step-grandmother."

Hailee whistled. "Did I ever."

Kenzi carried her plate to the sink. "Don't be coy. Spill."

"Did you know she grew up in Canada?"

"Yes."

"That she used to be a model?"

"Yes."

"That she had a butt job?"

Kenzi stopped short. "Okay, you got me there. A...what?"

"A Brazilian butt job. C'mon, Mom. They're all the rage."

"How on earth did you learn this?"

"Online, of course. Her doctor has a website page where he shows the happy faces—and butts—of his success stories. I found it using Face2Face. Candice isn't identified by name, but I can tell it's her."

"Face2Face? The program Morgan Moreno helped create? Didn't she shut it down?"

"She discontinued service, but...some of us figured out a way to keep it functioning on our laptops, even without creator support."

"Am I going to learn one day that you're some kind of master cybercriminal?"

Hailee hesitated. "I only use my powers for good."

"That's a relief. Okay, enough work. Bedtime."

"Don't blow off this doctor. I think it may be important."

"I already knew Candice was attentive to her appearance."

"But this is major. Like something only popstars and models and Kardashians get. So why?"

She shrugged. "To please...ugh." Her father. She didn't want to think about it.

"Are you saying my granddad is a butt man?"

"I am not saying anything. Bedtime."

"Will you talk to the doctor?"

"Fine. Maybe. If we have time. We have a lot to do. And many people to interview. Candice is counting on me. And your grandfather also seems very worried about it."

"She is still his wife."

"I suppose." She had a gnawing, nagging sensation in her gut. She didn't know what exactly was causing it. But she felt it, just the same. "I have to get to the bottom of this mess. Candice's life depends on it. And I'm beginning to think my father's life depends on it, too."

16

Emma stared up at the word imprinted on the canopy over the front door: HERA.

In smaller type, on a sign beside the door: Relationship and Counseling Services.

Certainly sounded legit. But Emma couldn't help but wonder, given that this was an escort service and possibly more, how Hera managed to get the clients she wanted with such an innocuous storefront.

Word-of-mouth, she supposed.

Kenzi said Emma was the best person to conduct this interview, since her lack of interest in relationships—that was a nice way of putting it—made her least likely to be swayed by pre-conceived stereotypes. Personally, she thought Kenzi just didn't want to do it. An escort service utilized by their father. No way this was going to be pleasant.

She pushed through the front door. A bell chimed. A moment later a substantial Black woman emerged. She appeared to be in her mid-fifties. Emma wasn't sure what to call the get-up she wore, but it was rose gold and frilly and looked comfortable. She wore the longest false eyelashes Emma had ever seen.

"Are you Emma Ortiz?"

"I am." Emma already felt awkward. Should she offer to shake hands? What did normal people do in a situation like this? Were normal people ever in a situation like this?

"Come inside my office, honey. Take a load off."

She followed Hera behind a curtain to an interior office. No chairs, but a comfortable sofa facing a smaller loveseat. Mannequins dotted the room, all wearing an array of supposedly sexy clothing. Not lingerie exactly, but certainly...comfortable. Like what Hera wore.

"We're trying out some new looks," Hera explained. "Spring lineup. Gotta change it up every now and again, don't you know? Can't be caught wearing the same thing over and over. People get bored."

Emma noted that she said "people." Not "men." "Just as a reminder, I represent Candice Rivera. The woman who's been charged with the murder of your former employee, Vanessa Collins. Venus."

"I know, sweetie. And you're Allie's daughter. What a pleasure to meet you."

"You don't mind talking to me?"

"I talked to the cops. They grilled me for half a day. I'm hoping you won't take so long."

"I can guarantee that." Emma didn't think she'd ever talked to anyone for half a day in her entire life. Maybe not even half an hour.

Hera sat on the sofa, so Emma took the loveseat. Given the environment, she wished she could think of a different name for it.

"Just so you know, honey, Venus was much more than an employee to me. I loved that girl. Loved her with all my heart and soul. I didn't always approve of what she did. But I loved her like a tiger momma."

Emma wondered if she should be taking notes. Probably not. A notepad or tape recorder might inhibit Hera, and in truth her memory was, if not quite eidetic, darn close. "How did you first meet her?"

"Her brother introduced us."

"That would be Icarus?"

Hera appeared impressed. "You've done your homework. The cops didn't know about him."

"Why did he bring his sister to your attention?"

"She was looking for work. He was helping her find something. They were both barely scraping along. They'd lost their parents. He'd lost his job. And he had some other problems."

"What kind?"

"The kind that goes down a hole in your arm. And results in every other kind of problem imaginable. They were practically starving when he came to me."

"Maybe this would be a good time to ask...what exactly you do here."

Hera gave her a coy look. "You saw the sign on the door, didn't you?"

"Yes. But I think there may be more to it."

"There always is. We do provide relationship and counseling services. But of a specialized nature. These days, you have to compete if you want to stay in business, don't you know? My main income stream comes from our escort service. We provide companions to well-to-do men."

"Forgive me for being blunt, but as I'm sure you know, in some quarters, 'escort service' is a euphemism for...sex work. Prostitution."

"And you think I'm a madam? Hera's Best Little Whorehouse in Seattle?"

"Well..."

"You're wrong. Mind you, if two people who meet through my service hit it off, they may decide to become intimate. But that's not what I'm selling."

"Maybe you should explain what you are selling."

Hera drew in her breath. "Let me give you the short version. About twenty years ago, after a series of failed relationships, I realized it had been more than three years since I'd been out on a date. And I started to wonder what my problem was. You ever been on a dry spell like that?"

Emma felt her face coloring. Technically, she'd never been on a date at all. And she was divorced. "Sure. Who hasn't?"

"Right. Although if I may say so, a change of wardrobe would do you wonders."

"Uh...what?"

"Heavens to Betsy. What's a pretty girl like you doing decked out in black? Men like a little color. Try some red. Maybe some mascara to highlight those gorgeous eyes of yours. And ditch the blunt cut. Please tell me you don't trim your own hair."

"Well..."

Hera covered her face. "Oh my goodness."

Emma cleared her throat. "Getting back to your story..."

"Right. So anyway, I'm not exactly shy, as you may have noticed. I have no problem taking the first step. Asking the man out, you know? But I never did. And eventually I realized...I never spent much time looking at men."

"You don't like men?"

"That wasn't it. I'm definitely straight. I started thinking back to when I was a kid. I'd hang with my peeps, you know? Me and my girl-friends. And they'd talk about how some boy was hot or had a chiseled jaw or a fabulous tooshie or whatever. I never thought that way. I never even noticed." Her eyes glistened. "That's when I realized I was demisexual."

"You were..." Emma liked to think she was liberal, tolerant, and well-read. But she had no idea what Hera was talking about.

"Demisexual, hon. It means I don't get turned on by physical appearances. I'm only attracted to someone after I develop an emotional connection to them. That's why I wasn't coming onto strangers. I mean, women talk about liking a man who makes them laugh, but that usually comes after they've been attracted to his floppy hair or washboard abs, right? Not for me. I liked guys who were fun, friendly, smart, interesting. Well-read, well-educated. Considerate. Liked to do the same things I like to do." She paused. "But that's much harder to find. And you're not likely to stumble across it in a singles bar."

Emma had no doubt about that. Not that she'd ever been to a singles bar.

"I thought back over my entire life and saw the same pattern. I liked kissing, but I never initiated it. I'd rather have a seven-hour conversation with someone than sex. Don't get me wrong. Sex is fun. For a few minutes. But it's no substitute for the stimulation I get from basking in the glow of someone whose personality turns me on. When

I meet someone new, I don't inventory their body parts. I want to see what's going on behind their eyes. And that takes a while."

Emma was beginning to connect the dots. "That's why you started this escort service."

"Exactly. I mean, think about how most people meet these days. In a bar. Or on some dating app. Are we really surprised when it goes sour? By definition, those relationships are initiated by appearances. I started a business that would allow busy people of means to spend time with someone in a low-pressure yet meaningful way. Business was slow at first, but once the buzz started, once we got people past their stereotypical assumption that 'escorts' was code for 'hookers,' it started catching on. Our customers love what we do."

"It is a brilliant idea. And something this world needs."

"I've found my calling. I'm like that lady in *Hello, Dolly!* I spread happiness by matching people up."

"Even married men?"

Hera leaned back. "I didn't know your father was married when he first contacted me. But we've had other men who were separated or estranged and I don't think it's my job to decide whether they should be dating. I'm not the moral judge of the universe. Then again, this isn't Taylor Petrie."

"Where he also went looking for women."

"But I belive he and Venus made a real connection. An emotional connection. They both loved Beethoven, did you know that? And they both loved Bollywood musicals. One thing led to another. Seemed like they were meeting all the time." She sighed. "And then your step-mama got involved."

"How did Candice find out?"

"I don't know. Can't you ask her? She's your client."

Presumably. But it never hurt to get a second opinion. "What do you think happened to Venus?"

"I wish I knew. She was such a warm, loving person. You meet her and two minutes later you love her, you know? That kind of gal."

"You don't have any clues about what happened? Hints? Wild speculations?"

Hera paused a moment, as if lost in thought. "I did have some indication that she might be having some money problems. She asked me once if I knew where she could score some money quickly. She wasn't panhandling. Just asking for ideas. Might have been asking on behalf of someone else."

"What did you suggest?"

"If I knew how to make money fast, I'd be doing it. I love this business I built, but it's not a get-rich-quick scheme. Even with clients like your daddy." She paused. "Come to think of it, given how well Venus and your daddy were getting along, you'd think he'd be the one she'd ask about money, wouldn't you?"

"Maybe she thought it would spoil the relationship. He'd think she was just a gold digger."

"Or maybe she asked and he said no. She was worried about something. I worried about her, those last few days. I thought she was in trouble. We lost another girl not too long before her, so I was taking all the warning signs seriously."

"What were the other warning signs?"

"Constantly checking her phone. Jumping when the doorbell chimed. I tried to play it cool. I thought we were good enough friends that she'd tell me in time. But...she ran out of time."

"I'm sorry. This must be very hard for you. Especially...given how it ended."

Hera's head drooped. "I knew she loved that meditation maze. Prayer maze, she called it. She found it calming. Walk the path, say a little prayer. Try to clear the clutter, you know? Who would've ever thought the thing she did for her mental health would end up being the death of her?" Hera pressed her hand against her forehead. "I hope she went quickly, before she had a chance to see how that maze betrayed her. She deserved so much better. That killer didn't just take her life. He took her safe place. I can't imagine anything more horrible than that."

17

K enzi had heard about Kelly's, but she'd never been there. Not because she was afraid of it. Not really. She just had no desire to visit. She wasn't sure why anyone would want to visit the joint that had a rep for being the #1 Sleaziest Dive Bar in Seattle—a city with a lot of competition in that category.

Not only did the storefront look like it should be raided (if not condemned), but also there was an actual paddy wagon parked across the street. She hoped that was just for atmosphere.

She opened the door and was inundated with waves of sensory impressions, all of them unpleasant. She was okay with the shamrocks and leprechauns and other faux-Irish accoutrements. She expected that in a place called Kelly's. But not the cheap rotting décor, the scruffy clientele. The aromatic blend of urine and vomit.

She hadn't taken two steps inside before the noisy bar was blanketed with a chilling silence. Heads turned.

They were all looking at her.

Why? Because she was halfway presentable? She'd made a point of leaving the designer jeans and Chanel Classic Flap purse at home. Was it just that her jeans had no holes? That she didn't smell like a sewer?

This neighborhood, Belltown, used to be the city's Skid Row, filled with junkies and hookers and panhandlers and miscreants. The park across the street was once an open-air drug marketplace. Now it was a doggie park. Slums were being rebuilt or replaced with tower apartments and fashionable restaurants. The area was getting upscaled—except here at Kelly's, the gnarly needle in a grim haystack.

Cracked vinyl barstools. Nicotine-stained walls. Reeking bathrooms. On the other hand, judging by the chalkboard behind the bar, the prices were reasonable. Maybe that explained the popularity. That, plus the fact that it was one of the few places in town that apparently still allowed patrons to smoke.

She continued strolling slowly down the main aisle, pretending she didn't feel the eyes following her.

"You the lawyer?"

Couldn't he have just called her name? She walked in the direction of the voice.

He looked whippet-thin, with straggly hair and a mountain-man beard. Even in low lighting, he had a pale, almost ghostly pallor. "You Icarus?"

He nodded.

She slid into the booth facing him. "You're Venus' brother?"

The mention of her name made him wince. "I was. Am."

"I'm sorry for your loss."

"Everyone is. But she's still gone."

Kenzi didn't take it personally. Platitudes probably seemed very hollow when you were grieving the loss of someone so close. She couldn't imagine how she'd react if she lost Emma. "You're two years older?"

"I'm her big bro. I was supposed to take care of her. That turned out well, huh?"

His head hung low, long hair drooping on both sides of his face, almost obscuring it. She detected major sorrow, more than his crappy drink could quell. But despite feeling sympathy, she couldn't escape the sense that there was something...dangerous about him. Something not quite right. "You were close to your sister?"

"We didn't have anyone else. Our parents died when we were young. I was eight. She was six."

"Wow. That's rough. I'm...sorry." Every word that came to mind seemed woefully inadequate. "What happened?"

"They left a fire burning on the hearth and went to bed. Gas leaked into their bedroom. Next morning, they were dead. Overnight, we became orphans."

"How did you survive?"

"Wasn't easy. Foster homes. Youth houses. Juvenile hall, for me. They constantly split us up, moved us. But we managed to stay in touch with one another. We had to. One set of foster parents were drunks. Nice people. But drunks. The next set couldn't pay their own bills, much less ours. When I turned sixteen I ran away."

"But you looked after your sister."

"Tried. Never had enough money. Couldn't seem to get ahead. I took a free course at the library and learned I had a talent for computer programming. But that just created more problems, not solutions."

"I hear you helped Venus find her...job."

"You mean with Hera? You don't have to be coy about it. I know what she did." He shrugged, trying to act nonchalant, but it wasn't convincing. "We had to eat. We needed a roof over our heads. And we were both developing...habits."

"She went to work as an escort, and the money bought your drugs?"

His eyes flared. "It wasn't just me. We were just trying to survive!"

Kenzi bit her tongue. She shouldn't be judgmental. "Hera trusted you enough to take your recommendation?"

"All Venus needed was an introduction. She's—she was—wonderful." His voice choked. "Did you ever see her? When she was alive?"

"No."

"Pity. She had a beauty within her. Not the kind of girl who would stop traffic, but she had an inner glow. Everyone wanted to be with her."

Including her father. "She must've had many clients."

"She did. Lots of repeat customers. Guys couldn't get enough of her. And as a result, some women couldn't stand her."

"Like Candice Rivera?"

"That's your stepmom, right?"

"Yup."

"You have any idea your daddy was messing around?"

"Nope."

"I bet your stepmom did. And I bet she didn't like it."

"I don't believe she killed your sister. Doesn't make sense. Even if she wanted to kill your sister, why do it in the middle of a park?"

"Don't know. Someone had a reason."

"And why use a mirror? Does that make any sense to you?"

He shrugged. "I've spent a lot of time with whacked-out women. Unfortunately. And you know what I've learned? Whacked-out women do whacked-out things."

Kenzi tried to mask how offended she was. "Did Venus have any other enemies? Maybe co-workers?"

"The other girls at Hera's place loved her."

"There must've been someone who was jealous. And there must've been other client wives. Or spurned suitors."

"Guys adored her."

"There's always an exception."

He did not immediately deny it. And that alone was a sort of answer. "I did hear that she got tangled up with someone...bad."

"Like who?"

"I don't know. She was seeing someone regularly. Someone who made weird requests. Had to have everything his way. Do it here, do it like this, that sort of thing."

"What was his name?"

"She never said. She might not have known."

"I need something to track. One name might lead to another."

He thought for a moment. "Does the name 'Kingsley' mean anything to you?"

"No."

"He probably knows you."

Something about the way he said it gave her a chill. "Why?"

"'Cause you were messed up with that Seattle Strangler business."

For a lowlife drug addict mourning the loss of his sister, this guy was remarkably well informed about her work. "And you think this Kingsley was involved with that?" After that case ended, the police shut down a Canadian sex trafficking outfit, but never learned who was behind it. If this was the guy...he'd be a ruthless and dangerous mob kingpin. "Does this case have something to do with sex trafficking?"

"I don't think so. But Kingsley has his hands in many fires. It could be something else just as bad. Or worse."

Worse than sex trafficking? She didn't even want to know. Except if she was going to help Candice, she had to know. "Where do I find this Kingsley?"

"You don't."

"But if I—"

"Listen to me. You don't want to and you couldn't find him if you did. Forget about it."

"Who works with Kingsley? There must be a...man on the street."

"You're getting into treacherous waters."

"Meaning you're not going to help me?"

"Consider it a favor. I know he's looking for me. Which is why I wanted to meet here."

"I have an obligation to my client. I have to find out who's behind this."

"You won't. These people are too smart. The cops couldn't find him and neither will you."

"Does this Kingsley have something to do with your sister's murder? Because if he did, I would think you'd want to go after him."

His voice broke, and all at once, tears streamed from his eyes. "Do you have any idea how much I loved my sister? Do you have any idea how much time and money I spent trying to protect her? And now—now she's gone." He covered his face. "If there was any way to get these people, I would. But there isn't."

He moved his hand and gave her a fierce look. "And if you keep poking your nose where it doesn't belong, you won't help your client. You'll just end up dead."

———

CROZIER WAITED on the docks near South Seaport in a secluded area. The night was dark and he didn't expect anyone could see them, not even FBI agents with night-scope cameras. Or competitors with sniper rifles.

Kingsley left his yacht and strolled toward him, big smile and extended hand. If you didn't know better, you'd think he was an insurance salesman. "Greetings, my friend."

Crozier took his hand. "Good to see you." He still couldn't place Kingsley's accent. He knew the man lived in Canada, but he clearly did not originate there.

They walked down the dock, sticking to the shadows. "Thank you for coming. We only have a few moments, so I will get directly to the point. It is not safe for me to be here."

Because of the murder? Because he feared he was being watched? Police? FBI? He decided not to ask. "It would be safer to meet in my office. I could get you in and out—"

"Too dangerous. There can be no connection between me and... what happened."

"You mean what happened to my colleague's young wife?"

Kingsley arched an eyebrow. "Colleague and arch-competitor, eh? I think your competition will soon disappear. You will be the Divorce King. A useful cover, no?"

Yes. "He might bounce back. No one's connecting him to the crime. I mean, it's his fault. But he didn't wield the mirror."

"He will not recover. He will fade away, like all tarnished heroes. But I am not concerned about him. I'm concerned about his daughter."

"Kenzi?" He assumed Kingsley wasn't referring to Emma. "Nothing to worry about there."

"So you say. But she was the one who discovered the so-called Slayer and the connection to my operation."

"She didn't so much solve it as...stumble across the solution."

"She ended a very profitable arrangement. I've had to abandon that income stream."

"No more trafficking?"

"I'm pursuing new opportunities. And that is because of your little lawyer friend. I told you to stop her."

"Tried to buy her off. Didn't work."

"I can think of a more expedient solution."

They reached the end of the dock. Kingsley pivoted and returned the way they came. Crozier suspected that once they returned to the yacht, the conversation would be over. "Let's not be extreme. That would only attract more attention and suspicion."

"If she learns the truth, she could destroy another income stream. I cannot afford that." He jabbed Crozier in the chest. "You are supposed to make sure these things do not happen."

"I'm doing my best—"

"That is not good enough!" He leaned into Crozier's face, almost growling. "You will end this threat. One way or another."

Crozier felt his throat go dry. "What do you want me to do?"

"First, find Sandy."

"I'm trying. He's hiding."

Kingsley shoved him so hard he fell backward into a post, driving splinters into his hand. "I do not want to hear about trying. Go to his office. Talk to his friends. Get it done!"

"Yes. I will. Of course."

"Do not allow this to interfere with my business."

Crozier pressed his bleeding hand against his mouth. "I'll see to it. I will."

"Sandy can find the brother. And make sure your friend's wife is convicted."

"I can't control the entire judicial—"

"You have connections. Use them!" His fists clenched.

"I will. You know I will."

"Make sure you do. Because if I lose more business, I will have to start making some cuts. Starting with your head."

———

KENZI FINISHED TAKING down all the names Icarus could give her. It wasn't much, but maybe if they turned over every rock he threw their way, eventually they'd get lucky.

The smoke and stench of this bar was making her nauseated. She would be glad to be out of here. "Thank you for your help. I appreciate you talking to me."

"If you find out who killed my sister, I want to know about it. Immediately."

"Understood." Her phone vibrated. She took a look. "Pardon me. I need to take this." She raised the phone to her ear. "Yes?"

"Kenzi? Shel Harrington. Sorry to bother you. But you need to get to my office right now."

"But it's—"

"Hey, you were the one complaining about us not sharing evidence in a timely fashion. So I'm calling you right off the bat. Come take a look."

At the least convenient time possible. Maybe that was part of his plan. "What could be so important that—"

"It's big, Kenzi. And ugly. And conclusive. Sorry to be the bearer of bad tidings, but we have discovered some shocking evidence. Of the ugliest possible kind."

"Shel, is this about the fiber? Because I already—"

"No, Kenzi." She heard a soft chuckle on the other end of the line. "This is about the sex tape."

18

Kenzi felt completely torn. She did not want to make this visit. And yet she had to make this visit.

Was it her imagination, or was her job beginning to seriously suck?

Maybe taking this case was a mistake. At any rate, she needed to get some help. Time was running out. Much too quickly.

The man at the front desk of the DA's office took her directly to Harrington's private suite. He greeted her, then closed the door behind them.

"I just want to emphasize," Harrington said, "that I do not have to do this. I could wait a good long time before I produced this. I'm giving it to you now because of my respect for the rules and my respect for your father."

"Where did you find it?"

"Email attachment. Anonymous source."

"And you trust that?"

"See for yourself. It is what it is. And...quite explicit."

"You can see both parties?"

"The camera is shooting over the top of a chair. The woman is in his lap. You can see everything about her, including her face, but precious little of him."

"So she could be with—"

"It isn't your father. Not nearly tall enough."

Kenzi squinted. "You've got a recording of Venus having sex with someone other than my father? Who cares?"

Harrington held his hands in the air, as if restraining her. "Hold on there. You're making some big assumptions."

"You said you had a sex tape."

"'Tape' may not be the right word. Video. Probably shot with someone's phone."

"Maybe Venus liked to keep souvenirs."

"You need to watch the recording." He swiveled his computer monitor around so she could see. "You've got this completely wrong."

"How so?"

"We don't know who the man in this video is." He paused, drew in his breath. "But there's no question about the identity of the woman having sex in front of the camera. It's not Venus. It's your stepmother. Candice."

———

CROZIER LEANED close to the third-floor apartment door. "I know you're in there. Open up!"

He did know Sandy was in there. And he also knew Sandy wouldn't be inclined to open the door. Was he capable of getting in anyway? Of course. But he didn't want to attract too much attention or instigate a call to the police. Or cause any permanent destruction.

He could hear stirring on the other side. Maybe, just maybe, that idiot would find the inner strength to let him in.

Crozier's voice dropped several notches. "I'm not going to kill you."

Not now, anyway.

The door opened, just a crack. Sandy's face appeared. He looked haggard. He obviously hadn't shaved for days. "What?"

"I need to talk to you."

"How do I know you won't kill me? The last time—"

Crozier pointed at himself, his two-thousand-dollar suit. "Do I look like an enforcer?"

"Someone has been trying to kill me. Someone working for you."

"If that were my goal, I would've already done it."

Apparently, that argument was persuasive. The door opened. He stepped inside.

The apartment looked like a rat's nest. How long had it been since Sandy went outside? Too long. "Look, you don't need the exposition, right? You already know what's going on."

"I know Kingsley put a hit out on me."

"Do you blame him? You owe a fortune."

"I've been paying it back."

"You've been paying off the interest. And now you're not even doing that."

"I've had an...interruption of services."

"Do you think Kingsley cares?"

"I can't give him anything if I'm dead."

"It would set an example."

"I just need more time. You know what happened. I lost Venus. I've lost Candice. And I can't go outside without some punk trying to kill me."

"Cry me a river. There's always a way. If you want it badly enough."

"What the hell is your interest, anyway? Haven't you already made a fortune, profiting off people's marital problems?"

Crozier smiled thinly. "I've had some setbacks. Made some poor investments. Which have required extraordinary measures."

Now it was Sandy's turn to smile. "You're into Kingsley, too. You're into him bad."

"That's neither here nor there. You have a debt. You need to settle it."

"Don't you think I want to? Do you think I enjoy living like this? Running, hiding? Always wondering if a hitman is hovering over my shoulder?"

Crozier came a few steps closer. "I can offer you a way out."

"You can?"

Crozier laid a hand on his shoulder. "We need help with this... current situation. If you're willing to assist, Kingsley will be grateful."

"He'll erase the debt?"

"He won't kill you. Do we have a deal?"

"Depends. What—"

Crozier's eyes burned a trail into Sandy's. He squeezed his shoulder. Hard. "Do we have a deal?"

Sandy swallowed. His head trembled. "What do you want me to do?"

———

KENZI BARRELED into Candice's apartment. She didn't care whether the woman liked it or not.

"Kenzi, is something—"

"Why the hell didn't you tell me you were having an affair too?"

"You heard what your father said at the settlement conference. I never denied it." Candice was obviously surprised, but she handled herself with an unexpected degree of calm. "What brings this on?"

"I saw it played out in living color. On the DA's computer monitor."

"Oh. They found the recording. I thought they might."

"Why would you make a sex tape?"

"I didn't. It was done without my knowledge. But I've seen it."

"You knew about it? But you didn't bother to mention it to me? Do you know how stupid that is?"

Candice lowered herself onto her sofa. "I'm sure you realize this is...very embarrassing for me."

"If you didn't make the video, who did? The man? Who is he?"

Candice drew in her breath. "Sandy."

"Sandy who?"

"I don't know his last name."

Kenzi rolled her eyes. "Mother of God. This just gets worse and worse. What, did you meet him at a singles bar?"

Candice looked up tentatively but didn't speak.

"Oh my God. You did meet him at a singles bar."

"I was lonely. Depressed. I didn't know what to do."

"So you had sex with a random stranger."

"I didn't know—" She breathed in short quick gasps. "He was kind to me. I was vulnerable."

"You had a one-night stand."

"Well..."

"More than one night?" Kenzi slapped her hand against her forehead. "I cannot believe this. I cannot *believe* this. You have seriously damaged your case."

Candice seemed puzzled. "I would think this would help."

"How would the DA getting your sex tape help?"

"Obviously, I was retaliating...in a different way. You should argue that I'd already exacted my vengeance against your father. I had no need to resort to murder. No justification, for that matter. Since I had also strayed."

"I get your point. But Harrington will use the video to trash you. To shame you. To prove you're a woman of bad character. Someone the jury wants to convict. It doesn't prove you committed murder. But there's no way to undercut the damage it will cause when a jury sees it. It was like watching a porno. You were really...emoting. Why would Sandy make this video?"

"I don't know. So he could relive the experience later? On his own?"

Kenzi pulled a face.

"Come to think of it," Candice said, "he was very particular. Manipulative. Always wanted to do it the same way. In that chair. Me on top. Facing him."

"Facing the camera."

"At the time, I just thought he was a control freak..."

"But now you realize he was positioning you for your closeup."

Candice sighed. "Can't you keep the recording out of court? It's not like it's a confession."

"I can try. But I don't know if the judge will suppress it. And even if it doesn't show up at trial, the press will get it. Or the internet. No one can keep secrets today. Which is why it's so important that you not keep secrets from your lawyer!"

Candice bit down on her lip. "Are you...are you going to quit?"

Kenzi paced back and forth across the living room. The thought had occurred to her. It would make her life so much easier...

But if nothing else, her father was counting on her.

"No, I'm not quitting. But if I ever find out again that you lied, or held back something important, I will. Understand? This is not an idle threat. I don't care if it's in the middle of the trial. I will leave you high and dry."

"I get it."

Kenzi closed in on her. "Is there anything else?"

"I—I don't—"

"Be sure. Don't lie to me. Tell me everything."

"I...take pills."

Great. "What kind? Ecstasy? Uppers? Downers?"

"Of course not. Prescription drugs. I have anxieties. They flare up sometimes."

"What exactly are you taking? The DA could use this to suggest that you're an unreliable witness."

"I take a mild antipsychotic. And an antidepressant."

Not great news, but at least they came from a doctor. "Fine. What else?"

"That's all there—"

"Think harder!" Kenzi shouted. "I want to know all the secrets."

Candice covered her face with her hand. Tears welled up in her eyes. "I met her. That woman. I knew her."

Kenzi's eyes bulged. "The victim? Venus? You met her?"

Candice nodded.

"You told the police you'd never seen her."

"I was...confused."

"That's not the word they'll use. Oh my God. Why did you meet her?"

"I wanted to see for myself. I wanted to know what my husband found so appealing."

"Where did you meet her?"

Candice drew in her breath. "We met more than once. Including... at that park. In the meditation maze."

Kenzi grabbed her by the shoulders. "You told the cops you'd never been there."

"I was scared. I wouldn't survive in prison..."

Kenzi wanted to pound her head against the wall. "You have torpedoed your own case. With lies and...and stupidity."

Tears trickled through Candice's fingers. "I'm sorry. I'm so so sorry. Is there some way I can make up for this?"

"No more lying!" Kenzi continued pacing, trying to map out a plan of action. "I'll call the DA. Explain that you were...confused. Better that we admit you didn't tell the truth now than watch them try to use this to impeach you at trial. I mean, they *will* use it to impeach you at trial, but at least we can say you already came clean."

"Whatever you think. Kenzi. I'm sorry I didn't tell you everything. But I did not kill Venus."

"So you say."

"We can still win this. Can't we? There's still hope?"

Kenzi grabbed her satchel and started for the door. "I don't know what to think anymore. Ask me in a week. I've got to start the damage control. And I've got a ton of work to do. We're going to need the best defense of all time. And right now—we've got nothing."

19

Emma crossed the street from Conrad Park to the apartment building. Like many of the older buildings in this part of Seattle, it was showing its age—crumbling brick, worn masonry, brown ivy that looked more dead than alive. Still, it was no slum, and living here would require some dependable income.

She didn't have to be buzzed inside. No one monitored the elevator bank. She rode to the third floor and rang the bell for Apartment 38.

The woman who opened the door wore a draped kaftan that masked her shape and added splashes of color to her otherwise gray appearance. She was at least sixty—probably older—wore too much makeup, and looked as if she'd been crying.

Emma tried to smile. It did not come easily, but she'd learned that people were more receptive to strangers who appeared friendly. "Hi. I'm Emma Ortiz. We talked on the phone."

"Of course. I'm Zelda Lehman. Please come in."

The apartment furnishings were adequate, if dated. The living room looked starved for attention. Emma took a seat on the sofa facing a large window that, if she had her bearings right, provided a lovely view of the park. Beside the window, she saw a small table and chair. The table bore an Apple MacBook Air. Hard to tell from this distance, but she thought it displayed a YouTube page.

"I've already spoken to the police. Repeatedly." Zelda let out a small groan. "I suppose you know how that is."

She had no idea, but it seemed smarter to appear sympathetic. "Repetitive?"

"Intentionally. You tell your story to one person. Then an hour later, they want you to tell it to someone else. I suppose they're looking for inconsistencies, or hoping you'll recall something new the fourth time around."

"Or hoping they can subtly shape your testimony with cues and prods and suggestions."

"I noticed some of that too."

"Can you tell me what you saw?"

"Your client emerged from the maze. There are trees that block the view when someone is in the maze. But I have a clear view of anyone going in or out."

"And you saw Candice coming out?"

Zelda nodded. "Covered with blood."

"It was dark. How can you be sure it was blood?"

"What else would it be? She was wiping it on her clothes, trying to get it off her hands. Like Lady Macbeth. Very upset. Running."

"Did you know her?"

Her voice rose almost an octave. "I don't know that I'd say I knew her. I knew of her, certainly. She frequented the apartment next to mine." Zelda pointed. "And sometimes she could be rather loud."

"You indicated to the police that you believed she was engaged in... amorous activities." Emma wanted to slap herself in the face. Why had she said that? This woman wasn't her mother. "Sex, to be specific."

"I don't know what else it would be. So much battering and banging. Sounded very violent."

"Who was she with?"

"I don't know his name."

Emma had already checked the records. Whoever leased that apartment did not use his real name. And when she knocked on the door, no one answered. "Can you tell me anything about him?"

Zelda thought for a moment. "He seems very bossy."

"How so?"

"Oh, you know. Sit here. Do this. They argued sometimes."

"You seem to have heard a lot."

Zelda laughed. "I'm not a nosy neighbor. But these walls are old and thin. And I'm home most days, now that I'm retired. And widowed. Worked as a hair stylist for more than thirty years. I think I've earned a little relaxation."

Emma's eyes roamed around the apartment. She noticed a liquor cabinet not far from the window. Looked like a gin bottle at the forefront. "Had you perhaps been drinking that night?"

Zelda's head pulled back. She looked offended. "Why would you ask that?"

"Just covering all the bases." She nodded toward the liquor. "I can see that you do indulge on occasion."

"That's mostly for guests. Would you like something?"

"I'm good, thanks. But I'm concerned about the combination of alcohol and darkness. And police pressuring you to say what they want you to say."

"I saw that woman leave the maze. Your client. Candice. There's no question about it. None whatsoever. I'd seen her picture in the paper. An article about her husband and that online dating service."

"You seem to spend a lot of time looking out your window."

"I suppose that's true."

"Any particular reason?"

"Only the obvious. I don't have that much to do here. It's a gorgeous view. Best thing about this apartment, really. The park, the trees, the moon. Wonderful when I have the tingles."

Emma tried not to react. "The...tingles?"

"You know."

"Pretty sure I don't."

"The tingles. ASMR."

"Still don't know what you're talking about."

A sly grin crossed Zelda's face. She walked to her laptop. "Then let me inform you. But prepare yourself. This is going to blow your mind."

————

KENZI SAT at a table in the coffeehouse drumming her fingers. She supposed she should be more patient. Sure, he was ten minutes late. But ten minutes wasn't that long a time in the larger scheme of things. Problem was, she didn't have the benefit of the larger scheme of things. All she had was a ticking clock ready to explode like a time bomb. The suppression hearing was imminent and she still didn't have a decent argument. Shortly thereafter they would begin the trial. If she was going to slow the prosecution juggernaut, she needed more information.

She supposed there were worse things than a few extra moments in a coffeeshop. Seattle was Coffee City, after all. Birthplace of Starbucks and Seattle's Best and several others. But rarely did she indulge herself with a few quiet moments savoring the aroma. She preferred something dark and rich so she could really taste the beans. She didn't use cream or milk or mocha or any of that kid stuff. If she wanted dessert, she'd go to Baskin-Robbins. If she was going to drink coffee, she wanted to taste the coffee.

A few minutes later, a tall man wearing a windbreaker and T-shirt entered. He scanned the shop, then came straight toward her.

"Hi." He extended his hand. "Alexander Grant. Apologies for being late."

She pointed toward the chair on the other side of the table. "No worries." She was too stressed to create stress, if that made any sense. Plus, the man was darned handsome. Cute, even. Trim but muscled. Obviously spent some time in the gym. Glasses. Beard. Great hair. Dressed well, too. In other words, her kind of guy. "Do you go by Alex?"

"Or Alexander. Whatever."

"My father has the same name. Well, the Spanish version. Alejandro. I'll call you Alex, if you don't mind. Just to avoid confusing myself."

"All good. Thanks for meeting me. I wasn't sure how you'd react when I called."

"As it happens, I was thinking about hiring a private detective, so this was major serendipity."

"One sec." He walked to the counter and placed an order. Dark. No froth, no cream. Almost exactly what she'd ordered. "Okay. I told you on the phone what I've been doing."

"Investigating the same case."

"Right. I can't say I've found much. But I do know a few things that might be of use to your client."

Kenzi felt a wave of relief rush through her body. She knew she didn't have enough to get Candice off the hook. Anything he brought her would be a godsend. "May I ask what inspired you to start investigating?"

"Oh. I'm sorry, I thought I told you. Venus hired me."

"Venus? The—The—"

"Yeah. The victim."

"You knew her?"

"I did. One moment she's talking to me every day, and the next, she's dead. In the most bizarre way imaginable."

"Do you have any insight on that? The mirror business, I mean?"

"No clue. Seems like a nutty way to kill someone. I'm a Zen Buddhist. We use mirrors as a metaphor for the mind that becomes unclean if untended, just as mirror collects dust. Some Buddhists ritualistically wash mirrors. The mind is also like a mirror because whatever comes before it is reflected within it."

"This killer was using the mirror as a deadly weapon, not a metaphor. Did you have any idea Venus was in danger?"

"Not to that degree. She thought someone was watching her. Maybe following her."

"Why would anyone be watching her?"

Alex shrugged. "Don't know."

"Venus must've had some theories."

"She really didn't. She speculated it might have something to do with her work. Like a jealous girlfriend or something. A customer who wanted more than she cared to give. But she had no names. It was just guesswork."

"Any other theories?"

"She had a brother."

"Yeah. I've talked to him."

"Did you ask him about the Canadian syndicate?"

"He mentioned it. Why?"

"Apparently Icarus is good with computers and he had a job working for a small outfit the syndicate controls."

She hadn't gotten that out of her interview. "He's in league with the mob?"

"It's possible he didn't know about the mob connection when he started. But something went wrong. He left the company and now they're after him." He collected his coffee. "Look, I'm going to continue investigating. My client is gone but I want to know what happened to her. I'm hoping we can work together."

"I have no problem with that at all."

"Let me tell you something else I know. Venus asked me to investigate her boss."

That took her by surprise. "Hera? Why?"

"Another one of Hera's employees, a woman named Athena, disappeared not long ago. Venus wanted to know what happened to her."

"Did she suspect Hera had done something to her?"

"I'm not sure. But Venus was worried about it. Worried that she'd be next."

———

EMMA LEANED over Zelda's shoulder while the woman clicked away at her laptop.

"I discovered ASMR a few years back," Zelda explained. "It changed my life. Don't expect me to explain the science. I'm not even sure there is any science. I just know it makes me feel...wonderful."

"Tingly?"

"Like you wouldn't believe. Like I've been charged with electricity. Like every cell in my body comes alive."

"You make it sound almost..."

"It's not sexual. It's a completely different sensation. Frankly, it's better. I had sex with my late husband for thirty-two years. Never that big a deal. But this is." She brought up a YouTube video. "ASMR stands for autonomous sensory meridian response. I have no idea what that means. But watch."

She played a short video that was nothing but a woman whispering into a camera. Her voice was melodic and she made some seemingly random hand movements. And that was it. She didn't move or dance or do anything Emma would call interesting.

Zelda whirled around. "Did you feel it?"

"Mmm. Maybe it takes a while to sink in."

"It didn't for me. I was mesmerized the very first time."

"Are all the videos like this?"

"No. Some are more involved. Some have people whispering about elaborate time-travel storylines or sci-fi roleplaying scenarios. Those are a little too Buck Rogers for me. I like to keep it simple."

"That one was pretty simple."

"You might prefer videos with more action. Some have women stirring soup, or crinkling wrapping paper, or spraying water. It doesn't matter. The whispering is what's important."

"I'm not sure this is ever going to do it for me."

"I suppose it's like everything else in life. Different strokes for different folks. We are not all alike."

That much was certain. "And you get a charge out of this?"

"Yes. But it's not like getting high. It's…soothing. Relaxing. Almost like a seizure, but a pleasant one. Calming."

Emma knew that the range of pleasure responses the human brain was capable of experiencing were vast and varied, but she'd never heard about this one before. She knew from an earlier case that some people got off on near-strangulation—autoerotic asphyxiation. She knew our brains supposedly reward us for activities likely to increase our probability of survival. That was the whole point of Darwinism, right? But she had a hard time understanding how listening to strange women whispering increased anyone's likelihood of survival.

Was it possible that neurodiversity had increased to such an extent that it no longer bore any relation to survival—or anything logical?

Or maybe there was a benefit to whispering. Maybe this was some sort of hypnosis. "Were you watching these ASMR videos the night Venus was murdered?"

"Yes. After a session, I always spend a long peaceful time gazing out the window. Enjoying the world."

So basically, she was in an altered state of consciousness when she witnessed whatever she witnessed. And she might have been drinking to boot. Kenzi could do a great deal with that on cross-examination.

"Thank you for showing me this."

"Don't dismiss it out of hand. There seems so little pure pleasure left in the world. If you can find something that makes you happy... what's wrong with that?"

"Nothing. But I'm good."

"Are you, though? You seem very closed. Uptight, we used to say."

"I may be private, but..."

"Are you afraid of what would happen if you allowed your emotions to express themselves?"

"I didn't say that."

"No. I saw that." She smiled. "I'm sorry. None of my business. I have a tendency to interfere. Old habits are hard to break." She let her voice drop to a whisper. "But allow yourself to be happy."

———

KENZI BLINKED RAPIDLY, trying to clear her brain enough to comprehend what Alex was telling her.

"Venus thought Hera might be out to get her?"

"Maybe."

"And she might disappear like Athena?"

"I don't know what sent Venus' mind down that dark path. But she was concerned enough to ask me to look into it."

"Are you still looking for this...Athena? And investigating Hera?"

"Absolutely. If I find anything, you'll be the first to know. If you want to know."

"I do. Would you object to coming to my office this afternoon? I have court in an hour, but afterward...maybe you could meet the rest of the team. I mean, meet my team. I didn't mean to assume—"

He laughed. "No worries. I know what you meant. I'd love to. And afterward, if you want...we could get dinner."

She blinked. "We could? I mean, yes, we could. Absolutely we could."

"But maybe leave the rest of the team at the office."

"Right." Was this going where she thought it was going? She should probably be avoiding distractions...but somehow, the thought of going out to dinner with him seemed very appealing. Like exactly the break she needed. "Okay, Alex, here's my Tinder profile. I'm thirty-seven, divorced, I have a daughter with ME, I have virtually no savings, I'm addicted to expensive clothes, I used to be a divorce lawyer but I'm expanding and I'm—"

"Cute as a bug?"

She flushed. "I was going to say, about to take a larger role in the management of my law firm. Which will probably be time-consuming. Also, I can't cook."

"Fortunately, I can. And just to reciprocate, I'm not rich but I make a decent living. I do have a little savings, I'm two years younger than you, I know everything there is to know about Star Wars, including all the different explanations for why Boba Fett survived the Sarlacc pit. I have no addictions, except maybe going to the gym—"

"That's a plus, not a minus."

"Glad you see it that way. And I'm not intimidated by a career woman who's good at what she does and tries to help people."

"Women. I only rep women."

"But...you like guys."

"Some more than others. But yes."

"I think that about covers it." He smiled. "I'm looking forward to dinner already."

"Me too. Can I pay for your coffee? It's a deductible business expense."

"No thanks. I can pay my own way." He winked. "I actually have some savings."

20

Kenzi sat on the far side of the round table in her private office, with the Battersbys on her left and the Le parents on her right. She knew how important this meeting was to all of them. It was important to her, too, but given everything she had on her plate right now, it was hard to shift gears. But she forced herself to do it. Now that the other couple in this drama had been identified, she had to devise a solution.

"Here's one thing I know for certain," Kenzi began. "You all love the children. But we have to find a path to move forward."

Julia Battersby looked even more stressed than she had in the courtroom. Kenzi wasn't surprised. The only thing that could possibly be worse than learning the child she was raising wasn't hers would be learning that her child was being raised by someone else. Someone she knew absolutely nothing about. Someone who might not want to give the child up.

"I want to see the one who's mine," Julia said, her voice aching. "How could I not?"

Amy Le spoke next. Discovery revealed that she had received the embryo that should have gone to Julia. "I don't know what I feel anymore. I loved my baby. Love, I mean. But I feel as if...everything has changed. I look at that child"—she raised her hands, as if hoping she might pluck the right words out of the air—"and I don't know who she is. I don't know who I am. I don't know who we are."

Her husband, Jaime Le, concurred. "It's as if everything we believed was a lie. A cruel lie." He pursed his lips. "An expensive lie."

Kenzi tried to sound comforting. "There are no lies here. Just errors. Terrible errors. A complete absence of essential protocols. I wonder if you might want to join the suit we've filed against the clinic."

"That clinic should reimburse me for the thousands I've spent raising a child who isn't mine," Jaime said.

"They'll argue that you would've spent the same amount of money if you'd gone home with your biological child."

"But I didn't!" His eyes flared. "This is like...fraud. They've destroyed the whole experience. Tarnished it. I don't think I can start over again. I just want to...forget it happened."

This situation was so far beyond what new parents expect it was probably difficult for anyone to know how they should feel. "I'll be happy to explore the civil possibilities with you at a later time. But for now, we have to find a solution to the problem at hand."

"I want to see my child," Julia said firmly. "I'm sure these people have formed an attachment to her. But that doesn't make me want to see her any less."

Kenzi watched Amy Le carefully, trying to judge her reaction. "I have a proposition for you. Let's change lobsters and dance."

All four looked at her as if she'd lost her mind.

After a few moments, Julia's eyes narrowed. "Are you saying what I think you're saying?"

"I am. Switch children."

"Just like that?"

"I'm not suggesting anything permanent. Trade children for a week. A temporary exploratory gesture. I know it will be hard on the kids, but they're young. They'll adapt."

Amy frowned. "And what do you think will come from this bizarre experiment?"

"It's possible that too much time has passed and you won't be able to bond with your biological children. Let's find out. After all, there's no point in arguing about how to get something you don't want."

"And what if we do?" Julia asked. "Won't that make the situation even worse?"

"Maybe. Honestly, I don't know. Nothing like this has ever come my way before. We're blazing new trails. But let's give it a try and see what happens. At the end of a week, I want you both to meet back here. We'll take it from there."

Julia's husband, Carl, spoke. "Are you going to have time? From what I read, you're about to become very busy."

"I made time for this meeting, didn't I?"

He granted her that.

"I'll find time for the next one too. Are we agreed? Swap babies for one week? Then we'll see where you want to go next."

Amy pressed a hand against her forehead. "Nothing is going to change."

"Tell me that in a week."

Julia grabbed her purse. "I'll have to write out instructions. Feeding time, sleeping times, music preferences, diapers, bedtime routines."

"I'll do the same," Amy said. "Vera can be downright cranky if you change her routine."

Julia nodded. "She gets that from me."

———

As KENZI RACED to the courtroom, she considered making a KenziKlan livestream. She was busy and stressed, but she knew Hailee would be unhappy if she let her social media following slide. She had to imagine there would be some interest, given that everyone online was posting about the jealous wife and the "A-Maze-ing Mirror Murder." But she resolved to keep it short. She had to stay focused on the hearing. If she lost this one, it would deal a painful, maybe decisive blow to Candice's case.

"Hey, KenziKlan." She held her phone at arm's length and talked as she walked. Hailee had turned her into an expert multitasker. "If you've been following my exploits of late, you know where I'm going today. Big hearing in the big case. It's a suppression hearing about a particularly nasty piece of evidence and probably our last get-together before the trial begins."

She crossed the street, dodging cars and pedestrians but never missing a beat. "If you've been online lately, you probably know what I'm trying to keep out of the trial. Given that it's all over YouTube, you may have seen it. But the jury does not need to see it. Even if they've already viewed it at home, they do not need to be reminded of it in the courtroom. They do not need to see it get the official imprimatur of the court, suggesting that this is relevant evidence with some bearing on the murder. My motion isn't about hiding incriminating evidence, because it doesn't speak one way or the other on the issue of guilt. This motion is about fairness."

She crossed another block. The courthouse was in sight. "But that's not what I wanted to talk to you about, people. I know you're fond of social media. That's why you subscribe to my channel. And I'm grateful. But when does a pleasant time-kill become an addiction? When do people live so much of their life virtually that they don't have a real life anymore? In my last big case, my client had to deal with sexting photos taken by an old boyfriend. Now my client has to deal with a sex video made without her knowledge. See the trend? It's pure slander. Make the defendant seem like a tramp and the jury loses sympathy. Which makes it a thousand times easier to convict. Even if she isn't guilty."

Kenzi pulled the phone closer. "She might be guilty of poor judgment about boyfriends, or guilty of having a sex life, but that is not the same as guilty of murder. I will fight hard to stop this patriarchal pattern of condemning women for doing the same thing good ol' boys brag about—namely, having sex."

She drew in her breath, then gave the screen one last bit of side-eye. "I hope you're getting the obvious takeaway here. If you're thinking about snapping sexy photos with your phone—don't. If you're thinking about making sexy videos—don't. If you're dating someone who wants to do that—drop him down a volcano. If you get the slightest hint that he might be doing something without your knowledge—confront him. You're too good for this kind of garbage. Don't let yourself become the next victim!"

———

ZELDA CHECKED herself in the large mirror beside the breakfront in her foyer. She did look rather good, didn't she? Sure, she would never see thirty again, or forty or fifty, for that matter. And she would never fit into her prom dress. But she didn't look her age. Did she? She'd had some rough years, but overall, she'd taken good care of herself.

Or maybe that was just the ASMR talking. She did love a little whispering first thing in the morning. Those delicious tingles made her head spin. Her life might be somewhat...restricted these days. But she found ways to keep her mind and spirit alive.

She'd always been a people watcher and didn't see why that should subject her to criticism. She refused to be thrust into some little-old-lady, nosy-neighbor stereotype. She was genuinely interested in people —what they did and why they did it. For decades now, she'd told herself she was gathering material for a Great American Novel. Maybe this was the year she sat down and wrote it. She certainly had enough material...

She had never for one minute imagined that she would become involved with a police matter of any kind, much less a murder. But it had been somewhat...thrilling. Didn't give her the same tingles as ASMR. But it wasn't bad. Made her feel important. Made her feel as if someone cared whether she lived or died.

And now they said she would be called to testify at trial. That she would be the prosecution's star witness. That was something special. No one could say her life was wasted after that.

She looked back into the mirror. She would need something to wear to court. Something that made her seem trustworthy. Like a reliable observer of the human condition. Maybe something from Saks...

She opened the door and stepped into the hallway, a smile on her face and a song in her heart. She was so inside herself that it took more than a few seconds before she spotted the person standing in the hallway, maybe ten feet away.

But that person spotted her.

She turned, raced back into her apartment and slammed the door behind her. She slid the chain into the slot, then turned the deadbolt.

A second later she heard a pounding on the door.

And the abuse, threats, and bribes that followed. But she didn't respond. And she certainly didn't open the door.

Should she call the police? She didn't want them to think their reliable witness was crackers.

She didn't know what to do. So she did nothing.

Except press her hand against her chest. Count to ten. Deep breath. Another deep breath.

Maybe the police didn't know as much as they thought they did.

———

KENZI TRIED to get into her aggro-litigator mindset. She knew her arguments backward and forward. But she also found herself thinking about the fertility clinic case. And when she felt her stomach rumble, she realized she'd much rather be having dinner with Alex.

Who she just met? Was she really having dinner with him tonight? Was she moving too fast? Then again, she didn't have any time to waste, because once the trial began, she would be even busier than she was now.

It was just dinner. They'd probably compare notes on the case. It wasn't really even a date.

At least that's what she told herself.

This was a positive development, right? Or the triumph of optimism over experience.

Whatever. She had to get her head in the game. She could not blow this hearing. If that sex video got in front of the jury, it would make her already impossible task even more impossible.

Candice wanted to attend, but Kenzi advised against it. Clients didn't normally come to pretrial hearings, and since her sex life was almost certain to be discussed, it seemed like an awkward scenario. Emma was in the gallery, and she would text updates to Candice whenever she thought there was something worth conveying. Candice had finally come clean and told her a lot about this case she didn't know, didn't even suspect. She felt like they were in a good place and she didn't want to mess it up.

Sharon had called friends and gathered as much information as possible about Judge Underhill. He was married, had four grown children, owned a boat, liked jazz, and collected baseball cards.

She wanted to like him. Then again, she'd rather listen to a police siren than jazz.

They were the only item on the court docket this morning. Underhill knew this case had attracted a lot of attention. He'd suggested holding the hearing in chambers, given the delicate nature of the recording in question, but Harrington wouldn't consent. Was he expecting reporters? Did he think this case could get him elected mayor? Or did he just want to create as much embarrassment and character damage as possible?

"Ms. Rivera, I believe this is your motion. Would you like to be heard first?"

"I would, your honor." Kenzi rose. "I know the court has had an opportunity to review my brief. Simply stated, this recording the prosecution wishes to admit at trial has no relevance to the murder charge. But the potential damage in terms of prejudice to my client is great."

Harrington rose. "We greatly disagree. It is relevant. Keenly relevant. Goes to pattern. And character. The jury has a right to know who to believe."

"Did you hear what he said?" Kenzi responded. "He practically confessed that he wants to use this recording to trash my client. To turn the jury against her. He's playing into ancient prejudices. When men have sex, that's ok. Boys will be boys. But if women have sex, they're sluts."

Underhill's eyebrows rose. Good. She'd chosen the word for dramatic effect. Surely he wouldn't want to be a part of such an overtly sexist attack.

The judge cleared this throat. "As I understand it, the prosecution believes this recording is relevant, not so much because your client is having sex as because..." He swallowed, frowned. "Because she's having sex with someone other than her husband."

"The prosecution's theory is that my client's husband was cheating and that made her insanely jealous and drove her to murder. But if she was having an affair too, that doesn't leave her much justification to be outraged."

"Counsel is being too logical," Harrington said. He was keeping cool, but Kenzi could see he really wanted to win this one. "These are matters of emotion, strong emotion, and people often don't think logically when they've been betrayed. More than anything else, this recording shows that the defendant is not who she purports to be. The jury should receive a balanced portrait, not one selectively edited by defense lawyers."

"Yadda, yadda, yadda. I feel certain the court can see through this blather. This video has nothing to do with providing a balanced portrait. The DA simply wants the jury to see my client having sex. To hear it. To see the expression on her face. After that's accomplished, the jury will never look at her the same way again. They probably won't be able to look at her at all."

Harrington shrugged. "We are all accountable for our actions. The woman had sex outside her marriage. And made a video."

"My client had nothing to do with that recording. It was done in secret without her knowledge or consent."

"Sure. That's what they all say."

"It's true."

"Then you can bring that out on cross. Let the jury decide."

"Which raises another evidentiary problem." Kenzi turned her attention back to the judge. "The DA has no sponsoring witness. He says he received this recording anonymously. He doesn't know who made it or under what circumstances. My client says it was done without her knowledge, so it violates wiretapping laws as well as common decency. Forgive me, but I don't think any prosecutor with a shred of decency would even consider submitting this so-called evidence. This is a desperate move by a desperate DA who jumped too fast to charge my client and now feels his entire career rests on convicting her."

"That's not remotely—"

Judge Underhill raised a hand. "That's enough of that. We don't need any name-calling or mudslinging. Maybe that plays in divorce court, but it won't get you anywhere with me."

Ouch. "I'm sorry, your honor, but this recording has nothing to do with the murder."

The judge tilted his head. "I can't make a judgment on that until I know more about the circumstances surrounding the murder. I am troubled by these evidentiary issues. Something that arrived anonymously in someone's email is not typically trustworthy enough to admit in open court. Email attachments are not self-authenticating. Especially with a charge as serious as this one, we have to enforce the evidentiary rules vigorously."

Kenzi clenched her fists. Sounding good...

Harrington jumped back into the fray. "This is a recording of two adults having sex, your honor. You can see why a concerned citizen might feel we needed to know about it—but might also be reluctant to have their name attached to it."

The courtroom fell silent. She could see that the judge was thinking. "My opponent is only underlining how potentially damaging, unfairly damaging, this recording is."

"That's not my intent. But I'm sure you're aware that this recording has leaked onto the internet. It's not as if it can't be seen by anyone who wants to see it."

"Yeah, and how did that happen, Mr. Harrington? So far as I know, only the people in your office had access. Who leaked it?"

"If you're suggesting for one minute—"

The judge raised his hand again, cutting Harrington off. "I'm going to deny the defendant's motion at this time. But the court is concerned about the provenance issues. If the defense can adduce evidence questioning the authenticity of this recording, the court will be willing to revisit this matter at a later date. Understood?"

Both lawyers nodded.

"Anything else?" Neither spoke. "Good. See you at trial. Court adjourned."

————

A FEW MOMENTS LATER, Kenzi saw Emma emerge from the gallery. "Did we lose?"

"Sorta kinda. For the moment. We can bring it up again if we have a good reason."

"The fact that Candice had sex with someone doesn't prove she's a murderer."

"This is about storytelling. Harrington doesn't want the jury to hear the story where Candice is a wronged woman. That might make her sympathetic—even to people who believe she committed murder. He wants her to be completely unsympathetic. He wants to prosecute a whore, not a victim. He wants to shame her. He wants to play on every ugly sexist stereotype available to him. And if this recording gets in, that is exactly what he will do."

———

ZELDA SAT on the sofa in her apartment. Her hands trembled and she couldn't stop them. She'd tried ASMR. It didn't help. She'd tried a large quantity of gin. It helped even less.

Hours had passed since she spotted that person in the hallway. The pounding on the door had ended, probably because it attracted too much attention. But she didn't kid herself.

She was not alone.

Suddenly, being the star witness in a big murder case was not nearly so appealing. She felt like she had a target on her back. She couldn't go outside. She didn't know if she should call the police. Or that district attorney. He said he'd take care of her, but...somehow, she didn't trust him.

She was trapped.

It was dark outside now. Very dark.

She tried to think clearly, but it got harder as time passed.

Her head jerked around. Did she hear footsteps outside? In the hallway? Again?

A cold chill froze her heart. What could she do?

She rose. Took a few steps toward the door.

What was that sound? A scraping? A squeal?

She was breathing fast, mouth closed, nostrils flared. She felt wobbly. Had she taken more gin than she realized? Flashbulbs went off before her eyes. The room seemed to swirl around her. At this rate, she would keel over before anyone got near her...

The crash came out of nowhere. She screamed. She fell to her knees.

The window. The window was broken. Shattered. Shards on the carpet.

But she was on the third floor...

She fell sideways. Her face flushed. She could barely breathe. Her heart pounded violently in her chest, so hard it hurt.

That person stood over her. The one from the hallway.

And—was that a mirror?

"Zelda, I think you have seen too much for one life. The time has come to close your eyes and rest. Permanently."

PART II

THE CURSE HAS COME
UPON ME

21

Kenzi felt massive guilt about taking personal time on the eve of trial, but hadn't she earned it? She had everything done, planned, outlined, ready to rock and roll. Her team was lined up and ready. Candice would not suffer because she had a nice dinner instead of reviewing her notes for the eighteenth time.

Scarlatti's was the best Italian in Seattle in her opinion. She had no idea what PIs made, but she doubted it was enough to afford this joint every night. Alex made a bold choice and signaled that he was taking this seriously. He was all in.

And he looked darn good, too. How often did he say he went to the gym? It showed.

"I'm looking under every rock in the city for this Sandy," Alex explained. He was wearing a white wool turtleneck with blue slacks. He looked like Adam Driver in *House of Gucci*. Dreamy. "But I wish I had more than the probably false first name Candice gave you."

"You and me both."

"But I'm convinced this relates to why Venus hired me. Why she thought she was in danger. She may have known this guy. Maybe he made videos of her too. I'm going to investigate the video from a different angle. Talk to some experts."

She took a bite of her trout almondine. It was delicious and she did not feel at all guilty. She'd tell Hailee she had fettuccine. "Experts in... amateur porn videos?"

"Sort of. This happens more often than you might imagine. Nasty boyfriends plant a GoPro in the bedroom."

She took another delicious bite. "This has become a nasty world we live in."

"It always was. Only the tech has improved. People are the same as ever."

He picked up the wine bottle and poured her another glass. Was he trying to loosen her up? She hoped so. "Please let me know when you've solved the mystery. I assume a real PI must have some skills."

He laughed. "Most of my mystery-solving skills I acquired from books. I love the Golden-Age mystery novels."

"I'm more a movie person," she confessed.

"Movies are cool, too. What have you learned from them?"

"Well, if this were a Scream movie, I should be watching out for you, right? It's always the...romantic interest."

He met her gaze. "If this were an Agatha Christie novel, I should be watching out for you. It's always the least-likely suspect. And the lead character is the least-likely suspect of all. In—"

"Don't tell me! I might read it someday!"

He grinned. "Maybe we should talk about something else."

———

KENZI TENDED to be an early riser, but never more so than when she was in trial. She was already thinking about getting out of bed when she heard her phone ring.

"Yeah?" She did her best to act as if she'd been awake for hours. "Sharon?"

"I'm with Kate. We need to talk. Face-to-face. We'll come to you."

"Does it have to be today? The trial starts—"

"Yes. Definitely today."

That was odd. And fairly frightening. "Ok. ETA?"

Sharon cleared her throat. "We're in the hallway outside your apartment."

This must be serious. She could ask how they got past security, but since Kate was a police detective, it probably wasn't hard. "I'll be right there."

She threw a robe over her nightie and flipped on some lights, stumbling toward the front door. Should she splash some water on her face? Yes. Quick bathroom stop, then back to open—

Hailee had beaten her to the door. She was in her pajamas, but she didn't seem to care. Sharon looked as tired as Kenzi felt. Kate looked like she'd been up all night.

"Is this about Candice's case?'

Kate nodded. "Big time." She gestured toward the kitchen table. "Can we sit?"

That sounded even more ominous. They all gathered around the table.

Kate looked hesitant, glancing at Hailee. "I'm not sure this presentation is rated for all audiences."

"Stop," Hailee said, before her mother had a chance to speak. "I'm almost fifteen. I have a YouTube account. I've seen it all."

Kate turned back to Kenzi, obviously seeking approval.

"It's okay."

Kate nodded. "I wanted to give you a heads up. Because I guarantee everyone at the courthouse will be buzzing about this. I wouldn't be surprised if your trial was continued to a later date."

"Enough with the suspense. What happened?"

Kate drew in her breath. "Zelda Lehman is dead."

"The prosecution's star witness? What happened?"

"She was found by a security guard. A neighbor heard a lot of noise and called it in. No one came to the door, so after a time, they forced their way inside."

She waited for the shoe to drop. "And...?"

"She was lying on the floor in her apartment. Dead."

"How?"

"That's the kicker." Kate licked her lips. "Someone smashed a mirror over her head."

Kenzi fell back in her chair. "Oh my God. Not again."

"'Fraid so. A big window in her apartment had been smashed, which was probably the source of the noise the neighbor heard. We assume that's how the assailant entered."

"On the third floor?" Hailee asked.

"Wouldn't be that hard. A tall ladder would do the trick. Or a rope, for someone who knew how to rappel."

"Maybe a grappling hook?"

"You've seen too many Batman movies."

"But—"

"I don't think the killer crawled up the wall like Spider-Man, either."

"Do you have any idea who's responsible?" Kenzi asked.

Kate grimaced. "I know what everyone thinks."

"And what would that be?"

"C'mon, Mom." Hailee looked at her as if she were still asleep. "The eyewitness dies hours before the trial begins?"

"That could mean many—"

"They think Candice did it."

"But she—she—" Was out on bail. With no monitoring anklet. Thanks to Kenzi.

"She is the most obvious suspect," Kate conceded.

"Which is exactly why she would never do it. She's too smart."

"Or maybe she's too desperate to be smart."

"You've already decided she's guilty? You and your cop buddies?"

Kate raised her hands. "Whoa. Stay chill. The only reason I'm here is because I know Sharon cares about you and I want to make sure your client gets a fair shake. No one has decided to bring charges yet. We don't want a premature arrest—"

"Right after the previous premature arrest."

Kate inhaled. " That might make it look like the DA has a vendetta. But I have to tell you, Kenzi. There's no doubt in the minds of the people back at the station. They all think Candice did it. Again. And as soon as they've gathered sufficient evidence, they'll bring charges, which will not make your life any easier. So be prepared for the worst."

KENZI WAS ALMOST DRESSED and out the door when her phone rang again. I don't have time for this, she thought. I'll just ignore it and maybe later—

She glanced at her phone. Alex.

Maybe she could carve out a minute.

She talked as she walked into the kitchen. Avocado toast? Oatmeal? Go-gurt?

"Kenzi? Alex. Have you heard yet?"

"About Zelda? Yeah. I got an early-morning briefing from a homicide detective."

"Really?" He whistled. "I had no idea they held you in such high esteem."

"Oh yeah. I got friends everywhere."

"I just heard and wanted to make sure you weren't blindsided in court." He paused. "By the way, I enjoyed dinner."

"Me too. Let's do it again. After the trial ends."

"Sounds good to me. Look, it's too soon to say anything, but I think I may be onto something useful about the video. I'll call back tonight, if that's okay."

"If you've got something that helps the defense case, believe me, I want to hear about it."

"Good. Knock 'em dead in court."

"Will do." She rang off, pivoted—

And saw her daughter staring at her. Grinning. "Was that the super-sexy PI by any chance?"

"What makes you think so?"

"The way your tired little eyes lit up as soon as you put the phone to your ear."

"Just business. He's helping on the case."

"I'll bet he is. Having dinner with him again any time soon?"

"Possibly. After the trial. Why? Do you want to come?"

"No. I want to design the 'Save the Date' postcards."

"Whoa. Slam the brakes. We're a long way from anything serious."

"This is what? Your first date in two years or something?"

"I've been focusing on business. Which is why you have a snazzy new MacBook Pro. So don't complain."

"I would never. That computer's going to get me into med school. May I make a suggestion?"

"Is there any chance I could stop you?"

"Don't go to Niagara Falls for your honeymoon. That's so cliché. The cool kids are going to Iceland. Think destination wedding."

Kenzi threw a pillow at her.

———

ONE LAST MIRROR check before she plunged into the outside world. Although given how this case was going, maybe she should avoid mirrors altogether.

She peered at her reflection. Good clothes, good foundation garments, expert makeup application. Worked wonders. Could you tell she was dragged out of bed at five in the morning? She didn't think so.

Could you tell she was scared to death? Probably.

Granted, this was not her first murder trial. But some things never got easier, and this was undoubtedly one of them. Especially not when she knew the defendant personally.

She gazed at the mirror. She knew the defendant...but didn't know her all that well. And in the past, didn't like her much.

Face it, she told the image in the mirror. You hated that woman. Absolutely hated her.

And now she's your client. Her life is in your hands. And if that isn't bizarre enough—she chose you to represent her because she thought you would do the best job. And her husband, your father, approved.

Life certainly has a fine sense of irony, doesn't it?

She gazed into her eyes. Can you do this? Can you be fair to this woman? Not just put on a show. Actually do the job. Give her the best defense possible.

She had to stare at those eyes for a long time before the answer came.

She could do it. Because she had to do it. Helping women in need is your driving impetus, she reminded herself. Sure, this client is not flawless. Like everyone else on Earth.

All that matters is that she needs help. And she chose you.

Kenzi grabbed her satchel. Time to get to work.

———

THE COURTROOM WAS chaotic and crowded. Harrington was already at his table when she arrived, flanked by four associates and a legal assistant. Candice sat alone at the defendant's table, probably wondering where her squadron was.

They had discussed her attire beforehand. In fact, Kenzi chose her outfits for the first five days of trial. She wanted Candice to look her best without appearing to be trying to look her best, if that made any sense. Jurors were like everyone else on earth—they made judgments based upon appearances. At the same time, they disliked people who appeared to be trying to impress. She had to find some kind of middle ground.

Emma sat in the gallery as she preferred, though she had agreed to join them for jury selection. Sharon was here too, and she'd seen Kate duck in and out. Probably had other things to do, given what had happened last night.

Speaking of which…

She sat beside Candice. "I suppose you've heard?"

Candice kept her voice flat, but she couldn't hide the panic in her eyes. "How could I not? It was all over the news. I suppose the police think I killed this woman, too?"

"They're still investigating." But yes.

"Will they arrest me in the middle of this trial? That will impress the jurors."

"I won't let that happen."

"You won't let them arrest me?"

She drew in her breath. "I'll make sure it doesn't happen here. If it happens at all." Pause. "I can't guarantee the DA won't make another stupid mistake."

"I hope I don't have to tell you this, but I did not kill the eyewitness."

"I know you didn't. Do you have an alibi?"

"No. I was at my place. Alone." Candice pressed a hand against her forehead. "When will it all end?"

"I don't know. But it will end. And if we have to defend you against another set of stupid charges—we will. I'm not going to let them railroad you. I won't let you become grist for Harrington's mayoral campaign."

Candice smiled a little. "I know you never liked me, Kenzi. I know you resented me for thrusting myself into your family."

"No, no, that's not—"

Candice waved it away. "Don't bother. I know. To some extent, it was mutual. But I'm really starting to like you."

"Glad to hear it."

She sighed. "And I'd like to take you to lunch sometime soon. So win this damn case, okay?"

———

JUDGE UNDERHILL CALLED Kenzi and Harrington into chambers to discuss the impact of Zelda's death on the case and whether he should continue the trial to a later date. He didn't want to. He wanted to stay on track and get this case off his docket. The big surprise was that Harrington, despite losing his star witness, didn't fight much.

"This has dealt the prosecution a serious blow," Harrington acknowledged. "But we do have the decedent's sworn witness statements. And if we proceed at this time, I assume the defense will not object if we read her statement at trial in lieu of calling her to the stand."

"I won't object," Kenzi said. This put her at a major disadvantage. You can't cross-examine a piece of paper. But under the circumstances, it seemed like the right thing to do.

"Good. Then we'll proceed as scheduled." The judge directed the court clerk to make a minute. "Let's not mention this new death during the trial. When the time comes, just say the eyewitness is unavailable."

"Most of the potential jurors already know," Kenzi said. "Or they will later today, as soon as they go home, disobey your instructions, and read up on the case."

Judge Underhill gave her a wry grin. "Perhaps. But I always like to give my jurors the benefit of the doubt. Let's find out who those lucky twelve people will be."

———

HARRINGTON STARTED THE VOIR DIRE, asked all the obvious questions, and little more. He resisted the temptation to preview his entire case with loaded jury examination questions.

Kenzi and Emma followed the procedure they'd developed during their previous homicide cases. It seemed to work, even if it made no sense. Emma took the lead. Somehow, the woman who never went anywhere and claimed to not understand people had a more objective approach to rooting out prejudice and bias. This left Kenzi free to watch people's eyes. If, as Shakespeare claimed, the eyes are a window to the soul, she would crawl through the window and stroll around, looking for anyone who might not be willing to give Candice a fair shake.

Judge Underhill kept a tight rein on the proceedings and didn't allow frivolous or repetitive questions. By the end of the morning, they had a jury.

"What do you think?" Kenzi asked Candice.

"I think if my whole future has to be in the hands of twelve people, I'd like to choose them personally. From my Christmas card list."

"Sadly, that is not an option."

"Only three of these twelve have been divorced. You think they'll hold it against me?"

"That you'll soon be divorced? Nah." But since eight of the twelve were married, they might not like the accusations of adultery. She had to thwart Harrington's efforts to portray Candice as a schemer, someone who destroyed one marriage and took drastic measures when the new one started falling apart.

"You think they'll hate me because I'm rich? Or was. Who knows what I'll be after this divorce."

"They're not going to see your tax returns."

"They'll know. Harrington will make sure."

Too true. And it didn't look like this jury had any millionaires. They rarely did. "Despite all the questioning, it's impossible to root out all prejudices. Humans are too complex, too multifaceted. But if I can convince them the prosecution didn't make its case, that will overcome even the most deeply rooted bias."

That was the way it was supposed to work anyway.

"Let's get lunch," she said, signaling Emma and Sharon to join them. "And yes, you are going to eat something. You need to maintain your strength. Because this afternoon, and the days that follow, are likely to be the worst times of your entire life."

22

K enzi had seen Harrington perform opening statements on previous occasions. And what a performance it was, full of dramatic pauses, rhetorical devices, emphatic gesticulation, and carefully planned omissions purposefully designed to create anticipation, to keep the jurors hanging on his every word.

She grudgingly had to admit that he was better at this than she was or ever would be. She liked to think that what the jurors did not get from her in theatrics, they would get in substance.

Despite his thespian skills, Kenzi felt her attention wandering. Of course, for the most part, she knew what he was going to say before he said it, but she liked to think the jury was equally bored. Her eyes wandered about the courtroom...

Hera, the doyenne of the escort service, sat in the gallery. She knew Hera felt close to Venus and mourned her loss. Still, she was surprised to find the woman in the courtroom.

Harrington's voice soared, recapturing her attention. "What kind of sick mind could conceive of such a thing? Stalking a victim who's engaged in prayer? Bashing her over the head with a mirror? What evil thoughts travelled through that diseased murderer's mind? Was she wreaking the most brutal, inhumane revenge imaginable against the woman she blamed for destroying her extremely profitable marriage?"

He grabbed the rail and leaned in closer, his eyes on fire. "There is no question about what happened here. The defendant first tried to take revenge against her husband by having a tawdry affair. When that didn't have the desired impact, she stalked the woman who was sleeping with her husband, found her alone, bashed her over the head with a mirror, then twisted the mirror back and forth like a saw on a block of wood, severing the carotid artery and cutting to the bone. The victim had no time to react, no time even to scream. A life all too soon snuffed out by one woman's rage."

He whirled around, his arm extended, his finger pointing at Candice. "This woman emerged from the maze covered with blood. An eyewitness saw her, guilt dripping from her fingertips."

He turned back to the jury. "You may feel sympathy for a woman betrayed by her husband. But if there is any justice left in this world, that sympathy will be eradicated by the grisly horror of what she did in response. There can be no excusing this kind of behavior. If we excuse this, no one is safe. I urge you—indeed, I implore you—to find Candice Rivera guilty of murder in the first degree."

Kenzi shook her head as Harrington made his way back to his seat. He was so extra, as Hailee would say. He must be prepping for the mayoral race. If high drama won votes, he was a shoo-in.

She pushed herself to her feet.

She was never going to match his level. Better that she didn't try. Instead, she would present herself as a deliberate contrast, a sober second thought, urging people to examine the evidence and do their duty without being swept away by emotions.

"There is no dispute about the fact that this was a horrific crime," she began, "but please do not let the horror of the crime become an excuse for ignoring the evidence—or lack thereof. There's been too much rush to justice in this case already. The DA seized upon the first available suspect when the police had barely begun to investigate. And now he's doubling down on that mistake, despite significant evidence suggesting that my client did not—and could not—commit this crime.

"Yes, Candice knew about her husband's affair. And yes, she was not happy about it and did some things that she later regretted. But this crime required far more than a wronged woman. Candice was already in divorce court, taking control of her life and dealing with her husband's infidelity in the logical, normal way. This murder gave her nothing. This murder was committed by a disturbed and damaged personality, and as you will see when she takes the stand, that is not Candice." She paused. "Yes, you heard me right. She will take the stand and tell you her story in her own words. Because she has nothing to hide."

Kenzi strolled beside the rail, keeping her eyes on the jurors, giving them a moment to think. "You have been put in the position of determining a human being's future. And you know what? That's a lot, as my daughter would say. A heavy burden to bear. The prosecution has assembled evidence that can be interpreted as indicating that Candice could have committed the murder, but they have nothing that absolutely proves that she did. And that is of crucial importance. Because this isn't a situation where you can convict someone if you think they probably did it. Or more than likely did it. As the judge will instruct you, you have to find that the evidence presented by the prosecution proves the defendant committed the crime beyond a reasonable doubt." She put heavy emphasis on each of the last four words. "That is an extremely high burden. It's meant to be. Better a thousand guilty men go free, Jefferson said, than a single innocent man is imprisoned."

She left them with a parting promise. "The prosecution will not be able to meet that high burden. Because my client did not commit this crime. And by the time this trial is over, you'll be just as certain of that as I am."

———

THE PROSECUTION'S first witness was the county medical examiner, Dr. Madison Chang. Harrington had to prove that a murder had occurred. Then he had to identify any evidence that pointed toward Candice.

Kenzi had dealt with Chang in court before. She knew the doc was smart and a prosecution team player, but not prone to exaggerate or make sketchy suppositions to please the boss. All in all, she was probably about as reasonable an expert witness as she could expect the prosecution to call.

After Harrington established Chang's credentials and expertise, he plunged into her findings. "Could you please describe the cause of death?"

"Yes. Death was due to exsanguination, which resulted in an immediate loss of oxygen to the brain. Death would've followed quickly."

"And the cause of the exsanguination?"

"To use the common parlance, the victim bled out. Her carotid artery was severed. The entire neck was severely damaged, but once the carotid is severed, death comes quickly. Five to fifteen seconds on average."

"And can you tell what severed the carotid?"

"Yes. I've seen photographs from the crime scene indicating that the victim was hit over the head by a large framed antique mirror. I've also had a chance to examine the mirror found at the scene of the crime. The victim's head went through the leaded glass. At that point, the assailant used a sawing motion, swinging the broken glass back and forth to cut the victim's neck."

"Is this something that could happen by accident?"

Chang shook her head. "No. Although the victim was likely stunned when her head went through the mirror, if the assailant had left it at that, she would have survived. It's the sawing motion that took her life. That demonstrates a deliberate intent to kill."

"Would that sawing motion cause the artery to spray blood?"

"Yes. With great force. Like a clogged pipe suddenly uncapped."

"You're saying the assailant might get blood on their person?"

"If the assailant was holding the mirror when the artery was cut, I don't see how it could be avoided."

Which fit the prosecution version of events, since Zelda claimed she saw Candice emerge from the maze with blood on her hands and clothes.

Harrington called another forensic witness, John Trenton, mostly to establish that the forensics team did a thorough job and the crime scene was not contaminated. He portrayed a meticulous, well-oiled, crack research team sifting through the evidence and determining what happened. He admitted the mirror into evidence as the murder weapon and also mentioned what Sharon had learned earlier from Kate —traces of opioids were found on the mirror frame.

What interested Kenzi most was not what the team found but what they didn't find. Although the mirror and its frame had been examined in every way possible, they didn't find any fingerprints. "The frame was ridged and thus not the most conducive surface for collecting prints," Trenton explained. "And the assailant might have worn gloves."

If the killer went to the trouble of lugging that mirror to the maze, there was a significant degree of forethought. Why not bring gloves too? Of course, the police had found gloves in Candice's apartment, but that didn't prove anything.

On cross, Kenzi drove her point home. "Is it unusual for a woman to own gloves?"

Trenton shrugged. "I wouldn't know."

"It does get cold sometimes here in Seattle, right?"

"It does."

"Do you have a pair of gloves at home?"

"Several."

"Was there anything about the gloves found in my client's closet that proved they had been used to hold the mirror?"

"No. We found no traces of blood, hair, or anything else specifically linked to the victim. Of course, we also did not find any bloodstained clothes. So presumably—"

"Objection," Kenzi said. "Speculation."

Judge Underhill nodded. "Sustained."

She knew Trenton wanted to argue that since Zelda saw Candice covered in blood but there were no bloodstained clothes in her apartment, she must've destroyed them. But the absence of evidence was not evidence. Not usually, anyway.

———

FOR HIS LAST witness of the day, Harrington called Valerie Powell, a Latina woman in her mid-forties who Kate said was the rising star of the hair and fiber department. Kenzi always worried about the so-called CSI Effect—the idea that because people watch so many forensic-driven crime shows, they tend to give forensic evidence disproportionate weight, considering it dispositive while giving less credence to other evidence.

As Harrington established Powell's background and credentials, Kenzi found even her cynical self impressed. This witness knew her stuff. She was articulate, direct, and convincing. She was able to explain what she knew and sell it, which was exactly what Harrington needed. She got the impression that if Powell hadn't been on the scene, that tiny fiber might have been missed altogether.

"Can you please explain your procedure?"

Powell smiled. "Of course. I was a member of the three-person hair and fiber team that arrived about forty minutes after the first officer on the scene. After photographs and videos were taken, we began our examination."

"What did you find?"

"Not as much as we'd like. This was an open-air maze in the middle of Conrad Park. Obviously the scene was contaminated by natural elements—leaves, twigs, insects, and other contaminants. But I discovered one thing on the victim's person that could not be explained by natural causes."

"What was that?"

"A green fiber. Almost invisible to the naked eye. But we found it."

Harrington went through the required process to introduce the fiber into evidence along with Powell's forensic report. Something any jurors suffering from the CSI Effect could use to amuse themselves.

"Were you able to determine where this fiber came from?"

"Yes. When the police searched the defendant's apartment, they found a green scarf. A muffler, to be precise. The sort of thing someone might wear out on a cold night."

"And the scarf had fibers similar to what you found on the victim?"

"Exactly the same. It's a perfect match. One hundred percent."

Harrington nodded, obviously pleased. "Thank you. Pass the witness."

Kenzi wasn't going to attack the witness' expertise. That wasn't likely to get her much. But there were a few details she felt Powell was omitting.

"Ms. Powell—"

"Dr. Powell," the witness corrected.

"Right. Dr. Powell. You testified that you found a green scarf at my client's apartment. I'm sure it was examined for bloodstains. Did you find any?"

"No."

"If someone wore the scarf while slicing the victim's arteries, shouldn't it be covered with blood?"

"I would expect the arterial spray to appear lower on the attacker's body. On the shirt or slacks."

"And you testified that the fiber was found on the victim's person. But that's not quite right, is it?"

"I don't understand."

"Isn't it true that the fiber was found on the victim's purse?"

"And the strap was in the victim's hand. Even after her death."

"I think most jurors would think 'on her person' meant touching some part of her body. Which the fiber wasn't, right?"

"It was on her purse. Tangled in the strap."

"Did your eyewitness see the victim enter the maze?"

"No."

"Then you can't be certain she carried the purse into the maze."

"The purse was right next to her body."

"Is it possible someone else brought the purse?"

"Why on earth—"

"To plant incriminating evidence, obviously."

"I think that highly—"

"I'm not interested in what you think. I asked whether it's possible."

Powell sighed. "I suppose it is remotely possible. Though—"

"Thank you for your refreshing honesty. By the way—that scarf you found in my client's closet after you turned the place upside down and made a gigantic mess of the place? Is it possible that could've been planted, too?"

"Why would anyone—"

"Same reason. To make the prosecution's case. Up until that time, you didn't have much."

"I am offended by the suggestion that any member of our police force would plant false evidence."

"But it has happened before, right?"

Powell's irritation was beginning to show. Good. The less implacable she seemed, the better. "I suppose that somewhere in the entire history of police investigations there have been some instances of planted evidence. But—"

"And it certainly seems coincidental, doesn't it? First you find the fiber. Then you find the scarf. Exactly where you wanted it to be."

"That's no coincidence. That's first-rate police work."

"Do you suppose that scarf is the only one of its kind in existence?"

"Now—what?"

"Are you claiming Candice crocheted it herself? 'Cause I can tell you with certainty that didn't happen."

"It was a name-brand scarf. Commercially available, but not common. Expensive."

"Are there others in existence?"

"I suppose."

"Someone else might've bought that same scarf."

"Undoubtedly."

"And therefore, someone else could have left that fiber."

"The odds of that are—"

"Did I ask you to calculate the odds? Is that your field of expertise?"

"No."

"Your expertise is fibers. And you identified the fiber. But you are not qualified to say where it came from. You focused exclusively on the possibility that best served your rush-to-judgment case. But that's not the only possibility out there."

23

Sharon didn't want this job, but they weren't able to track the doctor down till today, and Kenzi and Emma had a plausible excuse for passing the buck, since they were in the middle of a trial.

She supposed she couldn't complain. Well, she could complain, but what was the point? Just talk to the Brazilian butt doctor and get it over with.

She walked into the doctor's office, which did not look at all like a doctor's office. Wide open spaces, no receptionist's desk, posters of Disney World on the walls. A bookshelf instead of well-thumbed magazines. A mounted television that displayed YouTube videos. Some influencer she didn't recognize was offering moisturizing tricks to keep your skin clear and wrinkle-free. Sharon grimaced. What was wrong with a few wrinkles? She earned her wrinkles. Wouldn't adults rather be with a grownup than some wrinkle-free thing who looks like she still gets an allowance from Daddy?

She'd barely been there a minute before a middle-aged man emerged from a back office. He had black hair and barely a wrinkle, though Sharon immediately suspected that he'd had help with both.

"You must be Sharon. I'm Dr. Zabriskie."

Sharon shook his hand. "Thanks for taking time off from work."

"No problem. I don't normally work Mondays."

"I was admiring your office. It's...different."

"I hope you meant that in a good way. I was trying to break the old-school model of what a doctor's office should look like. Let's face it —that look instills dread and terror. Receptionists who make you sit around and wait. Crummy magazines perpetuating sexist ideals. Uncomfortable chairs. Sterile décor. I wanted a more humane environment." He waved his hands in the air. "But you didn't come to hear me rattle on. Would you like to step inside?"

She followed him. No cotton balls in jars or examination tables covered with rolls of crunchy paper. Instead—travel posters and recliners and a small putting green.

Zabriskie took a seat behind his desk. "I understand you're interested in Candice Rivera."

"We represent her in her pending litigation."

"I read about that. Hope it all works out."

"She's waived any physician-client privilege. You can talk freely to us."

"Yes. I received the waiver by email. How can I help?"

"It's my understanding that you performed a cosmetic surgery procedure on her."

"At her request."

"And that was..."

"I won't bore you with the medical terminology. What everyone calls it is a Brazilian butt lift."

"Are you Brazilian?"

He laughed. "No. Jewish. Brooklyn. The name comes from the area where the procedure was supposedly first popularized, though I'm not sure that's accurate."

"When did Candice have this procedure?"

"February. About three months before..."

"The murder?" The first murder.

"Right. Tragedy."

"What exactly is involved? I get that it's supposed to improve the appearance of your...posterior."

"Basically, I take fat from the abdomen and transplant it to the bottom. Creates that rounded peach-emoji look women want."

"The perfect pear-shaped figure." Why were women always compared to fruits?

The doctor nodded. "Even more popular than the button nose and the cat eyes. Butts built my swimming pool. This procedure has increased in popularity by seventy-seven percent in the last five years. It's the fastest growing cosmetic surgical procedure in the world."

"Everyone wants to look like Jessica Rabbit?"

"Oh, kids today don't even know who that is. They want to be Kim Kardashian. After getting shamed online, Kim posted an X-ray that supposedly proved she hadn't had butt implants. But a butt lift wouldn't show up on an X-ray, since no unnatural substances are inserted."

"Does it bother you that people are having surgery so they can conform with the internet's idea of what makes women attractive?"

"Fashion standards change all the time. Before the internet it was television, and before that the movies, and before that magazine illustrations. Not everyone has the imagination to create their own style. That's why these people are called influencers."

"Isn't Candice a little old for this?"

"Not at all. I don't think there's anything wrong with taking care of your figure at any age. I was just relieved she came to someone reputable."

"Meaning you?" She scanned the wall and saw a more-than-adequate number of diplomas from institutions of higher learning. "Do you specialize in...butts?"

He laughed. "It's not my only procedure. But it is my specialty. I have extensive experience and education in the area. Unlike many people performing this operation."

"I'm guessing you need some sort of...certification."

"Beyond medical school? No. Medical doctors can practice and treat patients in any field as long as they have consent from their patient. A newbie doc can set up a clinic and start selling liposuctions tomorrow even if they have no experience with liposuctions. It's completely legal and there's no higher board they have to answer to. A hospital might impose restrictions and oversight, but no doctor is forced to practice in a hospital."

"That doesn't seem right."

Zabriskie shrugged. "Historically, the medical field has policed itself. Most states have a board of medical examiners, but they rarely get involved in this sort of thing."

"Patients can sue. If something goes wrong."

"True. But that's a civil penalty, not a criminal one. That's why doctors carry insurance. And malpractice cases are difficult to prove. Doctors spin circles around juries, which tend to frown on people who seek cosmetic surgery. Like it serves 'em right if something goes wrong."

"You said you were glad Candice came to you."

"Definitely. This is a time-consuming, difficult, risky procedure, and some docs out there are doing eight of them a day."

"What? Why?"

"To make money. First they take some weekend course to learn how to do it. Then, to avoid the high cost of running an operating room, they rent space somewhere for one day a week. And try to cram as much into that day as possible. South Florida is a haven for this sort of thing—at least here in the US. You can get it cheaper in Mexico. Or Turkey. Or Thailand."

"Why Florida?"

"I don't know. You can wear your bikini all year, so if ever there was a place you wanted your butt to look good—"

"Candice lives in Seattle. Where it rains about half the year."

"Personally, I didn't think she needed it. But she was determined."

"What are the risks? Anesthesia and such?"

"That's the least of it. The fatality rate is about one in three thousand, which is much higher than for most surgical procedures. The problem is that your gluteus maximus has a lot of large blood vessels. Big as drinking straws, I heard a guy say once. If the doc accidentally injects a blood vessel with fat, it can travel to your lungs and cause a pulmonary embolism which will likely be fatal. I always put a strict limit on the amount of fat I'll transplant, but not all doctors do."

"No woman should feel like she has to take that kind of risk to feel pretty."

"Especially since the impact is often temporary. In some cases, the fat doesn't remain alive, so patients see their fabulous new butts shrink up over the following months. Which requires yet another procedure."

"Do you know how Candice found you?"

"Recommendation from a friend. Then she used an online site called certificationmatters.org that does what our profession does not. Allows patients to see if a doctor has the proper certification to perform the kind of surgery they need."

"Did she explain why she wanted this done?"

"I gathered that her husband was unfaithful. Personally, I don't think a butt job is going to do the trick if your husband is already straying. Better to just dump the creep."

"She probably didn't want her husband to know anything about this surgery."

"I don't know how he could fail to notice. Even the least attentive husband on earth could see the change."

"Do you know anything about what happened later?"

"You mean the divorce? I could've predicted that before it happened."

"I meant the murder."

"No." He paused. "Well, I knew the victim, of course."

Sharon leaned forward. "You knew Venus?"

"Of course. I worked on her before I worked on Candice."

"You mean—Venus also had a Brazilian butt lift?"

"Yes. In her line of work, appearances are everything."

"You knew about her line of work?"

"Of course. I've had many escorts and...similar professionals. Pole dancers. Models. Sex workers. For them, it's an investment. One that typically pays off."

"That's just...bizarre. Both Candice and Venus had the same procedure and coincidentally came—"

"No coincidence. Venus was the one who recommended me to Candice."

Sharon almost fell out of her chair. "What?"

"They came in together. Chatted amicably. I didn't think anything about it. Of course, at the time, I didn't know Venus was...the other woman. I just thought they were friends. Old high school chums or something." He pondered a moment. "I recall that at one point, they both stood in front of a mirror together, comparing one another's butts."

"A mirror?"

"They were laughing, touching. Complimentary. I got the impression they were quite close."

24

Kenzi slumped over the kitchen table, staring at the wall. Hailee hovered over the stovetop. She was prepping something for dinner and being much too chipper about it. Sharon and Emma were in the living room sorting through files and laying out exhibits for the next day.

Should she be helping? Somehow she felt she was doing her part, staring at the cracks in the paint and making sure she didn't drool.

Until Hailee started setting the table around her. "Sorry, Mom. We can't use your head as a placemat."

It took some effort, but Kenzi managed to sit upright. "I was lost in thought."

"Is that what it was?" Out the corner of her eye, she saw her daughter wink at Emma.

"What was that?"

Hailee smiled. "Nothing. You go on being morose."

Kenzi frowned. "I don't know if you reprobates noticed, but we took a drubbing in the courtroom today. I have a right to feel down."

Sharon laughed. "Oh, this has nothing to do with the courtroom, kiddo."

"Let's face it, this case is—"

"Hopeless?" Emma suggested.

"Yeah. And we don't—"

"Have a defense case?" Sharon completed.

"We're going down—"

"In flames," Emma said.

"The jury hates us," Hailee chipped in.

"My client depended on me," Sharon said, adopting a mournful tone. "And I let her down."

Kenzi put one fist on her hip. "Am I detecting a certain note of derision?"

Sharon pressed her hands against her chest. "From us? Perish the thought."

"I definitely get the impression I'm being made fun of. This is a dire situation, people. The prosecution holds all the cards and I didn't lay a glove on them today."

"We're not making fun of you. Exactly."

Emma shook her head. "We kind of are, actually."

Kenzi felt her teeth clenching. This was her trusted team of loyal associates?

"It's just that you do and say the same things every time, Kenzi."

"Every single time," Hailee added.

"What do we call this?" Emma asked. "Post-prosecution depression?"

Sharon pondered. "Bipolar advocacy syndrome?"

"My mommy being my mommy?" Hailee suggested.

"The point is," Sharon continued, "we've come to expect it. And we know you'll snap out of it eventually. We just wait for it to pass."

Somehow, this conversation was not abating her irritation. "I had no idea I was so predictable."

"That's because you don't have to deal with you. We do."

"And that's such a misery?"

"Only periodically," Emma assured her. "The first day of the trial is never a picnic for the defense. Harrington gets to be dramatic and impress the jury with the horror of the crime. Their experts put on evidence that's largely unassailable. And it will probably get worse, not better. But you'll have your chance later. After the prosecution is done. Just ride this out."

"The jurors keep glaring at the defense table. I can tell they don't like me. Maybe they don't like Candice either."

"You're being paranoid," Sharon said.

"Jurors don't like defense lawyers," Kenzi replied. "Criminal lawyers are more hated than anyone on earth."

Emma nodded. "Except divorce lawyers, of course."

"Thanks so much."

"But I was watching the jury carefully, and I didn't detect any particular animus toward you or Candice. In fact, I think they appreciated the fact that you kept your opening statement brief and factual, without employing Harrington's high-dudgeon dramatics."

"You're saying they liked that I was boring."

She craned her neck. "Sorta..."

Hailee pointed across the room. "Did you see my jury board! It's by the fireplace!"

Her daughter had filled a corkboard with juror photos, even arranging them to match their seating in the jury box. Beneath each photo, she'd used Post-It Notes to list the salient facts she'd unearthed about each of them.

"Impressive. You got this from social media?"

"Facebook, mostly. Though Juror Number Four has some amazing TikTok dances. And Number Seven has the cutest cat videos on Instagram."

"Does that mean she favors the prosecution or the defense?"

"It means she's a good person. All cat lovers are good people."

"I should mention cats a lot in my closing?"

"It couldn't hurt." Hailee laid down a big bowl of pasta and scooped it onto plates. "Lots of carbs to fuel your brains. And you'll sleep well afterward."

While she served, the doorbell rang. Kenzi frowned. "I don't want to be bothered by kids selling candy bars for the school soccer team."

Sharon popped up. "I'll get it."

Kenzi pushed her back down. "I'm a grownup. Usually. I'll go." She headed toward the front door. "But I'm not happy about it. The last thing I need right now is—"

She opened the door. Alex stood on the other side. "Is this a bad time?" he asked.

Kenzi stared at him. Took her several seconds to react. She stumbled and stuttered. "It—You—It—I mean—"

Alex smiled, a bit sheepishly. "I called but you didn't pick up."

"That's—Oh—I was—I put it in silent mode."

"No worries. I know you're in the middle of the trial. But I asked if I could come by, remember? Hey, I know I said this already, but I had a great time at dinner." Pause. She didn't speak. "Didn't you?"

"Well...yeah. I mean. It was...I was..." She stopped, then took a deep breath. Was her face flushing? "I'm not handling this very well, am I?"

He laughed. "You're under a lot of stress. But as soon as the trial is over, I think we should try it again. Dinner, I mean. Maybe this time even a movie."

She raised her hands. "Hold on, tiger. Let's not rush things."

"I'll let you pick the entertainment. After this trial, you'll deserve it."

She nodded, much too rapidly. "That would be...wonderful. Wait. I'm so stupid. I didn't mean to leave you standing in the hallway. Would you like to come in?"

He glanced over her shoulder. "Looks like you're busy. And you weren't expecting me for dinner. Rain check, okay? I would like to meet your daughter sometime."

He couldn't miss the shout coming through the open door. "She would like to meet you, too!"

He laughed. "After the trial."

"It's a date. I mean—I didn't mean—"

He looked into her eyes. "It's a date." He slapped his forehead. "I almost forgot. I found the expert I mentioned. And he has some info you need."

———

A FEW MINUTES LATER, Kenzi reentered her apartment. Her three cohorts were eating their pasta, but as soon as she drew close, all eyes were upon her.

"Brace yourself," she said. "This is going to rock your boat like you won't believe."

Sharon gave her a long look. "Looks to me like you're the one who got your boat rocked."

"Now...what?"

"A minute ago, you were so depressed you could barely see straight. Now you're lit up like a ball of fire."

"Almost like she saw someone she liked," Emma commented.

"Like a high school girl who finally got asked to the prom."

Emma rolled her eyes. "Every guy in high school wanted to take Kenzi to the prom."

"But now she's an adult who hasn't been on a date in two years."

Kenzi gaped. "It has not been two years."

"Three?"

"It—no—I've been taking a break."

"Did you tell Alex you were on a break?"

"I—Why—Alex?"

"You know. The guy you were having eye sex with out in the hallway."

"I was not—" She took a breath, then started again. "Look, he's doing some detective work for me."

"Undercover work?" Emma suggested.

"Would you stop? He's a PI. And he just turned up something none of you clowns did, so maybe you should have a listen." She sat at the end of the table. "That recording? The sex video? He thinks it's a deepfake."

"Candice has admitted she—"

"But that doesn't mean the video hasn't been altered."

"Why would anyone do that?"

"Because someone wants Candice to go away forever."

25

Kenzi had never seen a third party read the recorded testimony of a deceased witness. Of course, in divorce court, if one of the two litigants died, the divorce became moot. She agreed to let one of Harrington's legal assistants read Zelda's words. Being Harrington's underling, she shaded it to stress what Harrington wanted stressed, but overall she stuck to the script.

The judge spent a great deal of time explaining to the jury why someone other than the witness was appearing on the stand. The jurors appeared to take it in stride. Harrington had spliced together several interrogations, but the core was Zelda's identification of the defendant. "I just happened to be looking out my living-room window that night. The sky over the park was beautiful. Almost a midnight blue. Like in a Matisse or the best Spode china. Then I saw a female figure enter the park. I recognized Venus, of course. I'd seen her often enough in my building. She frequented the apartment next door. An extremely noisy visitor. Especially at night."

A few of the jurors smiled. Even without the woman there in person, they seemed able to conjure the image of the apartment busybody keeping tabs on everyone around her.

"I knew Candice Rivera on sight. Dark hair. Slender. Very attractive. Much younger than her husband, but I'm sure you know that already. I'd seen her photo in the paper. She wore some kind of sheer shirt, like an expensive blouse, and matching black pants. She could almost fade into the background, except her hair was a mess and there were splatters all over her."

The interrogator asked a specific question.

"Yes, of course it was blood. What else would it be? Don't you think I know blood when I see it? Candice was very upset. Turned one way then the other. Rubbed her hands against her pants, as if trying to rub something off. So upset. Agitated. Guilty, if you ask me. Then she seemed to get her head together and bolted across the street out of my view. I didn't know what to think. Eventually, I called the police and told them what I saw. I had no desire to get involved in this tawdry business. But I had no choice."

Kenzi could quibble about the testimony's validity—Zelda was not nearby, it was nighttime, and she made many assumptions. But the woman had been absolutely certain about what she'd seen. And the jurors would remember that.

————

SANDY KNEW HE SHOULDN'T, but he had a few shots before the meeting. They were in a bar, after all, and he assumed this isolated location hadn't been chosen for its charming ambiance. Because there wasn't any. The Angry Toad Bar & Grill. Seriously? But there was little chance of being spotted by anyone. Anyone sober enough to remember anyway.

Come to think of it, a third shot wouldn't be the worst thing, would it? Sure, vodka was poison, and any courage it seemed to provide was completely illusory. But his hands were shaking like he was in an earthquake zone. Knees weren't much better. Anything he could do to steady his nerves was probably a smart move.

He tried to comfort himself. He wasn't a coward. These feelings were completely natural.

It was hard to come face-to-face with the devil himself. Hard to confront the person you'd spent weeks running from.

When at last Kingsley arrived, he appeared to be alone. But Sandy wasn't stupid. He probably had thugs posted all over the place. Probably had accomplices who arrived hours before. For all he knew, the two losers at the next booth might be his goons. He had tendrils everywhere.

"We meet again, Sandy."

There it was, that deep growl of a voice, as he slid into the booth on the other side of the table. He had a trace of a foreign accent, though Sandy couldn't place it. "Thank you for agreeing to this meeting."

"Lou Crozier said you wanted to talk to me."

"I need to be sure we have a deal. In exchange for your assistance, you wish me to reduce your debt."

Son of a bitch. "I wish you to eliminate my debt."

"That I cannot do. It is too great."

"You can do anything you want."

"Not that, my friend. It would set a bad example."

"What's more important? Your business or your reputation?"

"Without reputation, there is no business."

Sandy gripped the edge of the table. This was going to be even harder than he'd imagined. Double trouble. Double deep dark despair. But there must be some way to bring it off. "I'm not going to agree to a mere reduction."

"It would be to your advantage."

"Would it, though? I've made payments. Over and over again. And yet, the debt never goes away."

"Because all you have done is pay down the interest."

"Because you set an impossible interest rate."

"You knew the terms. You accepted them."

"I had no choice."

Kingsley only smiled. "Everyone has a choice. We make choices every day. Perhaps you made a foolish one. But you made it. And now you must bear the consequences."

"Forever?"

"Until the debt is repaid."

Sandy leaned back, feigning a confidence he did not feel. "As you say, we all have choices. This is yours. If you want what I have, you'll erase the debt."

"Crozier tells me you've already begun looking. Without success."

"I'm not delivering until I know what I'm getting in return. Until I hear it from your mouth. Wipe the slate clean. Or forget about it."

Was that another smile on Kingsley's face? Or simply a sneer? "Look at you, Sandy. Not so much the sniveling loser I've dealt with in the past. Where is this confidence coming from?"

Vodka? "Guess I've finally seen the light. Take it or leave it, Kingsley. I'm more dangerous than you know."

"Is that a threat? Do you know how many of my people are watching you as you speak?"

No. But he could imagine. "Still waiting for your answer."

"Fine. I take it. Your debt will be erased. Your days of running and hiding are at an end. No more scraping together your pathetic dirty movies to keep the wolves at bay. You can start a new life."

Sandy almost spoke, but Kingsley cut him off.

"Provided." He chuckled. "Provided you give me what I want."

"I will."

"You are certain of this?"

"I am. I can give you Icarus. And I can make him do what you want him to do."

———

Kenzi knew Harrington's next witness would be her father, which only made her question whether she should've accepted this case in the first place. For the thousandth time. Candice didn't seem to be ruffled by her husband's presence at all. Perhaps that was just for show. The jury was watching for signs of enmity, disharmony. Motive.

Kenzi suspected this examination would be brief. Harrington and her father were old friends, after all, and there was no desire on either side to end a mutually profitable relationship. But he had to be put on the stand.

Her father looked elegant, well-groomed, well-dressed, and altogether distinguished as he took the witness chair. Maybe it was her imagination, but she thought she saw sadness in those eyes. Regret? Could he regain his lost luster? People tended to remember the worst, not the best.

Alejandro Rivera identified himself, his line of work, and most importantly, his relationship with the defendant. "We've been married for about six years now."

"When did the troubles begin?"

He sighed heavily. "About a year ago. Approximately."

"Was that when you began seeing...the victim? Vanessa Collins. The woman known as Venus?"

"It was."

"And how did that relationship begin?"

"A friend of mine...a friend at a rival law firm, told me about an escort service. Just to be clear, this was an escort service, not a front for something else. It helped people who wanted someone to accompany them on social occasions. People who don't have much time but want a pleasant, intelligent companion to share an evening."

"When you say it was not a front..."

"I'm saying it was not a bordello. Or anything like that. And the women there, including Venus, were not tramps."

Harrington cleared his throat. Kenzi was amazed by how delicately he was handling this. He appeared genuinely to be trying to minimize the embarrassment to his long-time friend. Perhaps the old-boy network ran deeper than she realized.

"You saw Venus more than once?"

"Yes. I liked her. We liked one another. The relationship clicked. I saw her again. And again. And in time, the relationship...progressed."

"You were still married to the defendant."

"I was."

"Did you tell your wife about this new relationship?"

Her father looked at Harrington as if he were the stupidest thing that ever crawled out from under a rock. "Of course not."

"But she found out?"

"Yes."

"How?"

"Ask her. All I know is that she confronted me one day and knew everything there was to know. Who the other woman was. Where we went regularly. She even knew Venus' brother's name."

"Can we assume she was not happy about this revelation?"

"She was not. She was angry. Loud. Threatening."

"What exactly did she threaten? Divorce?"

"Not at that time. She's not an idiot. If we divorced, I would have to give her something, but...she would not receive alimony. She would have to work. And that was not what she wanted. She channeled her anger in a different direction."

"Toward Venus. What did your wife say about her?"

"If you will permit me, I would prefer to not repeat the language she used. It was quite...foul. Suffice to say, she did not think Venus was an honorable woman."

"Did she make threats?"

"Yes. But I never thought—"

"Just give the jury the facts, please. We'll let them draw their own conclusions."

"I want to explain that I don't believe—"

"Sir, do you have personal knowledge of who killed Venus?"

"No."

"Then please do not offer opinions. As a lawyer, you know that's inappropriate. You're here to tell the jury what you saw or heard."

"Candice is not a bad person," he muttered. "A fiery temper, yes. But not mean or—"

"The two of you are in divorce court now, correct?"

He sighed. "Yes. She filed. We were trying to settle it when Candice was arrested. That of course changed everything."

"What is the status of the divorce?"

"Pending. Held in abeyance until this murder case is resolved. Let me say—"

"Please wait for a question. And only answer the question. You've mentioned that your wife has a temper. And that she was angry when she learned of your extramarital relationship. And that she made threats against the woman who is now dead." Thank you so much for the self-serving summary, Harrington. "I'm sure you feel some guilt about this matter and you—"

"Wait." This time, her father cut Harrington off. "I do not feel guilt. I could have handled this better. Much better. But I do not feel guilty about it."

Harrington squinted his eyes. "You admit you were stepping out—"

"But Candice was cheating long before."

The whole room seemed suspended. No sound. No movement.

Kenzi glanced at Candice. She was looking at the witness stand. Candice and her father exchanged a long look.

"You're saying..."

"I caught Candice red-handed. And she never denied it. And her lover...unlike Venus...was not an intelligent or elegant person. He was scum. After I found out...well, you can imagine how I felt. I was devastated. I considered divorce right then and there. I ultimately decided against it. I'm not a young man and I didn't welcome the disruption that would cause. But I had little to do with Candice after that. We slept in separate bedrooms. Eventually she moved out. I don't see how I can be criticized for seeking solace elsewhere."

Harrington acted as if he were genuinely surprised. "You have proof that your wife was unfaithful?"

"You've seen the video, haven't you? Believe me, that's the most devastating thing that could pop out of a man's inbox. Cheating is bad enough. But making a porno film?" The jurors were stirring, shifting from side to side, looking at one another, and of course, looking at Candice. "I think I showed admirable restraint, all in all. If I'd filed for divorce at that time, I don't believe the court would've given her a cent."

Harrington shuffled papers. He looked as if he'd lost his place. "There is one other matter. The eyewitness mentioned that, on the night of the murder, the defendant wore a silk blouse and matching black slacks."

"I know exactly what she's describing. I bought that outfit for Candice. We were on vacation in Italy. Bought it in Rome, in fact. At the foot of the Spanish Steps."

"Do you know where that outfit is now?"

"No. After I read the account in the papers, I looked for it in

Candice's closet. It was gone. It's possible she took it with her when she moved out. It wasn't at the dry cleaners, either."

"You checked?"

"That was the logical place to look. You wouldn't put something like that in the washing machine. Couldn't even hand wash it at home. It requires special treatment." His voice dropped a notch. "Especially if you need to remove blood stains."

26

Kenzi declined to cross-examine for a wide variety of reasons. For starters, the man was her father, and interrogating her father about infidelity was likely to give everyone the creeps. If the jury didn't hate her already, they certainly would after that.

But the truth was, she had little to say. When Harrington finished his direct, she scribbled a note on the legal pad between Candice and herself.

TRUE?

Candice scribbled her reply. TOLD YOU. HAD LOVER.

BEFORE HUSBAND?

Candice took a few moments before she scrawled her reply. MAYBE.

DURING THE BREAK, Kate approached her. "Is Sharon here?"

"Sorry. She's tracking down a new lead."

"That's okay. This really concerns you more."

That caught her attention. "Something about this case?"

"Indirectly. Probably. I don't know." Kate pulled a small notepad out of her back pocket. "I've come from the medical examiner's office."

"Something about Zelda?"

"Exactly. Chang finished her tests. Probable cause of death? Heart attack."

"Now—what?"

"You heard me right. Natural causes. Not a head wound."

"Then...her death was just a bizarre coincidence?"

"I didn't say that. Remember how she was found."

"With a mirror around her neck. But—I don't think she did that to herself."

"Someone could conceivably have shown up with a mirror after she died. I asked the examiner to look into it, to see if she can determine how closely the time of death corresponds to the time of the...bashing."

"Could someone have used the mirror to suggest Zelda was killed by the first murderer—even though she wasn't?"

"That is the question, as Hamlet would say. For that matter, it's not impossible that the mirror preceded the heart attack."

"Maybe it induced the heart attack?"

"Maybe. Which is why I'm concerned about your murder trial."

"Because...?"

"Because the only thing I know for certain is that there's a lot about this case we don't know yet. In fact, I think there's more we don't know than we do."

———

SHARON DESCENDED the steps to what looked more like a bunker than a basement. More like a dungeon than a workplace. One padded reclining chair in the middle of the room. No seating for visitors, which suggested that her host never had any visitors. The only illumination was the glow emanating from more than a dozen widescreen monitors mounted in a semi-circular arrangement.

"Cool office, huh?"

"Just what I was thinking," Sharon replied. "You must be a mind reader."

She had some qualms about entering the mancave of Stanley Ventrillo. His home was in a low-rent neighborhood and gave off a serious serial-killer vibe. Stanley himself was short, portly, and bore a beard that looked as if it hadn't been trimmed since...well, ever. Mid-thirties, she guessed, but with all that hair it was hard to be sure. His pale skin suggested that he spent most of his life in this room staring at screens.

"Thanks for seeing me. Alex says you're the best in the field."

"He's right."

No false modesty there. "Not to be rude, but when I performed an internet search on your name, I got nothing."

"Only fools use their real names on the internet. You wouldn't if you knew everything going on out there. Next time, search for Deep-FakePhil."

She made a mental note. "All run together? No spaces?"

"Exactly. Only Alex and a handful of others know my real name. At this point, I think my mother may have forgotten my real name."

"And your specialty is..."

"Like the moniker suggests. Deepfakes." He took a seat—the only seat—and swiveled around to face her. "Sit down."

"There's no other chair."

He grinned, then pressed a button on his armrest. She heard a hydraulic whirring sound, followed by a click.

A portion of the floor slid away, revealing a sizable opening.

Another chair, just like his, slowly rose.

"Is that the coolest thing ever or what?" he said. "Cost a fortune, but so worth it."

"No doubt." Once the whirring ended, she tested the seat with her hand. Seemed secure. She slowly lowered herself into it. "And here I thought you were antisocial."

"Are you kidding? I got two other pop-up chairs on the other side. For gaming nights."

"Video gamers?"

"Natch. No one can beat me. But they still make futile efforts. Foolish mortals. I am the king of Rainbow Red Siege."

"Tell me more about the deepfakes. Alex doesn't think the video the prosecution plans to use at trial is real."

"Oh, it's real all right." Ventrillo stroked his beard knowingly. "The question is whether it's really your client. Or whether they're really having sex. Or something else has been altered. Do you know what a deepfake is?"

Not really, but she didn't feel like admitting it. "I gather it's kinda like...Photoshopping."

"Not at all. Photoshop is for still photos. And frankly, Photoshops are relatively easy to identify, if you know what to look for. Deepfakes are the next gen. Deepfakes are digitally altered videos that use AI to make someone appear to be doing or saying...whatever you want them to do or say. The key is artificial intelligence. That's what makes it so difficult to detect."

"How does that work?"

"AI algorithms use a dataset of videos and images to create a virtual model of an individual's face. That model can be altered, manipulated, or superimposed to create whatever you want. Hollywood does it all the time. That's how Princess Leia appeared at the end of *Rogue One*."

"Or how Candice appeared in a porno?"

He tilted his head. "Look, creeps have always been with us. But once upon a time, forging a realistic image of someone took a lot of time, skill, and effort. Today, any jerkoff with an internet connection, software, and a powerful PC can do it. The first deepfake videos involved celebrities. That Wonder Woman actress' head stuck on a porn actress' body, that sort of thing. A video like that can be sold to losers everywhere. But the video in this case is different."

"Because Candice isn't famous?"

He nodded. "Maybe her head was put on another woman's body. But that's not the only possibility. It could be her but transplanted to a different location or situation. It's possible the male figure was replaced. Or disguised. There's not much a good deepfaker can't manage these days."

"Isn't there anything that can be done to stop this?"

"No. At least, not yet. As you probably know, misogyny runs deep on the dark web. And in the extreme right. Sadly, those two groups have a sharp correspondence. It isn't all ex-boyfriends seeking revenge. Some men flat-out hate women. That's triggering a lot of gun violence these days, too, but that's not my area of expertise. A DEEPFAKES Accountability Act was introduced in Congress, but it didn't go anywhere. So deepfake porn thrives. You can even download free apps that allow you to 'nudify' the pics on your phone. To effectively remove a woman's clothing and then post the photo, claiming someone was sexting when in fact the photo has been faked."

"Unbelievable."

"Nasty people do nasty things. Revenge porn, or nonconsensual porn, has skyrocketed. A vindictive hacker doesn't need sex tapes of a woman who spurned him. He just needs her Facebook or Instagram photos to insert into one of the zillions of public-domain porn movies available online. Combine a search engine with a deepfake app and you can cause a lot of misery. There are even forums where men post paid requests for videos of a specific woman, then share links to the woman's social media."

"That should be illegal."

"Should be but isn't. Section 230."

"Right."

"A few platforms have taken steps to stop this voluntarily. Facebook has blocked people posting URLs for those deepfake digital undressing sites."

"But not the photos themselves?"

"Depends on the platform. YouTube has family-friendly divisions that don't like nudes at all. But of course, there are some legit reasons to post nudes—famous works of art, classic photos of Marilyn Monroe. And many women deliberately post sexy pictures of themselves. Maybe not complete nudes, but very revealing. That's how they build their followings. So how can a platform distinguish a legit nude from a faked one?"

"I think Section 230 needs to be repealed. Or seriously rewritten."

"You're not the only one. It's a decades-old law. But revision doesn't seem to be high on anyone's legislative agenda. And social media platforms aren't looking for more work. Even the ones that have policies forbidding sexually explicit content do a poor job of enforcing their rules. It's just not a priority. You'd have more luck getting them to take down illegally posted copyrighted material than you would getting them to take down a deepfake photo."

"If it's so hard to discern fakes, how can you be sure about the video the prosecution is using?"

"Because I have software most people don't. Software no one is supposed to have. I hacked it from DARPA."

"Uhh..."

"Department of Defense. Defense Advanced Research Projects Agency. They've got the best stuff in the world. They've developed learning algorithms that can detect manipulated videos, including deepfakes. Of course, the software gets more sophisticated all the time. The DOD has to work double-time to keep up."

"You're certain the prosecution's recording has been altered?"

"Correctimundo. But as for how exactly it's been altered—I can't be sure."

"Would you be willing to testify?"

He gestured around the room. "Does this look like the abode of someone who wants to go public? I'm in the webhead subculture. We like to keep a low profile."

"Surely you can make an exception. Candice could go to prison for the rest of her life."

"For all I know, she deserves to go to prison for the rest of her life."

"I can subpoena you, you know."

"You'll be sorry if you do. You won't get what you want."

Sharon's fingernails dug into the armrest. "There must be some way I can convince you. This is very important."

His head slowly turned. "How important?"

She didn't like the sound of that. "What are you gettin' at?"

"You look like a super-cool woman. And unlike some of the losers on the internet, I like women."

"I'm not going to sleep with you."

He sat up straight. "I was just thinking...you know...maybe coffee."

"I'm not going to date you to get your cooperation."

He looked so crestfallen, she couldn't help softening the blow. "Besides, I'm in a relationship. With a woman."

"Oh. Sorry. I had no idea. I didn't get that vibe."

She pressed her lips together. "And what vibe would that be?"

"I mean, I just—"

"'Cause I don't have a butch haircut and a flannel shirt? Maybe big boots and an overloaded keyring?"

"I'm sorry. I just thought you were cool and wanted to spend more time with you. I don't get many women down here in the cave. Could you at least give me...thirty minutes of gaming? I mean, you're already in the chair."

She knew she should not feel sorry for this chump. But he looked as if he were about to cry. "You got MarioKart on one of these machines?"

"Of course. I have all the classics."

"Then boot it up, pistol. I don't know much about video games, but I know how to drive." She grinned. "Buckle your seatbelt. I'm about to take you for the ride of your life."

27

Next day, Kenzi endured a morning full of prosecution witnesses. They were dry as dust, and she didn't think the jury was nearly as interested in the mysterious green fiber as Harrington was. On the other hand, the witnesses did make their points, and who was she to judge what might turn the tide?

It took him three witnesses to accomplish the task, but Harrington managed to establish an evidentiary chain from Candice's purchase of the scarf to the appearance of the fiber on Venus' purse. With a combination of retail testimony and commercial thread experts (yes, they exist), he established the link. The fiber came from the scarf purchased by Candice, which was so expensive it was hard to imagine many people walking the streets of the city with it.

Harrington's forensic fiber expert was a middle-aged balding man named Ian Yarrow. Kate had warned her that Yarrow might look weak but was in fact extremely smart and would stand his ground.

On cross, Kenzi asked, "Can you itemize the factors that allowed you to positively identify this fiber and tie it to my client's scarf?"

"Absolutely. Color, texture, and type. In this case, we have a match on all three."

"You know, I was given an opportunity to examine the fiber. In a concealed evidence bag. I had a hard time even seeing it. Saying that it positively came from a particular scarf would've been impossible."

"For you." He offered a small smile. "Which is why we have people like myself who specialize in this field. We know what to look for and we have the tools to find it."

"What kind of equipment do you use?"

"In this case, I used both a stereomicroscope and a polarized light microscope. They can both be useful. The first is better for judging color, the latter is better for texture. When you're looking at these fibers on the microscopic level, even the slightest difference is readily detectable. Of course, I first performed a burn test."

"What exactly is that?"

"Pretty much just what it sounds like. Light a Bunsen burner, bring the sample close, though not close enough to set it on fire, and record your observations."

"Such as what?"

"The odor can provide a great deal of information about the fiber. It's how we distinguish a natural fiber from a manmade fiber, or a blend, or for that matter, a human hair. Even designers and fabric stores use this test to make sure they have the fiber content they want. If it smells like burning hair, it's probably silk or wool. If it smells like burning paper, it's probably cotton, rayon, or perhaps linen. If it melts and beads, it's acetate or nylon. If it doesn't burn, it's probably polyester or asbestos."

"Sounds like this test only narrows the range of possibilities."

"Which is why I do much more. The burn test is a starting point, not an end. By performing many chemical tests, we eventually narrow the possibilities down to something specific. Which is why I can state conclusively that the fiber in question came from that scarf."

"Or another one just like it."

"That is tremendously unlikely."

"But it's possible."

"It wouldn't explain the cross transfer."

Kenzi hadn't expected that response. She glanced at Harrington.

He was grinning. Yup. He'd left a trap for her. And she fell into it.

But the jury was listening. She couldn't stop now. "What do you mean?"

"The green fiber from the scarf was found on the victim's purse. But we also found a fiber on the defendant that matches what the victim was wearing when she was killed."

"What would that be?"

"A piece of pink cotton. The victim was wearing a pink sweater when she entered the meditation maze. It was in the defendant's hair."

"You cannot possibly say with certainty that this cotton came from Venus."

"I can say that it completely conforms with the clothing the victim wore when her body was found at the murder scene. Color, fabric, type. Perfect match."

"But—this could just be an...unfortunate coincidence."

Yarrow raised an eyebrow. "Getting to be a lot of those, aren't there? Like, beyond the realm of reasonable doubt."

———

DURING THE NEXT BREAK, Kenzi met Julia Battersby in the courtroom corridor. She felt bad about dragging Julia downtown, but she had insisted that they meet. Kenzi didn't need to hear the words to understand how upset Julia was. All she had to do was listen to the distraught tone of her voice.

"You and the Le parents did the baby swap, right?"

"We did."

"And?"

Her eyes widened. Tears sprang out so quickly it was almost frightening. "She's my baby!"

Her husband Carl stood beside her, propping her up. "I always knew something was off. I'm not saying I didn't love Ellie. But—this is entirely different. This baby is a part of me."

"I felt the same way," Julia said, wiping her eyes. "This child is mine. I knew it the first instant I held her in my arms. Mine, mine, all mine."

"Plus she looks like us," Carl said. "She looks like my mother. She's a member of this family. She shares our heritage."

"I didn't have to work to feel a connection," Julia said. "It was already there."

"Have you talked to the other couple? How do they feel?"

Julia and Carl looked at one another. "Differently."

"But—if you could tell instantly that this was your biological child—"

"You'd think they would experience the same connection. But apparently they don't. It's like they shut the child off."

"I think this has been very stressful for them," Carl explained. "Amy doesn't seem entirely rational."

"What do you mean?" Kenzi asked.

"I'm not qualified to make a diagnosis. But I think she's having some kind of breakdown. She can't even discuss it rationally. Apparently she's going to some kind of facility to get help."

"And the baby?"

"Her husband isn't going to raise a child without his wife. I get the impression they want all this trauma to just...go away."

"It's been stressful for all of us!" Julia said.

"I know, I know." He wrapped his arm around her and patted her shoulder. "But they've walled themselves off. They just can't do it. They're spent."

"They don't want to switch babies permanently?"

"They do not. They aren't capable right now. He's going to have his hands full taking care of his wife."

"Do they object to you adopting the baby they've been raising?"

"Not at all. They've already brought her back to us."

"Then this is a great opportunity for you. Keep them both. It's a bonus. Two beautiful babies for one pregnancy."

The couple looked at one another. Neither spoke.

"I'm sure it will be a strain on you," Kenzi continued. "At least at first. But in time—"

Carl had to be the one to say it. "We can't do that."

"But why?"

"We can't afford it, for one thing. I told you that before. We're barely getting by as it is. And the strain on Julia..." He shook his head.

Kenzi looked into her client's eyes. This whole business had been so much more draining than anything she'd imagined or bargained for. It needed to be resolved before she went completely around the bend.

Kenzi spoke quietly. "I will remind you that this whole situation began because you were having trouble conceiving. Since that's unlikely to change in the future, you might welcome the opportunity to have an additional child who is the same age as your own child. They'll be like twins."

"I think adoption is a wonderful thing," Julia said. "When it's voluntary. Adoption was always an option for us. We chose the in-vitro procedure because we wanted a child who was biologically related to us."

"But still—"

"We're not doing it," Carl said flatly.

Kenzi stared at him wordlessly. She couldn't believe what she was hearing. "We still have a civil suit pending. We might be able to get a settlement that would ease the financial strain."

"You're not hearing me. Our plan was to raise one child. We're sticking to our plan."

Kenzi was stunned and didn't know what to do about it. She'd thought the hard part would be persuading them to give up the child they'd cared for so many months. "Look, I'm in the middle of this murder trial. Can you keep both babies a few more days? Then we'll try to figure something out."

"One week," he said. "Max."

She sighed. "One week."

———

KENZI WATCHED CAREFULLY as Madison Morrisey testified. He was an older man, late sixties at least, bald at the top with tufts of graying hair shooting out from either side of his head. He spoke with a cultured accent, almost British, just enough to sound refined and possibly a bit elitist. He wore gold wire-frame glasses and a pocket square.

"I've been trading in antiquities since the Eighties," he explained. "At first I worked out of my home. Now I own a large shop downtown. No internet presence at all. Can't stand all that online bickering, don't you know? No one can truly decide whether they wish to own a treasure until they've held it in their hands."

"Where's your shop?" Harrington asked.

"On Fifth. But don't bother dropping by. It's not open to the public."

"You have a shop that isn't open to the public?"

"Showings by appointment only."

"Doesn't that restrict your customer base?"

"Oh, no. It increases it. If people want to rub shoulders with the Great Unwashed, they can go to Walmart. People come to me for a different kind of experience."

"Who are your customers?"

"My clients, you mean. My clients are the creme de la crème. Serious collectors from many states. Even other countries."

"How do you find them?"

"My dear boy. They find me. Word of mouth, don't you know? People who travel in the best circles talk. Word gets around."

"And would one of your clients be the defendant?"

"Yes. I've placed many fine pieces with Mrs. Rivera. She specializes in works of Hispanic art. Though she is not Hispanic herself, I believe her husband is, and he has been collecting for some time."

"What have you sold the defendant?"

"Many wonderful things." He lowered his gaze. "But I expect what you want to hear about is the mirror."

That got the jurors' attention. "What kind of mirror?"

"Spanish colonial. Mid-eighteenth century. Red lacquered with mercury glass and a golden border."

Kenzi didn't have to be an expert to realize that sounded exactly like the mirror admitted into evidence as the murder weapon.

"How much was the mirror worth?"

When the witness answered, there was an audible gasp from the gallery.

Harrington shook his head. "I guess that's not something you'd buy just to check your makeup."

The witness chuckled. "I wouldn't think you'd bash someone over the head with it, either. But there's no explaining people."

"Am I correct in my belief that the mirror you sold the defendant sounds like the one that was used to kill the victim in this case?"

"There is no other mirror like that one in the entire world. It's one-of-a-kind. Or was."

"Then—"

"The mirror I sold Candice is the one that was used as a murder weapon. Indisputably."

"You're certain about that?"

"I am."

Harrington quickly admitted documents establishing the mirror's provenance and value.

"I looked for another mirror like that one," Morrisey explained, "after I realized it had been destroyed. I could find other Spanish mirrors from the same time frame. Other mirrors with mercury glass. Even similar mirrors with different frames—giltwood frames and octagonal frames and such. But one just like this one? It doesn't exist."

"So you're certain that the mirror you sold the defendant was used to kill Venus Collins."

"There is no question about it."

"Thank you. Pass the witness."

Kenzi marched to the witness stand. She didn't think she was likely to intimidate this witness. But Candice had given her enough information to throw him for a loop or two.

"You've sold work to both Mr. and Ms. Rivera, haven't you?"

Morrisey took out a handkerchief and dabbed his forehead. "I have had that pleasure."

"Who buys the most?"

He pondered a moment. "Who buys more items, or who spends more money?"

"More money."

"That would be the husband. I rarely—" He hesitated, then smiled. "Wait—that's your father, isn't it?"

"Please answer the question."

"Perhaps you recall seeing the mirror yourself."

"I'm not a witness. Answer the question."

"Mr. Rivera I see perhaps once a year or so. Usually when he's redecorating his office or a room in his home. He favors fine art rather than decorative art. Paintings and sculpture. And that, when you're talking about well-known artists, tends to be more expensive."

"His wife doesn't spend nearly so much money with you, right?"

"No. Though she is no piker. But my impression was that she had a more...restricted allowance."

"And you're aware that the two are currently in the process of divorcing?"

"I am. So sad. What a world we live in."

"In the foreseeable future, my client is unlikely to buy much from you. Whereas Mr. Rivera might well spend millions on your fancy gewgaws."

"I'm afraid I don't see—"

"I'm saying her husband is the one who butters your bread, so it is very much in your interest to do what you think will please him. Even if it means throwing Candice to the wolves."

Harrington stood. "Argumentative."

"Sustained."

No biggie. The jury heard what she said. "Have you spoken to Mr. Rivera recently?"

"Just a few days ago. He was interested in a small Fernando Botero. A Columbian artist. Already quite collectible and I believe the value of his work will skyrocket in the years to come."

"Six figures or seven?"

The witness pursed his lips. "Seven."

"Did you close the deal?"

"No. He was interested but said he needed to wait to see what the outcome of this trial might be."

Kenzi smiled. "And he said this knowing full well you would be taking the witness stand."

"Yes, but if you're implying—"

Kenzi walked away. "Don't bother. The jury gets the drift. No more questions."

28

After lunch, Kenzi told Candice to brace herself for the worst. Not that any of this had been fun.

But now it was time for the sex video. Although she had renewed all her arguments, she had not been able to keep it from the jury. And that wasn't the only invasion of privacy on the horizon.

Harrington called yet another member of the police department to the witness stand. Peter Zola, head of the cybercrimes department, who led the quest to hack into the cellphone seized shortly after Candice was arrested.

Zola described the arduous process they followed to get inside Candice's phone.

"Getting past the superficial ID lock is not the main problem. We did have access to the defendant's face, though we might've needed a subpoena to force her to look at her iPhone. But six-digit encryption is not particularly daunting. If you try every number combination in order, you can find the right one in, on average, about eleven hours. We have a computer program that inputs the numbers for us and over-rides the failed-attempts lockout, so we don't have to do it manually. We just initiate the program and wait."

"You were able to get inside the defendant's phone?"

"Yes. But we wanted more information than what was immediately available. We wanted access to files that might have been deleted. We wanted inside her email and text accounts. We wanted into her cloud backup files. We also wanted to search files that were no longer present on the phone due to their age. Apple has chosen not to assist law enforcement, citing their customers' needs for privacy."

"But you didn't let that stop you."

"Of course not. The first time Apple refused to help, the FBI organized a task force of cyber-experts, which they loan out when schedules permit. They don't need Apple anymore. Best for all parties concerned. But if you think anything on your phone is private, you're kidding yourself."

"I believe you found some video of interest?"

"Yes. It appears the defendant received a video by email and viewed it on her phone. The sender was anonymous and untraceable, apparently a fake account created on a public library computer to send this video. And the defendant appears to have deleted both the email and the video shortly after she received it. We would never have found it but for the extraordinary data-recovery measures we took."

This was the key to Harrington getting the video admitted into evidence. He couldn't authenticate a video anonymously sent to him, but anything acquired from the defendant was self-authenticating. Kenzi couldn't help but be suspicious about any complex recovery procedure that led to the prosecution getting exactly what it wanted.

"What can you tell us about this recording?"

"The defendant appears in it. Her face is completely visible. She's much more...excited than she appears now in the courtroom."

"And who is she with?"

"That we don't know. As you will see, the man is facing away from the camera. And in shadow."

"Thank you. With the court's permission, I would now like to show the recording."

Judge Underhill nodded. The bailiff dimmed the lights. The monitor on the wall became a movie screen.

And the courtroom became a porn parlor.

The movie was not as explicit as some of the filth readily available on the internet—but it was bad enough. Candice was completely naked. She was straddling the man's lap, bouncing up and down, visibly enjoying herself. Harrington had the volume turned up full blast, so the jury was treated to loud wails of pleasure, waves of ecstasy.

The man never turned his head. And never made a sound. In fact, he never moved much at all. Candice was doing all the work. Of course, the man probably knew he was on candid camera.

After a full minute of gyrating, she bore down on the man's shoulders and accelerated her pace. Her hip thrusts and grinding accelerated. Her head flipped back and the sounds emerging were guttural, almost animal. Eventually she let out an ear-piercing scream.

The jury breathed a communal sigh of relief when it finally ended. Kenzi could see them looking at one another. She wasn't sure what they were thinking. But she was certain that the jurors' opinions of Candice had been permanently altered.

Candice seemed undisturbed, as if she hadn't been watching. If the jurors were looking for embarrassment, they didn't find it. Nor did she appear particularly guilt-ridden. Given a choice between covering her head or acting defiant, she chose a middle ground that was difficult to read.

Harrington let a few moments pass before he spoke again. He probably wanted the jury to keep the video in their heads for a while. Let it have impact. Before he moved on.

"You don't know who the man is?"

"No." Zola paused. "But it isn't her husband. Alejandro Rivera is much taller. Wider also."

"I see." Harrington took a step back, wiping his mouth. He was putting on a show, acting as if he hated to press forward because this was all so tawdry and unpleasant. But darn it, he had a job to do. "Did you discover anything else of interest on the defendant's phone?"

"Two things. First, the defendant had Location Services activated on her iPhone. She used Google Maps. The phone kept track of her movements. As a result, we know that she—or at the very least, her phone—was at the maze where the victim was murdered. About the time of the murder."

"That's certainly noteworthy. Was there something else?"

"Yes. Texts."

"The defendant was texting people?"

"Lots of people. Constantly. Not unusual these days. We ultimately unearthed more than ten thousand texts from her account just from the past year."

"How many of those are relevant to this case?"

"Only a few. I would draw your attention to a few text exchanges with her husband, and then a few with"—he paused, obviously building suspense—"the victim. Venus."

The jurors appeared surprised. The defendant texted the victim? They knew Candice met Venus before her death. But they didn't expect them to be digital pen pals.

"Let's start with her husband," Kenzi continued. "I'm sure no one is surprised that the defendant texted her husband."

"You might be more surprised if you realized there were only seven texts to him during the previous six months. And those were pretty frosty. Judging from these texts, the two were not getting along well. But in the week before the murder, their texting became angry."

"What were they discussing?"

"That's not always clear. But they were arguing about something. They were angry—"

Kenzi rose. "Objection. There's no probative value in the witness' summary. If he has the texts, let the jurors read them for themselves." Not that the texts were going to do Candice any good. But there was no reason to have the witness magnifying the damage. These texts didn't need a spin doctor.

"Fair enough," the judge replied. "You're planning to enter these texts into evidence, aren't you, Mr. Harrington?"

"Yes, your honor." He looked like a little boy who'd lost his favorite marble. "We can do that. If you wish." He turned toward the screen and brought up a screenshot of the first series of texts. "Mr. Zola, can you please tell the jury what we're looking at?"

"This is an exchange between the defendant and her husband. I excerpted these myself, so I can authenticate them and testify that what you're seeing was on the defendant's phone. The only changes I've made is to remove texts that do not pertain to the case."

Before trial, Kenzi had objected to this redaction on grounds that it created a false portrait, since all the jury would see were the texts that fed the prosecution's case. The judge overruled her objection.

Zola used a handheld remote to scroll through the texts and to highlight what he was discussing. "This is a text exchange initiated by the defendant. She writes, 'I know what you did.'" Zola scrolled a bit more. "The reply, which came almost immediately, according to the phone's internal clock, is, 'I know what you did, too. I've seen it.'"

"Just to be clear," Harrington said, "did the video the jury just viewed exist at this time?"

"Yes. The defendant had received it before this exchange took place."

"Could he be referring to the sex video?" Harrington had cleverly avoided an objection by using the word "could."

"We know it had been sent to the defendant, so it's entirely plausible that it was sent to her husband as well."

Kenzi eye-checked Candice. No reaction. Nothing at all.

"Why do you say that?"

"Look at the next part of the exchange." He scrolled down a little lower. "'You have no moral ground to stand on.' And then she replies, 'And you do?' About ten minutes pass. Then he responds. 'You've had your petty revenge. It's finished. Let it go.'"

"He seems to be hoping for...some kind of reconciliation."

"But look at the reply." He moved the screen down. "'Finished? I've barely begun.'"

A rustling from the jury box. More shifting around in seats. In many ways, an ambiguous comment like that was better than a confession. It allowed their imaginations to go wild with possibilities. That remark could mean anything, but the way the prosecution presented it made it sound like a threat.

Zola sat up straight. "And that's the end of the exchange. So far as we can tell, the parties never texted again. Not from that moment to when the police confiscated her cellphone."

"Very interesting." Harrington stroked his chin, then turned a page in his notebook. "And I believe you mentioned another text exchange of interest."

"Yes. This was between the defendant and her victim. I'm sorry. The victim. Venus."

"Objection," Kenzi said. "All this man is doing is reading texts. He doesn't know who wrote them."

Harrington jumped in. "We've verified the number."

"Then at best," Kenzi said, "assuming you did your work right, you know whose phone the messages came from. You can't prove the owner of the phone composed the texts. You didn't see it happen."

"Is learned counsel suggesting that someone else grabbed the defendant's phone and sent messages without her knowledge?" He laughed out loud. "If so, she's even more desperate than she seems."

"What I'm suggesting," Kenzi said, "is that the district attorney and his witnesses should stop exaggerating what little they know. Given how much they've interfered with my client's phone, it isn't hard to imagine someone else could do the same. We live in a world in which digital data is manipulated every day. Half the things people see online turn out to be false."

"Are you saying these texts are fake news?"

"I'm saying, stop overplaying your hand. You found these texts on a phone. And that's all you know about it."

She was doing her best to instill doubt, but today, everyone relied on their phones, and in many cases, spent far too much time staring at their phones. They had learned to trust them.

"I'm going to overrule the motion," the judge said, "but I will caution the witness to restrict his testimony to his field of expertise. Don't make assumptions. And don't assert facts unless you know them to be facts."

"Yes, your honor," Zola said. "Of course."

"And now that we've gotten that out of the way," Harrington said, bristling, "could we please hear about the other texts you mentioned? Between the defendant and the murder victim."

Zola pushed a button on his remote and brought up another series of texts. "Here's the first exchange. The defendant—" He stopped himself. "The texter using the defendant's phone initiated the contact. It's clear that they've met, but so far as I can tell, this was the first time they texted. The first message reads, 'I'm coming for you.'"

He scrolled quickly through the messages. "After some time passes, the victim replied, 'Leave me alone. I'm working.' The reply? 'Flat on your back, I bet.'"

Kenzi pressed her lips together.

"A few minutes later, another response from Venus' phone. 'Jealous?' And here's the reply." He pushed a button that highlighted and enlarged the text. "'You skanky whore. You need to be punished.' The victim replies, 'You'd like that, wouldn't you?' The defendant comes right back with, 'Damn straight. I'm going to take you down, bitch. I'm going to have fun making you hurt.'"

He paused, presumably to give the jury a moment to catch up. "The exchange continues. Venus texts, 'You wouldn't dare.' The defendant answers. 'The hell I wouldn't. Maybe I'll come over right now and mess you up but good.'"

A somber tone filled the courtroom. Didn't matter what Kenzi argued now. That sounded like a threat.

"Just one more message I want to bring to your attention." Zola scrolled down. "The defendant texted, 'You need to take a long hard look in the mirror, slut. Maybe I could help you with that.'"

PART III

OUT FLEW THE WEB AND FLOATED WIDE

29

W hat Kenzi really wanted was a quiet firelit dinner with Alex someplace no one was watching where she could indulge in completely decadent behavior. But that wasn't going to happen anytime soon.

She still kinda hoped he'd drop by, though.

Her team had gathered at her apartment to rehash the day's trial and determine what they should do next. "Any chance we're going to see Candice?" Sharon asked.

"No. I invited her. But apparently she doesn't want company."

"I don't think she should be alone tonight," Hailee shouted from the kitchen. "She must be worried sick."

"We're all worried sick. But she's facing a prison sentence. Possibly for the rest of her life."

"Some of this is her fault," Emma said. "It would've helped if she'd told us everything. At the start."

True. But that wasn't helpful. "We need to focus on how we're going to rehabilitate our client."

"Candice could've given us the inside track," Emma insisted. "Instead, she left us trailing the prosecution, eating their dirt." She pointed toward the fireplace. "Hailee even had to redo her murder board."

Kenzi glanced at the hearth. Hailee had assembled a large bulletin board with photos of the key players, evidence photocopies, time-place stamps, and yarn indicating the interconnections. It was a monumental effort. Not something she could introduce in court, but helpful when trying to make sense of a case with too many players and unanswered questions.

"Here's where we stand," Emma said. "Candice had an affair— apparently before Daddy did. With or without her knowledge, someone recorded her having sex. Candice knew about Daddy's relationship with Venus. Candice texted remarks to Venus that could be taken as threats and made a veiled reference to a mirror. Forensic evidence places her at the scene of the crime."

"You left out the most incriminating fact," Sharon said.

"And that would be?"

"She had a Brazilian butt job. I mean, who does that?"

"Maybe she wanted it to look good in the video."

"That skinny little thing? She didn't need butt work."

"Maybe she was doing it to keep her husband."

"If she wanted to keep her husband, she shouldn't have been screwing other men and making porn videos. And palling around with her husband's mistress. Who, if I may remind you, also had a butt job. Suggesting that your daddy is a major butt man."

Emma clamped her hands over her ears. "I do not want to hear this."

"By the by," Sharon said, "did you spot the butt doc in the court-room yesterday?"

Kenzi's head rose. "I did not. When was he there?"

"Mid-morning. Stayed most of the day."

"I guess I was too busy to notice. Are you sure it was him?"

"I couldn't mistake him for anyone else. He saw me, too. Kept looking at me weirdly."

"Maybe he wants to ask you to dinner."

"More likely he wants to plump my butt." Sharon patted her back-side. "As if it weren't plump enough already."

"Apparently you can never have too much."

"Too much for your daddy, you mean."

Emma slapped hands over her ears again.

"Okay, you clowns need a break." Hailee stepped out of the kitchen. "Come eat some pasta. I've been slaving away on this for hours."

Possibly an exaggeration. But what caught Kenzi's attention was that Hailee was out of her wheelchair. And carrying a heavy platter. She almost cautioned Hailee not to overexert herself—then stopped. She knew that would embarrass her.

"I have another surprise," Hailee said, resting the platter on the table. She swirled her arms around. "Abracadabra. Presto chango appearo."

Alex stepped out of the kitchen.

Sharon whistled. "Now that is a damn fine parlor trick."

Alex waggled his fingers. "Hey, Kenzi."

"Well...hey." She felt a sudden rush of blood to her face.

"Sorry about the surprise. Your daughter called. She assured me I wouldn't be intruding."

Kenzi squinted. "And how did my daughter get your number?"

Hailee answered. "From your phone."

"You hacked my phone?"

"Are you kidding? You've used the same code on everything since before I was born."

"But I never reveal the code."

"Mom, it's your birthday."

"Well..." She walked toward Alex. "Can you stay?"

"I was promised dinner." He glanced toward the others. "I hope that's okay. You can talk about the case."

"Honey," Sharon said, "that's all we've been talking about."

"That, and Brazilian butt doctors," Emma murmured.

Alex hesitated. "I...don't know too much about that."

"No worries. We can enlighten you."

They sat around the table. Alex waited till the women were seated, then took the chair beside Kenzi. Which the others had left for him.

"I've been working with Ventrillo," Alex explained. "I think he's ready to testify. I wish he could say more. But he can impugn the credibility of the video."

"That sounds good." Kenzi took her first bite. And swooned. "Hailee, this is delicious."

Hailee fanned her face. "Thank you, Mother dear."

"How did you make the cream sauce?"

"A magician never reveals her secrets."

"But chefs share recipes."

"I'm waiting for a million-dollar book contract."

Couldn't fault that.

"I've lined up another witness you might want to call," he said. "In a similar vein."

"What does he do?"

"He's a...uh...film distributor."

"What, like MGM?"

"Not exactly."

"What a minute," Sharon said. "Are you talking about some porn movie sleazebag?"

"I'm afraid I am."

Kenzi's brow creased. "What would this guy say?"

"That video hasn't been screening exclusively in the courtroom. It's been sold on the internet. For profit."

Kenzi pressed her hand against her forehead. "I knew it had leaked but—someone's making money off it?"

"Apparently this is scary common. Big business."

"Sounds like mob big business," Sharon said.

"And you are totally on the nose."

Kenzi got an unpleasant tingling sensation. "We had Canadian syndicate connections in our last case. How many mobs are there?"

"More than you realize. But most still focus on narcotics. Prostitution. Sex trafficking. Porn is plenty lucrative, though."

"Porn is the new black?"

"No. That would be bank fraud."

"The mob is involved in bank fraud? I thought that was all Wall Street preppies."

Alex shook his head. "The world is going digital and the mob has to keep up. Some of the old mainstays are fading. Extortion. Kidnapping. They don't make nearly as much money as a good hack can. Law enforcement clampdowns have put a dent in the human trafficking market. It's harder, riskier. Requires transporting people across borders. So some criminal organizations are getting involved in bank fraud. Hacking. It doesn't require crossing borders. Just a few brainiacs with low morals."

"I've seen *The Sopranos*," Sharon said. "Those guys aren't smart enough to be hackers."

"They find people who are. Apparently computer whizzes are so valuable now that mobsters pay big money for them. It's a whole new business model, if that's the right word. The new mob weapon isn't switchblades. It's code."

"Computer code?"

"Right. In the past, most hackers copied and pasted code devised by the Russian and Eastern-European eggheads behind the cyberattacks you've probably read about. Now some Latin Americans are getting into the game. And Canadians. They're cooking up their own code and selling it abroad. Like Walter White used to cook meth."

"That's it," Sharon said. "I'm taking all my money out of the bank and stuffing it inside my mattress."

"You'll probably make about the same interest rate," Emma noted.

"There's a cartel called Amavaldo whose masterminds invented a particularly vicious trojan virus targeting banks. They've entered banks' online domains and drained user accounts. The word on the street is that next they're coming after your cellphones."

"Nooooooo!" Sharon screamed. "Anything but that!"

"On a slightly tangential note," Emma said, "could these people... plant fake texts?"

"I don't see why not," Alex replied.

Kenzi swallowed another bite. "Why do I keep getting involved in mob schemes?"

Alex tilted his head. "It suggests that someone in your circle is involved with the mob."

"I think it's Emma," Sharon said. "So quiet. Always thinking. Plotting."

Emma shook her head. "I think it's Hailee. Let's face it. She's smarter than the rest of us combined."

"Me?" Hailee looked appalled—then started laughing. "Me as the secret mastermind no one suspects because of my clever disguise as a chairbound middle-school student?" She beamed. "I kinda love that."

"If it's okay," Alex said, "I'll bring this film distributor to meet you tomorrow morning. And I'll tell him to keep his schedule clear. I think he'll be a good witness for you, but he's kind of a...a..."

"Sleaze," Sharon completed.

"Well...yeah."

"I can handle that," Kenzi said.

He gave her a long look. "Like it or not, Kenzi Rivera, we're going to be spending a lot of time together."

Kenzi looked deeply into his eyes. "I can live with that."

30

I carus felt an itching on his arm, one that was impossible to ignore. He kept clicking away at his laptop, but there weren't enough websites in the world to distract him forever. The demon was always with him. The monkey was always on his back.

It had been weeks since he last shot up. And he missed it. Surely he could be excused for a few slips, given what happened. But it was all a slippery slope, wasn't it? He missed the palpable rush that helped keep the ravens at bay.

Venus had always said it would get the best of him.

She'd been right.

And now she was dead.

He felt entirely on his own, isolated from his real life. He hadn't even been able to go to his sister's funeral. Instead, he watched from a distance, a sad pathetic ceremony with a whopping six people in attendance, counting the preacher.

Venus deserved so much more than he had ever been able to provide.

He wanted to go out. He was sick of this disgusting rooming house and the spiders and the couple fighting upstairs. But he knew they were looking for him.

He stood slowly, pushing himself up on wobbly feet. He couldn't start thinking like that. He had always courted depression. The only way to beat it back was to refuse to give in, to drown out the dark voice. The ravens.

He walked to the window, careful to keep his distance.

There was a whole big city out there—funny, scary, bright, dark, pretty, ugly, busy, beautiful. So many people with so many agendas, all living in their own personal worlds. But also intersecting. Like ants in an anthill crawling from one mound to the next, willing to do almost anything to get another crumb from the rich man's table...

He leaned into the glass—then stopped himself. He didn't want to be seen. He pulled back, but adjusted the shutters to shield his face while he peered through...

Sandy. He was almost certain of it. Hadn't seen the bastard for weeks, and his vision was far from perfect...

But it was Sandy. And he was with that other man. Not Kingsley. The lawyer. Couldn't remember his name, but it was him. He'd seen the guy on television a few times. Looked like someone who shouldn't be trusted.

And they were in his neighborhood. Hunting for something. Or someone.

All at once, Sandy looked up. Straight at him.

Icarus rocketed backward, stumbling over a chair, crashing down on the floor.

Had Sandy seen him?

He waited, motionless, listening. Seconds seemed like hours. Sweat dripped down his face.

No sounds on the steps. No pounding at the door.

Maybe he'd gotten lucky. Maybe he'd escaped. But they were nearby. And they weren't going away till they found what they wanted.

He had to get out of here. Fast. He'd throw everything into a backpack, leave no trace...

And go where exactly?

The borders were closing. The trap was tightening. Soon there would be nowhere left to run.

He'd tried everything and everyone. No one wanted to help.

What about the lawyer? The other one. The one who met him in the bar. That had been a miserable interview. He was coming down hard and could barely see straight, but he faked it.

She said she'd take care of him if he would testify.

What he knew could blow her case wide open.

But if Kingsley found out, that bastard would blow him wide open.

———

KENZI KNEW she was the center of attention as the judge directed her to begin the defense case. The jury must be curious to know what she could possibly do or say after that avalanche of prosecution evidence.

For Kenzi's first witness, she recalled Ian Yarrow. She knew leading with a repeat forensic expert would be anticlimactic and she thought that was just fine. Let the jury suffer from dashed expectations, leading to diminished expectations...leading to startling surprises yet-to-come.

"When you testified for the prosecution, you stated that you felt the green fiber entwined on the victim's purse came from my client's scarf. Correct?"

"I didn't feel it to be so," the witness corrected. "I know it to be so. Based upon exhaustive scientific analysis."

"Right, right. And you didn't think it could've come from another scarf. Even another scarf of the same kind from the same manufacturer."

"The odds against that are enormous. Even a fiber from the same type of scarf might not be as perfect a match."

"I was wondering...can you tell from your exhaustive analysis when the fiber travelled from my client's scarf to the victim's purse?"

"The logical assumption—"

Kenzi raised a finger, stopping him cold. "I didn't ask for your assumptions. Do you know when the fiber made its way to that purse?"

"I doubt it would remain on the purse forever."

"Didn't you testify that it was entwined on the strap?"

"Well...yes."

"And you testified that it was all but invisible to the naked eye, correct?"

"True."

"So even though it was there, Venus would not pull it off. Since she couldn't see it."

"I suppose."

"The problem," Kenzi said, "is that we've all assumed that the night of the murder was the only time Venus and Candice met. But the district attorney has admitted evidence suggesting that they knew each other before that fateful night. And if they met before, the fiber could have been transferred at an earlier date."

"There's still the eyewitness who—"

"Yes. The elderly woman who claimed she saw Candice in the middle of the night wearing clothes no one has been able to find. But if the fiber transferred to the victim's purse on an earlier occasion, then it doesn't prove Candice had anything to do with the murder, does it?"

Yarrow stared at her, lips pursed, not answering. He didn't need to. Everyone in the courtroom could answer for him.

———

KENZI WAS NEVER comfortable calling someone to the stand she hadn't spent much time with. She was never happy calling someone who appeared sketchy at best and criminal at worst. Of course, not everyone associated with the porn industry was necessarily a crook. But she suspected many of the people sitting on the jury would not make that distinction.

Ernie Arkin was wiry, short, and way too fond of himself. His clothes appeared to be at least thirty years out of fashion—boots, bell-bottoms, silk shirt with flared cuffs, aviator glasses. Tinted-lens aviator glasses. He might as well have a big tattoo on his forehead reading: DON'T TRUST ME.

But then again, if he came across like a Boy Scout, it might be hard to believe he knew anything about porn. If nothing else, he had credibility in his chosen field.

"Please explain to the jury what you do for a living."

"I'm in the adult film industry."

"And when you say adult film, you mean..."

"Sexually explicit flicks. What we used to call stag-party films. Except today, it would be more accurate to call them kids-on-the-internet films."

Kenzi waited a few moments for that coin to drop, and then, once she thought the jury had absorbed it, she asked, "Would you also tell us about the job you had before you took on your current occupation?"

"No prob. I was an FBI agent."

Most of the jurors kept their emotions in check, but they still looked like they'd been smacked in the face. Good. Now she had their attention.

"What did you do for the FBI?"

"My last assignment was in the interstate vice division. Mostly undercover work. And yes, that included porn films."

"The FBI polices pornographic movies?"

"Less than you might expect. Porn isn't necessarily illegal these days, so long as the rules are followed. There are a few things you can't do, but as long as it's consenting adults having normal sexual intercourse, most jurisdictions don't think it's worth messing around with. Protected by the First Amendment and all that."

"What was the focus of your investigation?"

"The FBI is concerned about organized crime. In the last few years, we've seen a sharp increase in mob activity. Mob, syndicate, cartels, call it what you will. All variations on a theme. The internet has changed everything."

Kenzi eye-checked the jurors. Most of them were over forty, and she wanted to make sure they were following. "How so?"

"There are still a few porn parlors around, but they're dying fast because it's so easy to get that stuff on the internet. Kids know where to find it, and they know how to pay for it even if they don't have a credit card."

"If it's all over the internet...what's the problem?"

"It's big business, and people can make millions, even billions of dollars—if they have the content. More and more content. Like a drug addict, they can never get enough. It's a constant craving. More porn is more money. And you know what that means."

"What?"

"Distributors can afford to pay their suppliers lots of dough for content. So you get lowlifes creeping around makin' these movies any way they can."

Harrington rose. "Your honor, objection. Relevance. While I'm sure the jury is grateful to defense counsel for illuminating them about repulsive obscenity, I don't see any connection to this case."

"That's hard for me to imagine," Kenzi said. "He introduced a porn film into evidence."

"A film starring the defendant."

"Who knew nothing about it. And that's why I've called this witness. We—"

Judge Underhill raised his hand. "I see where this is going. I'll allow it a bit longer. But I do expect this to tie into the case. As soon as possible."

"It will, your honor." She turned back to the witness. "What was the FBI's cause for concern?"

"With the upswing in demand for pornography, we've also seen an upswing in what we call sneak-peeks. People making movies without the knowledge or consent of those involved. Cellphones have augmented this. You can make a damn fine film with your iPhone. Just plant it in the right place, start it, and get something going with your girlfriend. Or some drunk chick you picked up at a bar. Whatever. Insto-presto. Porn film."

"What does the FBI do to prevent this practice?"

"Damn little. But to be fair, what can you do? Sleaze will be sleaze. You can't stop people from being terrible human beings. Payments are typically made in cash. And organized crime figures are notoriously hard to nail down. Usually, the FBI targets the man at the top of the syndicate on the theory that if you cut off the head, the snake dies. But the last few decades have proven that it doesn't always work that way. Organized crime isn't a snake. It's a multi-headed hydra. You cut off the head—and three more spring up in its place. Very frustrating."

"And that's why you quit the FBI?"

"In part. After years of banging my head against the wall, accomplishing absolutely nothing, I noticed that my bank account was empty. I had nothing to show for my efforts, professionally or financially." He spread his hands wide. "Look, I got five kids. The oldest is about to start college. She wants to go to Stanford and she's smart enough to do it. But who's gonna pay the bills? The FBI? I don't think so."

"You needed a more lucrative line of work."

"Big time. And as it turns out, the feds have educated me in this field. I know the business inside out. I know the traps and pitfalls. I won't work with criminals. I run a business that's completely legit. You may not care for it. I get that. I wouldn't let my daughter anywhere near this stuff. But it's not illegal and I'm not taking advantage of anyone."

She didn't like seeing any woman reduced to appearing in smut. But she grasped his point. He was one of the good porn dealers.

"Could you describe for the jury what you do?"

"I distribute adult films. I don't make them. I have people who make them for me on a contract basis. Just like the big Hollywood studios do. I approve the script, then the production team, then the actors. I review a budget. Then I give them some money to make the flick. If they go over budget, that's their problem."

"How does this differ from how...say, a Canadian syndicate might make porn movies?"

"Objection," Harrington said. "Calls for speculation."

The judge tilted his head. "I think the witness has established his expertise in the area. I'll overrule the objection."

"Then...I object based on relevance."

The judge smiled. "You're getting warmer. But counsel has promised she's going to tie this into the case. I'm going to give her maybe two more minutes to do that."

Kenzi nodded. I hear and obey. "Please answer the question."

Arkin obliged. "Syndicates don't pay anyone, or if they do, they don't pay fairly. They trap people and force them to produce content. They take advantage of drug addicts and debtors. I, on the other hand, don't deal with anyone unless I know who they are and where the content came from. No sneak-peeks. Everyone who appears in one of my films has signed a contract. No kids, no addicts, no unwitting girl-friends. I also police the operation to make sure there's no sexism on the set or violence in the pictures. I'm well aware that some people think pornography fuels violence against women. I don't agree—when it's done properly. There's nothing wrong with a little sexual excitement not intended to fuel anger or gender-based violence." He raised his hands. "I'm not gonna make out like I'm Mother Teresa or anything. But I'm not a criminal and I don't work with anyone who is."

Okay. Time for the payoff. "Sir, have you had a chance to look at the film that plays a large role in the prosecution's case against my client?"

"I have."

"What do you think?"

"Based upon my expertise in the area, I would say it has all the classic hallmarks of a sneak-peek."

"And by that you mean...?"

"Looks to me like the woman in the movie had no idea she was making a movie."

Kenzi saw the jury stirring. Were they buying it? "Why?"

"Look how it's staged. Only the woman is identifiable. There's no script, no story. She's not in costume, not made up. Typically, guys making these sneak-peeks get very demanding. You must sit in that chair. We must do it this way. They've set up the camera in advance, in secret, so it has to go down as planned. Note that not only is the guy's face not visible—you don't hear a peep out of him. He's just a prop."

"Then this film may not reflect on the woman's character?"

"Not unless you're condemning a woman for being sexually active."

"The prosecution will note that she's having sex with someone who isn't her husband."

"If that were illegal, the prisons would overflow. I don't know who sent this movie to the district attorney, but I can tell you this. When the prosecution decided to make this an important part of their case, they played right into some scumbag's hands."

31

Kenzi called Stanley Ventrillo, aka DeepFakePhil, to the witness stand. He looked less scruffy than he had when Sharon interviewed him. She supposed she could thank Alex for that.

She led him through the introductory parts of his testimony as quickly as possible. She knew the jurors were becoming impatient with this parade of witnesses that didn't interest them that much. But the sex video was the most titillating part of an increasingly bizarre murder trial, so they probably wouldn't mind too terribly if she didn't waste time. Yes, here was another expert witness with far too much knowledge of the adult film industry, but as soon as he started talking about the digital manipulation of images, most of the jurors discerned why this testimony was important.

"People would be astounded at how easily video can be manipulated these days. Computers can collect footage of an individual and use it to create a database—a matrix, if you will. Drawing from that matrix, the computer can create footage that seems entirely credible. Sound files can be manipulated just as easily—in fact, more easily. A significant amount of the video on the internet right now, on social media platforms and particularly on the dark web, has been manipulated."

"You're saying large numbers of people are being fooled?"

"Every day. As it turns out, some people are pretty easy to fool. Especially when they want to be fooled. Confirmation bias makes morons of us all. When the message is something the recipient wants to believe, is predisposed to believe, they're much more likely to be tricked."

"Who would be able to make these so-called deepfakes?"

"These days? Your average grade-school kid with a souped-up laptop. I'm not exaggerating. It's not that hard and there are software programs readily available to help. You don't have to write the code yourself to pull this off."

"Are a lot of people using this software?"

"Thousands. Maybe tens of thousands. Creating clickbait or sucker magnets. They sell memberships, merch, access. Tap their marks' sense of patriotism. They target suckers who haven't done as much with their lives as they should've and convince them they can make a difference by supporting some cause. And sell it with fake video."

Kenzi could see Harrington was antsy. Probably getting ready to object. But she couldn't help but wonder if there wasn't maybe another reason for his discomfort.

"Let's turn to the present case. The jury is all too familiar with a recording that appears to present two people in a sexual act. And one of them appears to be my client. Have you seen this video?"

"I have."

"Where did you get it?"

"I have two sources. The prosecution turned over a copy of the recording they showed, which came from the defendant's cellphone. But after some effort, I also managed to get them to forward the original anonymous email attachement they received."

"Have you performed an analysis?"

"That's why I'm here."

"And your conclusion?"

He looked straight into the jury box. "It's been altered."

"You're sure?"

"No doubt about it. It may not be completely fake. But it has been manipulated."

"How do you know that?"

"By comparing the two versions of the video. By analyzing their digital signature. Computer animation, sound-tracking, and image manipulation have all become more advanced. But even with the best equipment and high-level rendering, there are still skid marks on the digital highway. Close frame-by-frame analysis reveals blurring. Occasional jerkiness. Background fuzz."

"How specifically has the video been altered?"

"I can't tell you that. I can tell you there are many possibilities. I do not believe the film is a complete digital creation. I think this started as a recording of...something. But it's been altered. Someone else's head could have been added or removed. It's possible that a more innocent situation was manipulated to make it appear sexual. I know for a fact that a lot of the moans and groans have been dubbed and I suspect—"

"Objection," Harrington said, cutting him off. "Speculation."

Ventrillo tilted his head. "Sorry. I'll withdraw that. But I am not speculating when I say someone has tampered with the film. That's a fact."

Kenzi took a breath before she proceeded. She wanted to make sure the jury was prepared to deal with Ventrillo's latest surprise. "Do you have any idea when this digital manipulation took place?"

"I know when at least some of it took place," he replied. "Remember, I have two versions of the film. What the prosecution originally received, and what they sent to the defense, saying it came from the defendant's phone. And guess what? They are not identical."

This time, she could see the jurors react. Several pulled back, brows creased, concerned. It was one thing to hear that a piece of evidence had been altered. It was something altogether different to hear that the prosecution was in on the fix.

"How do they differ?"

"Again, impossible for me to know what's been done with complete certainty. I can see that the audio has been altered. That could just be turning up the volume or eliminating static, both of which are standard prosecutor procedures when they prepare video evidence for trial. But am I the only one who thinks the woman in the video seems to be moving...somewhat oddly? All the writhing and twisting. Flipping her head back. Does anyone really do that? The prosecutor's office may not have access to the best people and equipment—"

"Objection!" Harrington said, rising to his feet. "This is outrageous. This man is suggesting that my office was engaged in evidence tampering."

"I'm not just suggesting it," Ventrillo said. "It's a fact. No question about it."

"Your honor, I move that this man's evidence be completely stricken from the record."

Judge Underhill frowned. "On what grounds?"

"It's—It's libelous."

"Only if false. Anything else?"

"It's the lowest most underhanded form of defense trickery—"

The judge raised his hand. "Stop. We don't need any name-calling. Everyone is well aware that you and the defense have opposing points of view. That's why we have trials. If you hear something you think is incorrect, you'll have a chance to fix it on cross-examination."

"This goes far beyond legitimate impeachment of—"

The judge stopped him again. "On cross-examination, counsel."

"But your honor! This—should not be allowed."

"Because you don't like it?"

"Because it undermines the integrity of the district attorney's office."

"Forgive me for saying so, counsel, but the only people who can do that are the people in the office. If they're found to have engaged in unacceptable conduct, they should be called to account for it."

Kenzi suppressed a smile. Despite Harrington's protestations, the judge was not ruling out the possibility that the prosecution manipulated this evidence. And the jury was listening.

Harrington slumped into his chair, obviously angry. But now silent.

Kenzi continued. "Just to be clear, is there any question in your expert opinion about whether the film has been altered?"

"None. I may not be able to give chapter and verse on what

changes have been made, but I can state with certainty that changes have been made. Moreover, I can say that changes were made to the film after it was initially received by the district attorney."

"Thank you. No more questions."

Harrington leapt to his feet, but once there, paused for what seemed an eternity before he spoke. Kenzi understood the problem. He was fueled by outrage, a feeling that he had been personally impugned, which was not a good look for someone planning to run for mayor. Most of this talk about digital manipulation probably went over his head and he didn't have a computer geek handy to explain it to him.

"You say the film changed between the time when my office received it and when it was shared with the defense."

"Precisely."

"But you can't say who made the changes?"

"I have no way of identifying the individual who made the changes."

"Then you can't say why it was done."

"Not beyond the obvious. Someone wanted the film to appear differently than it appeared originally."

"You don't know the who or the why or the where or the when—"

Ventrillo raised his finger. "That's not true. I know when. After you got it. And I've found copies of this video leaked to the internet, including on for-pay pornography sites. In each case, the film matches what you sent out—not what you received. Which suggests that someone at your office leaked or sold—"

"Objection!" Harrington's face reddened. "Your honor, I'm going to ask for sanctions. This witness continually attacks my office with no justification."

Ventrillo's face scrunched. "I'm going to be sanctioned for telling the truth?"

The judge held out his hands, as if trying to separate two fighters in the ring. "No one is going to be sanctioned. Mr. Prosecutor, if you have more questions, ask them. But you need to stop acting as if the defense is not allowed to question your evidence. That is literally why the adversarial system exists."

"They can defend their client without engaging in slander."

The judge drew in his breath. He looked as if he was losing patience. "If the defense believes evidence has been tampered with, they are permitted to say so. And at this point, they have presented credible evidence that the film you fought so hard to get into evidence has been altered. This is something the jury needs to know."

Harrington whipped his head around. He looked as if he were about to explode. "You admit that you have no idea what was changed. It could be something small. Trivial. Inconsequential."

"Perhaps. But if that's the case—why bother?"

"It could be just...someone renamed the file."

"No. This is an alteration of the video itself."

"You have no reason to doubt that it is in fact the defendant in that video having sex with someone other than her husband."

"To the contrary, I have every reason to doubt it. Common sense tells me that no one would risk altering the film if it was already accomplishing what they wanted it to do." He paused for a moment. "I remember something my father told me years ago. We were watching a football game and the team was going for a two-point conversion. Seemed like a poor idea to me, but time was running out. My dad said something I will never forget." He took a breath before continuing. "Desperate people do desperate things."

32

During the next break, Kenzi walked to the back of the gallery to speak to her father.

"Hey, *Papi*."

He nodded. "Nice work on that last witness."

She shrugged. "My investigator found him."

He arched an eyebrow. "Your investigator?"

"Yeah. I have an investigator now. To dig up info."

"Is he the muscular bearded fellow I saw at the office? Handsome man."

"Is he? I hadn't noticed."

He smiled. "I appreciate how well you're handling this case."

"I'm doing the best I can."

"A few days ago, I didn't think you had a prayer. Of course, Harrington always acts as if he has a slam dunk." A slight smile crept across his face. "And yet, my girl always seems to trounce him."

"I want to get to the bottom of this. Expose all the secrets."

"Maybe not all the secrets." To her surprise, he reached out and took her hand. "Just get Candice acquitted. Leave the rest alone."

KENZI TRIED NOT to be overly optimistic as she gave Candice her final instructions, but it was hard. After Harrington's virtual meltdown during the previous cross, everything she'd been saying about the DA and his mad rush to judgment seemed more credible. She had no idea what the jury was thinking, but to her, Harrington looked like a man with something to hide.

"The jury has been waiting this entire trial to hear what you have to say, Candice. You must convince them that the circumstantial prosecution evidence doesn't amount to a hill of beans. Tell them you did not commit this crime, would never commit this crime, had no desire to hurt Venus."

"And when they find out that Venus and I really did...know each other..."

"They'll feel the same way I did when you told me."

"As I recall, you had a hard time believing it."

"Initially." She steered her client toward the courtroom door. "It will make sense to them. It's the final piece of the puzzle. Once they understand—once they believe it—everything should fall into place. For the first time ever."

———

A HUSH FELL over the courtroom as Candice approached the witness stand. It was almost like a perp walk, or someone inexorably advancing to the electric chair.

Kenzi realized, even more powerfully than she had before, that everything depended upon this testimony. This case was Candice's to win or lose.

"Would you please state your name for the jury?"

"Candice Elana Rivera."

"Are you married?"

"Yes. To Alejandro Rivera."

"What's the status of that marriage?"

"We're in the midst of divorce proceedings. They were put on hold when I was arrested on this charge. This false charge," she added.

"How long have you been married?"

"About six years."

"Forgive me for breaching unpleasant subjects, but as you know, the prosecution's theory of motive is based on you taking revenge against your husband's paramour."

"Which is completely untrue."

Kenzi raised her hand. Give me a moment. We'll get there. "I'm explaining why I have to address uncomfortable subjects that you'd probably rather not talk about."

"That's fine," Candice said. "I want everyone to know the truth. The whole truth. These tidbits the DA has sprinkled can be easily manipulated. Misinterpreted. If people know the whole story, they'll understand how preposterous it is to think I would harm Venus. Or anyone else."

"You mentioned the victim, Venus. Your husband was in a relationship with her. There have also been allegations that you were in an extramarital relationship."

"And it's true. I was. In fact..." She drew in her breath. Her face was firm but resolute. Not proud, but not ashamed either. "More than one."

"Please tell the jury about that."

She turned slightly, as if bringing the jury into her view without making anyone uncomfortable. "Our marriage was not a happy one. I didn't know exactly why. I assumed it was my fault. That I was somehow...inadequate. I've always suffered from low self-esteem. And depression. When Alejandro married me, I felt he wanted a trophy wife. You know what I mean. Arm candy. But soon after the marriage, I began to doubt he was truly...attracted to me. In love with me. And I blamed myself for that."

"When you say he wasn't attracted to you—"

"We were not sexually active. At least not often. Even from the very beginning. He admitted that when he was on the stand. He was always at the office, or off with friends and clients. We never talked, not in the morning, not in the evening. Unless he wanted something. He took me to social gatherings. Charity balls. Bar association meetings. But the rest of the time, he seemed to prefer the company of others."

"Like Venus?"

"I don't know if she was the first...outside interest he had during our marriage. I doubt it. I mean, we had so little to do with one another. He's a healthy virile man. I don't know if he was seeking sex or merely companionship. But I know he was not getting either from me."

"How did that make you feel?"

"How do you think? I felt lonely, isolated. Unloved. I was working in a bookstore before we married but he insisted that I quit. It would be a blemish on his public persona, I guess, if his wife worked. So I didn't. But that left me with precious little to do. I wanted children. I still do. But my husband already had three children and didn't want any more. What else did I have? You can only spend so much time shopping. Or binge-watching television shows. I wanted my life to matter. I wanted to be someone's Number One. I tried to talk to Alejandro about my unhappiness, but he was...emotionally unavailable." She leaned forward. "Don't get me wrong. I'm not saying he's a bad person. He's not. But he's very old school. Attending to his wife's emotional needs is not really in his wheelhouse. He thought as long as he paid the bills and kept me in fake fur, he was performing his marital function."

"Were you concerned about the...dearth of sex in your marriage?"

"Not at first. Let me tell you another unpleasant truth. I didn't think I was a very sexual person. I'd had sex before of course but... never really understood what the big deal was. I don't think I'd ever had an orgasm with a man. Even after I discovered what that was, the only time I had them was when I was...with myself. Truth is, I was never entirely comfortable in any sexual situation when other people were around."

"Any idea why that might be?"

Candice paused, breaking the rhythm. She'd already dug deeper than anyone likely expected her to go, and now she seemed to be plumbing even greater depths. "I did not have the happiest childhood. I grew up in one of the poorer parts of Seattle. My mother was...different. She started talking to me about sexual matters at a very early age. Scary early. Sick early, some would say. She would...touch me. In a way no mother should."

In the jury box, Kenzi could see the reaction, see the distaste. This could backfire. But she was committed to giving them a full portrait. If they were going to judge whether Candice should spend the rest of her life in jail, they should at least know who they were condemning. "How often did this happen?"

"All the time. Starting at age five and ending at ten, when my mother died. Almost every night, the same disgusting thing." Candice drew in her breath, eyelids fluttering. "Sometimes she'd bring an audience."

Someone in the gallery gasped.

"Older men. Way older than me. Older than her, even. To watch, not to participate, thank God."

"How often did that happen?"

"Too often. I've blocked it out of my mind so much it's hard for me to answer that question. I was a little kid. I didn't keep a calendar. But it was...constant." She inhaled deeply. "And there were also the parties."

Press onward. Even when it's the last thing in the world you want to do. "What happened at the parties?"

"More adults. Watching. Mostly men but some women. Mother would do her usual routine. Sometimes she told me to...touch myself."

Kenzi steadied herself against the podium. "And you did this?"

"I was a child. I did what my mommy told me to do. And regretted it ever since. I've been in therapy for years. I don't know if I'll ever get past it."

"Given your background," Kenzi suggested, "it's perhaps not surprising that you were not comfortable in sexual situations."

"I felt cheap. Worthless. I wanted to be a good wife, but...that obviously wasn't happening. Maybe it was my fault. Maybe my lingering remorse was impacting the marriage. Maybe I just wasn't that interested. Or he wasn't. I don't know that he was particularly unhappy. He got the arm candy he wanted. And if he wanted sex..."

"He went somewhere else?"

Candice's head lowered. "I suppose."

"Are you still in therapy?"

"Yes. Probably always will be."

"Are you on any medications?"

"Yes. Something for anxiety. Something stronger for depression. Something to deal with bipolar mood disorder."

"But you're functional. You understand what's going on around you?"

"Of course. I'm medicated. Not intoxicated."

"You're capable of having...intimate relationships?"

"Yes. I was having extramarital relationships. I was desperately lonely. And bored. I started going to bars. Not to drink. To meet men. My therapist says I could only have self-debasing sex. Because I was punishing myself. I went home with strangers."

"There's been a great deal of talk about a video that appears to be you engaged with another man. Have you seen that video?"

"Yes."

"Is it you?"

"Honestly? I don't know. It could be. I know this—I never authorized anyone to make a sex video. Not in a million years would I do that. But as we heard, some people are making these films in secret, without the knowledge of the other party. I can't rule out that possibility."

"Does anything in that recording look familiar?"

Candice steadied herself by holding the rail in front of her. "Yes. Guy I met at a bar. He called himself Sandy. He had an apartment in the same building as Zelda. And I recall that he was very particular about how and where we did it. He wanted us in a chair. And he wanted me on top. Not a position I would've chosen myself."

"We've heard a witness testify that the film has been altered."

"I don't know anything about that. Maybe someone stitched my head onto another body. I can't tell. I'm sure all that moaning and rapturous ecstasy isn't me. I've never made noises like that in my life."

She thought the jury had heard enough about this. Time to turn the page. "When did you find out about Venus?"

"A few weeks before she died. I was pulling my husband's cellphone off its charger because I wanted to plug mine in. The screen lit up and displayed a text from Venus, obviously setting up a rendezvous. I knew his password, so it wasn't hard to get her number. I just called her."

"You met Venus before her death?"

"Many times. Maybe that seems weird, but I wanted to know more about this woman who was giving my husband what I could not. I wasn't even angry, which is what makes the whole prosecution theory of motive so absurd. I wasn't mad at her. I wanted to know more about her. What she did. How she did it. Maybe she had some pointers for improving my marriage. And my life."

"Did she agree to meet with you?"

"She did. And I know I wore that green scarf on at least one occasion, so I'm guessing that's when the fiber got attached to her purse."

"You two hit it off?"

"We did. She was a bit nervous at first, but we had something in common, after all. Or someone. Venus told me she'd had cosmetic surgery to give her the rear end men seem to like. I confess, as soon as I heard that, I asked Venus all about it. If that was what my husband wanted, I was going to get it. Pretty soon we were...I don't know. Having a good time together. Like two high school girls swapping stories about boys. Except I never did that in high school. This was a first for me, on many levels. Venus and I got along wonderfully well."

"You liked her?"

"I loved her. With all the love I had to give. And I believe she loved me."

"When you say you...loved her, people are going to wonder..."

"If it was strictly platonic? Let me appease your curiosity." She took another deep breath. "It wasn't."

Even if there was no gasping, Kenzi could feel ripples racing through the courtroom.

"You had a sexual relationship with Venus?"

"Yes. And forgive me for being blunt, but it was the best sex of my life. For some reason, when I was with her, all the discomfort and anxiety melted away. And I got some insight into why being with a man wasn't doing it for me. Sure, my childhood screwed me up, but...I was simply happier and more comfortable with a woman. Some of it I'm sure was that Venus knew what she was doing. Wasn't just focused on pleasing herself. But there was more to it than that. I was anxious to explore these new feelings. Almost...ravenous. Toward the end, I was seeing her every day, which was hard to explain and interfering with her business."

"Like what?"

"Like she had a regular appointment with that guy in Zelda's building. The one I was with once. Sandy. She knew him too and he paid her decently. But I was getting selfish. I wanted her all to myself. I met her afterward once and we crossed the street to the park and walked through the maze together. She loved that park. Loved the meditation maze. The lovely labyrinth, she called it. She was much more spiritual than I am."

"I apologize for bringing this up, but you heard the testimony of the expert who hacked into your cellphone."

"Right. A complete invasion of privacy."

"But he found some texts that made it sound as if you hated Venus. As if you were threatening her."

A slow smile crept across Candice's face. "Those were my texts. But it wasn't anger. It was roleplaying."

Kenzi blinked. "Can you explain that?"

"Sex play. Which I would've thought was obvious, given how many texts that witness must've read. But of course, he only showed the jurors the ones he thought helped the prosecution case and he read them out of context."

"Please explain what you mean by roleplaying."

"She pretended to be a misbehaving scamp. I pretended to be angry and promised to give her a spanking or whatever. Come on. Those texts are totally over the top. 'You skanky whore. I think you need to be punished.' And then she says, 'You'd like that, wouldn't you?' We're just playing. 'Maybe I'll come over right now and mess you up but good.' Does anyone really talk like that? There's one passing reference to a mirror, and the prosecution acts like it's a confession." For the first time, Candice smiled. "Maybe it sounds deranged, but I'm telling you—this was hot stuff. I'd start the drama by text and then we'd continue it in person." Her shoulders bounced a bit. "Still gives me shivers."

"So those texts were not angry?"

"Not at all." At the prosecution table, Harrington clicked his tongue and rolled his eyes. "Let the jurors decide for themselves. Read those texts. *All* the texts. In context. Knowing what I just told you. Seeing that they're surrounded by other texts where we arrange to meet each other." She turned toward the jury. "I think you'll realize the prosecution is trying to dupe you. But I'll leave it to you. Make up your own minds. Based on all the information. Not a carefully curated selection."

Fair enough. "Given what you've said, I hardly feel the need to even ask this question, but—"

"I did not kill Venus. I would never. I wanted to see her again. I adored her. We were supposed to meet that night. That's the reason I went to Conrad Park and that maze. It was a tryst. But when I got there, Venus was already dead. I couldn't believe it. I grabbed her and shook her, as if I might wake her from a deep sleep. She was covered with blood, mostly around the neck and torso. I guess that's how the blood and that pink cotton got on me." Her hand went to her forehead, covering her eyes. "And she still had that horrible mirror around her head."

"Someone suggested that was your mirror."

"Maybe it was, I don't know. Mine is missing. But there have been so many law enforcement people invading my living space—anything is possible."

"You must've been shocked when you found her. Dead."

"You don't know." Tears were visible in Candice's eyes. "You just don't know. I'd finally found someone who could make me happy. For the first time in my life. And then I lost her. In the most gruesome, horrible way possible." Her voice choked. "I don't know what happened to my clothes but, given all the other hinky stuff that happened after the cops ransacked my house, I can't help but think they had something to do with the disappearance. Doesn't matter. I would've destroyed them. I wouldn't want to wear that outfit again."

"What did you do afterward?"

"I didn't know what to do. I staggered outside. I assume that's when Zelda saw me. I was dazed, in shock, and I don't remember a lot about what happened for the next hour or so. I made it home and eventually fell asleep. Or passed out. Woke up the next morning, went to that meeting where I was arrested. I should've called the police but given the circumstances...I didn't. I think I would've in time but, as it turned out, I never had the chance." She wiped her eyes and gave the jury a steely expression. "But I did not kill Venus. I loved Venus. And I miss her. Every single day."

———

KENZI STEPPED ASIDE and Harrington began his cross-examination. He seemed not only skeptical but angry, as if he was offended that Candice had attempted to defend herself.

"Ms. Rivera, are you on drugs at this very moment?"

"Objection." Kenzi rose to her feet. That didn't take long. "My client has already acknowledged that she has prescriptions for pharmaceutical drugs."

"That's what I'm getting at," Harrington said. "The jury has a right to know if the witness is medicating. Or thinking clearly. Or an addict."

"And I object to his misleading effort to portray my client as a drug addict. Her doctor prescribed medications to help her. There's no shame in that."

"The question," Harrington said, teeth clenched, "is whether she's of sound mind and body. Can her testimony be relied upon? Is she recalling what happened or hallucinating? Fantasizing?" At this point, he wasn't arguing to the judge. He was previewing his closing argument for the jury.

The judge waved both lawyers to the bench and covered the mic. "First of all, counsel, objections should be addressed to me. And no one else. I don't like speaking objections. Or performative objections."

"I don't like anything that's happened in the last hour," Harrington shot back. "That testimony was a pack of lies."

"You are entitled to cross-examine to expose falsehoods."

"Cross-ex questions won't expose whether her mind is clouded by drugs."

Judge Underhill tilted his head. "We've heard the witness testify for an extended period of time. She does not appear to be impaired."

"The biggest addicts learn to hide it."

Kenzi kept quiet. So far as she could tell, Harrington was losing his argument for himself.

The judge tapped his fingers on the bench. "Ms. Rivera, your objection is overruled. The prosecution is allowed to inquire about whether a witness is taking any potentially mind-altering medications."

"Because she's suffering from mental illness."

Harrington snorted. "Which the jury also has a right to know about."

"Which my client openly acknowledged," Kenzi shot back. "Your honor, can't you see how questions of this nature create an aura of shame? A culture of secrecy? Mental issues like depression and anxiety, mood swings—these are relatively commonplace. No one should feel embarrassed to talk about it. To the contrary, people should be encouraged to be honest and to seek help. The prosecution's questions—his whole attitude—basically punish the witness for having problems. Which, given her tragic childhood, is far too understandable. This kind of assault discourages people from getting the help they need to be healthier and happier."

"I hear what you're saying," the judge replied, "but my ruling stands. Let's get on with this. I'm still hoping we might finish today."

Harrington returned to the witness. "Let me ask you again. Are you medicated today?"

"I've taken my physician-prescribed medications," Candice answered. "It would be extremely foolish not to do so."

"I believe you also take hydrocodone, correct?"

"Not anymore. I had a surgical procedure not long ago, and the doctor prescribed that while I recovered."

"Was that a cosmetic surgical procedure?"

Kenzi jumped up. "Objection. Relevance."

The judge nodded. "Sustained."

Harrington smirked. "That's all right. The point I wanted to make was...hydrocodone is an opioid, right?"

"I believe so."

"And our forensic expert testified to finding opioid traces on the mirror. The murder weapon." He leaned into Candice's face. "Those opioid traces came from you, didn't they? When you used your own mirror to kill your husband's lover!"

"No! I—I mean—it may have been my mirror. Maybe I...touched it one day after taking my meds. Or maybe it happened when I found Venus in the maze and embraced her."

"Please. How much do you expect the jury to believe? Madam, you are a liar."

"I told the truth."

"Excuse me, but isn't it true that you initially told the police you'd never met Venus?"

Candice was breathing hard and fast. "I was confused."

"Now you say you saw Venus repeatedly and the two of you were lovers. Are you lying now or were you lying then?"

"I'm sorry." Candice said, her voice breaking. "I didn't know what to do."

"Didn't you also initially tell the police you'd never been to the meditation maze?"

"I was scared. I didn't want to go to prison."

"So you lied."

"I admitted the truth later, long before this trial. I wasn't thinking straight. I was in shock and everything happened so fast—"

"You were lying. And you know what? I think you're still lying."

———

KENZI OBJECTED, but Harrington continued in this vein for three more hours. Candice held it together as best she could and stood her ground. Kenzi thought that while Harrington may have dented her story here and there, he couldn't disprove anything. She'd given the jury an alternative interpretation and explanation for everything that happened. She'd explained away the evidence against her, while also giving the jury compelling reasons to believe she wouldn't kill Venus.

Kenzi rested her case.

When it finally came time for closing arguments, it felt anticlimactic and unnecessary. They'd said everything that needed to be said. Now it was time for the jury to decide.

"Are you going to sit still and listen to this pack of lies?" Harrington had calmed down a bit, but not nearly enough, Kenzi thought, for someone who wanted to be perceived as a level-headed, objective advocate. "We're supposed to believe that suddenly, out of nowhere, this defendant struck up a friendship with her husband's lover? Sure she did. Because that happens all the time. We're supposed to ignore her completely shameless, immoral behavior. And those texts she sent threatening to murder Venus? Turns out she was just getting frisky. Because all women like being threatened." He blew air through his lips. "Give me a break."

Harrington went on like that for what seemed an eternity and Kenzi never objected once. She didn't think he was helping his case. To the contrary, as she watched the jury, she thought they were turned off by his self-serving tirade. It was like he thought this case was about him, not the defendant, and not justice.

When it was her turn, she took a decidedly different approach.

"During my opponent's closing, on five different occasions, you heard him say, 'Do you believe this?' But here's the truth. It doesn't matter what you believe. The only relevant question is whether the prosecution proved its case beyond a reasonable doubt. If you harbor a reasonable doubt, as the court instructed you, you cannot find my client guilty. Regardless of what you think might've happened. If they did not prove guilt beyond a reasonable doubt, you must acquit."

She stood about a foot from the rail, close enough to hold their attention, but not breathing down their throats. "Let's think about that for a moment. Do you have any cause for doubt? You've heard Candice offer an explanation for everything the prosecution threw at her. She was not mad at her husband. She was not mad at Venus. She loved Venus. The texts were playful, not angry. There are many occasions when the green fiber could've attached itself to Venus' purse— before the murder occurred. Candice tried to revive Venus, which explains how she came to be covered with blood. She was in shock afterward. She would've gone to the police in time, but she never had a chance because they arrested her before she'd had time to think clearly."

She took a step closer. "Is Candice's explanation the only possible explanation for what happened? No. But is it possible? Could it have happened that way? Is it sufficient to create a reasonable doubt?" She gave them a firm look. "Absolutely.

"You may have wondered why Candice was arrested before she had a chance to think straight, when the police had barely begun to investigate. Now consider what else you've learned. The recording introduced by the prosecution, even though it proves nothing about the murder, was doctored. After the DA received it. The texts found on my client's phone were introduced in an incomplete, deceptive way to give you a false impression of what happened. Why are they resorting to this kind of behavior?" She paused. "And most importantly, can you trust evidence coming from someone so determined to convict at any cost? Excuse me, but you not only have significant reason to doubt that my client is guilty, you have significant reason to doubt that the prosecutor has acted in good faith. It might be helpful for a prosecutor's future prospects to get a conviction in a high-profile case, but that's no reason to put an innocent woman in jail for the rest of her life. That's no reason to do anything. Except, of course, to find Candice Rivera not guilty."

And with that, the case was submitted to the jury.

33

Kenzi realized she should probably stretch her legs or grab dinner—or anything, really, other than sitting around the courtroom. But somehow, she couldn't get her legs to locomote. Candice didn't seem to have the wanderlust, either. It made no sense. The jury could be out for hours, even days. After being stuck in this courtroom so long, you'd think she'd be ready to be anywhere else.

But it's hard to put down the book when the story isn't over, right?

"How you holding up?" she asked Candice. Seemed like the tritest question imaginable when a group of twelve people were in a nearby room deciding how you were going to spend the next twenty to thirty years of your life, but that was all she could come up with.

"I'm good. Better than you might expect." Candice contemplated for a moment. "Better than I've felt in some time. Probably since this whole fiasco began."

"You deserve it."

"It felt good to finally get my story out. The good and the bad. I don't think I have anything to be ashamed about."

"You did a terrific job on the witness stand."

"I just explained what happened."

"Which is always more difficult than people realize if they've never done it. You had a tough story to tell. And you held up well under questioning."

She waved a dismissive hand in the air. "What a blowhard Harrington is. I see now why your father always kept him at a distance. He's not going anywhere. He just thinks he is."

Really? News to her. "He was trying to challenge your testimony with his righteous outrage. Since he didn't have proof."

"He was trying to intimidate me. It's a typical power move for insecure men. Shout at the little woman so she'll back off." Her lip curled slightly. "Didn't work."

"It did not. And I watched the jury. I don't think they bought it. They wondered why he was taking it all personally, why he seemed so determined to convince them of matters he couldn't prove. That's why I made prosecutorial conduct one of the main themes of my closing."

"You have good instincts. For that matter, you're a damn good lawyer, Kenzi. You actually care about your clients. It shows. And it translates into hard work." She smiled. "Everything your father told me about you turns out to be true."

Her head twitched. "My father said something nice about me?"

She laughed. "All the time. He knows you're the jewel in the crown. That's why I wanted you to represent me."

"Then—" She caught herself, careful not to sound angry. "Why did he make Gabe managing partner?"

"Gabe needed it. He's never going to be a superstar attorney like you. But he can administrate, which I don't think would interest you. He can go to the bar meetings and country clubs and gladhand. Drum up clientele. But you belong in the courtroom."

"There's more to being managing partner than gladhanding. Someone has to...set the tone."

"You might have a conversation with your father about that. He's trying to draw you into the firm leadership, right?"

"We did have a conversation."

"Follow up. I hope you don't mind if I'm blunt. You're wasted in divorce court. I know those cases are important. I know your father built his firm on those cases. But you could be helping women on many fronts, not just one. That's your calling."

K ENZI   EXPECTED Sharon and Emma to return with snacks—but instead she saw Hailee wheeling herself down the corridor and Alex close behind her, carrying a brown bag. Did Hailee never run out of energy or enthusiasm? Soon the girl would be telling her she'd scheduled a pickleball match.

Hailee gave her mother a hug. "Congrats on your closing. I heard it was fabulous."

"Adequate. Harrington's the orator, not me. I just stumble along."

"I heard you were incredible and Harrington looked like he was about to disintegrate."

"What I heard, too," Alex said. He bent down and, to her surprise, gave her a kiss on the cheek. "Someone in the gallery has been live-tweeting all day. According to judicial_kite347, you doubled down on Harrington's unethical shenanigans. Blew him out of the water. Created so much doubt the jury can't possibly convict —unless they've already decided the defendant is guilty and don't care about evidence." He glanced toward Candice. "Sorry about that."

She shook her head. "I'm not going to kill the messenger. You're not telling me anything I didn't already know."

"If what I read online is even half true, you've exposed enough potential prosecutorial misconduct to instigate an inquiry. I wouldn't be surprised if Harrington is forced to resign. Which could seriously mess up his mayoral plans."

Hailee pulled out her phone. "He's already defense-tweeting. At this time of night. While the jury is still out. Which means he's running scared."

"The internet can ruin reputations in the blink of an eye," Kenzi noted.

"Or make them." Hailee scanned her phone scrolling with her thumb. "Harrington is blaming the defense. Which of course means you, Mom. He says you've engaged in underhanded defense-lawyer tricks." More scanning. "He says you're trying to win by distracting the jury. Dirty tricks."

"He's accusing *you* of dirty tricks?" Alex whistled. "He needs to take a good long look in the mirror."

"Again with the mirrors," Kenzi said. "What you mean is, you think some introspection could be beneficial."

"I'm a Zen Buddhist, remember? I'd spend all day introspecting if I could."

"What does Harrington hope to gain?" Hailee asked. "The jury is sequestered. They can't see his tweets."

"The tweets aren't for the jury. They're for the voters." She picked up her phone and texted Sharon. "Since you appear to already have snacks, I'm going to send Sharon on a different mission." She glanced at her watch. Eleven o'clock. The judge hoped to get this finished tonight but said he wouldn't keep people past midnight. "How much longer can the jury think about this?" She frowned. "Is there food in that bag you're carrying?"

Alex smiled. "Asian. I hear you like a good pad Thai."

"I would do anything for a good pad Thai."

"Anything?"

She snatched the bag, grinning. "Within reason."

———

JUST BEFORE ELEVEN THIRTY, Kenzi received a text inviting her to return to the courtroom.

She placed her hand on Candice's arm. "The jury has reached a verdict."

"I don't suppose your text tells you what that verdict is."

"No. That would be too efficient. We have to go through a lot of dramatic rigamarole before we get to the punchline. I know, it sounds archaic. Some judges are streamlining the process—but not Underhill."

"I've waited this long. I can wait a little longer." Candice pressed the heels of her hands against her forehead. "But I'll be glad when this is over."

The courtroom reassembled, just the judge, the clerk, and a few bailiffs. Two guys from the sheriff's office, just in case Candice decided to bolt. Or to haul her away if she was convicted.

Her father was also there. Sitting in the back. Waiting.

Kenzi tried to read the faces of the jurors as they filed back into the box, but she didn't get much. She wasn't surprised. This was the moment when the spotlight shifted to them. For a few brief moments, they were the power players. It was only natural to want to maintain the mystery, to be the center of attention as long as possible.

The bailiff brought the written verdict to the judge, who reviewed it for technical defects. But he wouldn't steal the jury's thunder. He passed it back to the bailiff, who took it to the elderly man on the back row who served as foreperson.

"The jury will now read the verdict," Judge Underhill said.

The man cleared his throat. "On the charge of first-degree murder, we find the defendant...not guilty."

Not guilty. *Not guilty!* She gripped Candice's hand.

The verdict was the same on the lesser charges. The judge summed it all up with a rapid-fire series of charges and admonitions. He thanked the jury and warned them to avoid the media. Then he looked at Candice and said, "Ms. Rivera, you are free to go."

Candice wrapped herself around Kenzi. "Thank you. Thank you." She squeezed so tightly it pushed the air out of Kenzi's lungs. But she still managed to squeeze back.

The rest of the team surrounded them, hugging and laughing and congratulating.

Kenzi barely noticed. Her eyes were focused on the back of the courtroom.

Her father stayed away. But as soon as they locked eyes, he mouthed, "Thank you."

And as if that weren't enough, he gave her a big thumbs-up.

34

After all the work was done, Kenzi accepted Alex's invitation to join him at his place for a nightcap. Candice was anxious to sleep. Emma volunteered to see that Hailee got home safely.

Alex's apartment was simple but adequate. A bit messy, but she supposed that was not unexpected. He threw a coat in the closet and gestured toward the sofa. "Please make yourself at home."

She did.

"I hope you can tell how glad I am you decided to come over. I know this trial was important, but..." He grinned. "It kinda got in the way."

"Of your seduction plans?"

He corrected. "Courtship plans."

"That sounds much better."

"Would you like a drink?"

"Sure, thanks."

"I'm gonna get a beer."

"Sounds good. Bring me one too. Are you surprised I came over?"

"A little. You must be exhausted."

"But very ready to blow off some steam. You have no idea how stressful that was."

"I can imagine."

"You probably can't. Having someone's future resting on what you do or say...that's a level of stress no one needs. I wouldn't be sorry if I never had to deal with something like that ever again."

He returned, beers in hands, and sat on the opposite side of the sofa. "I'm glad I was able to play a small part in your success."

"You played a big part."

"I doubt it. Smart girl like you. If I hadn't brought you my deepfake expert, Emma would've found one for you."

"Maybe." She stretched out on the sofa, tossing her arms back. "The key was realizing that we needed a deepfake expert. That the film had been surreptitiously made for the underground porno circuit." She picked up her beer and brought it to her lips. "How did you figure that out, anyway?"

He shrugged. "I've had to deal with all the slimiest people imaginable. Probably no crime I haven't seen. I'd like to think I spend all my time helping single women in need, like the PIs on television, but it's mostly slime service. Getting the goods on wayward spouses. Making deliveries of packages that contain God knows what." He scooted a little closer to her. "Are we going to talk about business all night?"

She grinned. "Not all night. Just the next ten minutes or so. Let me unwind."

"As you say. How's the beer?"

"Excellent. I think it's already going to my head."

"Did you eat tonight?"

"Sure. You brought Asian and I—" She paused. "Oh wow. I never ate any of it, did I?"

"Not that I saw. Want a snack?"

"I'm good. Let's just chill." She blinked several times rapidly. "I must be getting tired. I can barely keep my eyes open." She hesitated. "Do you feel the room spinning?"

"No." He inched closer to her. "But then, I didn't put the Rohypnol in my beer. Just yours."

Her face tensed. "The—the what?"

She tried to get up, but he pushed her back against the sofa. With one finger.

"Don't bother trying to leave. You're not going anywhere."

"You—You drugged me."

"True. But you've figured it out, haven't you? Even if you haven't, I can't take the risk. You've got to go."

"You—You—" She pushed one way, then the other. "I'm getting out of here."

He pushed her back down. "No, you're not."

"Then I'm going to scream."

"I doubt you can muster the energy. But if you try, I'll knock you across the room. So please don't."

"You—You—" Kenzi licked her lips. Her eyelids fluttered. "You killed Venus."

He didn't deny it.

"And Zelda?"

He shrugged. "Zelda stroked out."

"After you scared her to death."

"True."

"You're—You're a sick... crazy..."

"I'm a desperate man who got himself in way too deep. I didn't want to hurt anyone. But I had no choice. Now I'm closing up shop and moving away. Once my debt is paid there will be a new job waiting for me in Canada. New name, papers, everything. A chance to start over again." He placed his hand around her throat. "Once I've taken care of you."

"People will notice if I disappear. They'll remember that I went home with you."

"They'll remember a fake name and a guy with a beard and glasses, all of which I will soon lose. They'll never find me. Especially not in another country."

"But—if I'm—murdered—"

"I plan to make it look like a suicide. Once I strangle you into unconsciousness, I'm going to string you up in your office. Everyone knows you've been stressed. Erratic. Will anyone really be surprised if you decide to off yourself?"

"You—lied—to me."

"Repeatedly. And you bought it, you egotistical bitch. You made my life very uncomfortable for a while." His lips curled, and all at once, he reared back his hand and slapped her hard across the face.

Her head whipped to one side. "Please...don't."

"I'm gonna do a hell of a lot more than that. Did you really think I was attracted to you? Your vanity blinded you."

Kenzi blinked. "I'm...surprised..."

"No doubt."

"But you... are going to be surprised too." The stuttering disappeared.

She knocked his hand away from her throat then stood, shoving him to the sofa. "You have many surprises coming. For one thing, I put that beer to my lips, but I never drank it. I'm not an idiot."

His face flushed. He sprang toward her, hands extended, grasping for her throat.

She grabbed his hands and struggled, but she knew he was bigger and stronger. "I didn't come here alone. *Kate*! My life is being threatened!"

Less than a second later, the front door burst open. Kate stepped through, gun at the ready.

Alex started to run. Kate blocked his path.

"Freeze," Kate said. "You're under arrest. If you move, I will shoot." She glanced at Kenzi. "Thanks for shouting me some probable cause."

"My pleasure. Please take this murderer away. And congrats on solving the case."

"You solved it. But I'll be happy to share credit. I assume you have a confession. Like we planned."

Kenzi nodded. "Recorded the whole convo on my phone. Including the threats."

"That should prove useful." Kate glared at Alex, cowering in the corner. "Guess what? You're going away for a long time."

Alex raised his hands. "I'll talk. I can give you chapter and verse. Everything you want to know about the Canadian syndicate."

"That's what we're counting on." Kate pulled out her handcuffs. "Let's go downtown."

"Wait," Kenzi said. "Before you do that?"

"Yes?"

Kenzi swung her fist around and clocked Alex so hard he fell to his knees. "I owe you that, loser. For hitting me. And lying to me. And—" Her voice choked. "Making me care about you. Making me feel like a fool."

She drew in a deep breath and tried to steady her voice.. "Kate, you didn't see that punch."

Kate shook her head. "Nope. Jerk probably hurt himself trying to escape."

"I wouldn't be a bit surprised."

35

Two weeks later, Kenzi assembled the two strangest gatherings of her career. She needed both of the firm's corner conference rooms just to hold all the players.

She stopped at Sharon's desk. "Think you can direct traffic for a while?"

"Got it all under control. You go, girl."

"By the way, thanks again for sending Kate to back me up."

"She was happy to do it."

"I don't know if I've mentioned this yet, but—I really like Kate."

"Coincidentally, so do I."

"You're going to move in with her?"

"Already done."

"Excellent."

She found Emma outside the first conference room. "Ready to rock and roll?"

"Yes. But they're nervous. Not sure why you called them."

"Understandable. Have I thanked you yet for all your help?"

"Do you ever?"

"C'mon, little sis. You know I love you."

"'Know' might be pushing it."

Without a word of warning, Kenzi leaned in and gave her sister a big hug. "Know it, Emma. We Rivera girls stick together."

Emma stiffened, then slowly relaxed. "Someone's got to."

Kenzi looked into her eyes. "I think there are about to be some big changes at this firm. And I want you to know that...you don't have to stay in the basement. You don't have to do divorce work, either."

"What am I going to do?"

"Whatever makes you happy. Be the person you want to be."

"And if the male patriarchy running this firm, all of whom are related to us, don't like it?"

She jabbed a thumb into her chest. "Then they'll have to answer to me."

———

KENZI WONDERED if Hera and Icarus minded being in the same room with Candice. By now, they'd surely heard that Candice had been completely exonerated. Still, it could be an awkward gathering.

"Thank you for coming. I wanted to make sure you knew what was happening. And I wanted you to meet Candice. I know all three of you loved Venus very much."

"Loved her and failed her," Icarus said. "Again and again."

"Don't beat yourself up. You had some difficult situations to deal with. We're none of us perfect." She turned. "And you, Hera, worked with her and were probably more aware of her day-to-day activities than anyone else."

"I should've done more," Hera said, shaking her head. "But I did love that girl."

"I think she loved you as well." Kenzi paused. "I should tell you that this little get-together was Candice's idea."

"It's time for healing," Candice explained. "We've all made mistakes. But what happened to Venus was not your fault. Or mine. Let's let the past go and focus on the future."

"Sounds good," Icarus said. "But I'm not sure how to do that. What have the police learned so far?"

"More than you might imagine," Kenzi replied. "Alex—the man you knew as Sandy—is talking up a storm. Trying to save his own neck."

"Bastard," Icarus muttered. "I feel like an idiot. I let him fool me. I've known him forever. He was the one who gave us these mythological nicknames. Hera because she was the top goddess. Venus because she was beautiful and loving. Icarus because he thought I was...I don't know. A brash idiot. He was totally obsessed with those Greek and Roman stories. And I always thought he was kind of crazy. I just didn't realize...how crazy."

"Should've known he thought he was better than everyone else," Hera said. "After all, he dubbed himself Alexander. As in, Alexander the Great."

"I should've known he was the killer," Icarus said.

"We could all blame ourselves for being slow on the uptake," Kenzi said. "Sandy was short for Alexander, but I never realized that one person played two roles in this drama."

"He disguised himself," Candice explained. "Glasses, wig, fake beard. I didn't recognize him. And I'd...seen him up close."

"Apparently his dual identities went beyond the glasses and hair and other external alterations. He'd developed something resembling a dual personality. He was obsessed with doubles, twinning. He may have dissociative identity disorder. Maybe that explains the obsession with mirrors. That's where he saw his other self."

"Why did he do it?" Hera asked. "I mean, I knew he and Venus went out, but—"

"It was more than that," Kenzi explained. "Sandy really was a private detective. But he didn't make much money at it. Which led him to doing work for people he should've stayed clear of."

"This Canadian syndicate?"

"Exactly. Worst people in the world. People you don't want to cross. He botched a job. One of those deliveries he mentioned. Probably drugs. It went south and the boss said he owed them for the loss. Hundreds of thousands of dollars, which Sandy couldn't possibly pay back. So he started making these surreptitious porno movies."

"Why did he have to do it in secret?" Hera asked. "I know how desperate some women get. He could surely find someone somewhere who would make his dirty pictures for a little money."

"Apparently getting good porn actresses is harder than you might imagine. Drug addicts come off flat and unenthusiastic. If you want the optimal talent, you have to pay for it. Sandy needed to make money, not spend it. He stumbled onto this trick of making porn movies without the women in question knowing about it. He'd set up the camera and mic in advance, make sure the women did it where he wanted them, and recorded the whole thing."

"Disgusting," Hera muttered.

"You'll get no argument from me. But it worked. Better than he expected. His movies looked real—because they were. They had the exuberance of truth, I guess."

"So that's how he paid off his debt."

"Tried. All he really did was create an insatiable demand for more movies. Although he paid down the interest, he never made much of a dent in the principal."

"They owned him."

"Right. He couldn't find enough women to make his movies. He had a specific type he liked. Short, petite. He could get extra money by passing them off as underage. He also liked that pear-shaped, Brazilian butt look. Hera, I believe you knew a woman who appeared in one of his earliest film epics. And then disappeared."

"Athena?" Hera said, horrified.

"Yes. Sorry. The cops found a body in Conrad Park, long before Venus died, that they've now identified her as the woman you called Athena. They think she was the first woman Sandy killed. Then he made several flicks with Venus without her knowledge. That held the wolves at bay for a time. But eventually, his audience wanted fresh blood."

"He made one with me," Candice said. "As I guess everyone knows now. Before I met Venus and...well. Realized my tastes went in a different direction."

Hera reached out. "I'm so happy for you, honey. And I'm glad Venus found a little happiness too. Before it all ended for her." She looked back at Kenzi. "Why did he kill her?"

"Venus found out what he was doing. Apparently one of her other customers saw a sneak-peek featuring her online and told her about it. Venus was outraged. She confronted Sandy. He says he tried to reason with her. Argued that being an escort—and sometimes a prostitute—was no better than being a porn actress. But she wasn't having it. He stole the mirror from Candice's apartment. He wanted Venus to peer inside her own soul and realize she was no better than him—and therefore shouldn't be complaining. But she wouldn't back off—so he killed her. He claims to be a Buddhist and believes that mirrors provide insight into the soul. I should've suspected him when he first told me that, but I was too distracted by his good looks—until he said it again, while we were waiting for the jury to return. Something about it seemed off. Too coincidental."

"I had a girl once who hated mirrors," Hera said. "Thought they were the devil's peepholes."

"Mirrors are considered dangerous in many belief systems. That's why people turn them backward at funerals. That's why breaking one is bad luck. Sandy is obsessed with Greek mythology and particularly with harbingers of fate, destiny, death. Mirrors play a huge role in these myths and legends."

"So Sandy took the mirror to the maze planning to kill Venus?"

"He claims there was no plan. He met her in the maze and tried to talk her down. Unsuccessfully. But what we know for sure is that he bashed that mirror over her head and killed her."

"And then I showed up," Candice added.

"After Sandy left. And Zelda saw you, which is why we had that big trial."

"That man was everywhere. All over the singles bars. I'm not surprised Venus and I both crossed his path."

"Apparently the PI cover worked well. He could introduce himself to women claiming he was working on a case. That he made up. Better than asking women about their sign."

"Jesus God that's disgusting. Why did he go after Zelda?"

"He stayed away from the apartment in Zelda's building for a while because he missed a payment and the syndicate was after him. He didn't want to be seen in any of the usual places. But a syndicate goon found him and slipped a threatening note under his door, so he fled from his hiding place. He eventually went back to Zelda's building. She spotted him and realized he was the man she'd seen—and heard—with Venus."

"So he had to kill her."

"Getting to a third-story window was no big trick for that gym boy. He grabbed her mirror and attacked her more or less the same way he did Venus, to throw the cops off his scent. He claims he just wanted to talk to her, too, but I don't believe it. I think he would've killed her, but the stroke eliminated the need."

"I was hiding, too," Icarus said.

"I know. Because the syndicate wanted you to work for them as a hacker."

His head hung low. "I worked for this company I thought was legit. Turned out they were owned by the syndicate. I developed code that broke new ground. Let me hack into ATM machines and transfer money. It was strictly for my own use—we were desperate. But the syndicate found out and they wanted it. They tried to steal it, but I designed it so if anyone tried to copy it or hack into my computer and download it, the program would delete itself. I thought that would keep them away. What it really did was make them desperate to find me. I knew if I worked for them it would just be a matter of time before I was dead. So I hid."

"They finally caught Sandy," Kenzi explained. "Some guy named Kingsley—probably not his real name—is apparently the local point man. Sandy saved his neck by offering them Icarus. Seems they just lost a big income stream and they wanted to replace it with something else. The porn films were just a stopgap. As Sandy himself told me, the big money is in bank fraud. Digital hacking. I should've realized he wouldn't be so knowledgeable about the syndicate unless he was involved." She shook her head. "That's why he came to my doorstep and started helping me. He thought since I was gathering info about Venus, I might learn something that would help him find you, Icarus." She paused. "Let me give you some advice. Get a job with the government. Hack for the FBI. Once you're a fed, you'll be better protected."

Hera reached across the table. "How did you capture Sandy?"

"When he made that remark at the courthouse about Buddhism, it made me suspicious. I texted Sharon and asked her to show a pic I snapped of Alex around Zelda's building. Zelda was dead, of course, but others remembered seeing him there. That's when I realized he must be the missing link. The killer. So I set him up. Went over to his place—"

"And put your own life in danger," Candice said, as if she were scolding her.

"It was worth it. And now we need to get to the main reason for this gathering."

"I want to create some kind of memorial," Candice explained. "I don't want Venus to be forgotten. She was too wonderful. Too loving. I owe her too much. And I think you two knew her better than anyone else. I want to work with you to create something worthy. Maybe a shelter for women who find themselves in trouble. So they don't have to do what Venus did."

"I wanted to do something for her," Icarus said. "But I'm broke."

"I've got money," Candice said. "And I'm about to have more. We've reached a settlement in my divorce case. I can't think of a better way to spend some of it."

Hera took Candice's hand. Her eyes were misting. "You know what? All during that trial, I was hating on you. I thought you took my Venus away from me. But I was wrong. So wrong." She gave Candice a squeeze. "You're giving her back to me. You're good people."

"Not yet," Candice said. Her eyes appeared misty too. "But I'm trying."

———

A few minutes later, Kenzi switched to the other conference room. Candice followed her and Kenzi introduced her to the Battersbys.

"Here's the situation as I see it. Julia, you and Carl want your biological daughter. I know you love Ellie, the baby you've cared for these past months, but you can't afford to raise two. The Le family doesn't want either baby. I just checked—Amy Le is still under care. She isn't going to be capable of raising a child for some time and her husband can't do it alone. The fertility clinic doesn't accept returns. So Ellie will be going up for adoption."

Carl lowered his head. "I feel terrible about this. But we have to be realistic."

Kenzi nodded. "Adoption is a blessing that has brought joy to many lives. And in this case, I know someone who wants to adopt. I know we'll have to make it good with Child Services, but I have a lot of influence there and I think they'll agree that the child should be with someone who can afford her and will be a very good mother. Someone who lives near you and will welcome you any time you want to visit."

Julia's voice caught. "That—would be perfect."

"Thought so." She swiveled around. "Meet Candice Rivera. Newly divorced. Childless. And ready to turn over a new page in her life."

"I know you've probably heard terrible things about me," Candice said. "And some of them are true. I have made some serious errors of judgment. But I've always wanted children. I think a lot of my mistakes happened because I was...bored. Unloved. Unfulfilled. Didn't have anything meaningful to do."

"That's about to change," Kenzi said. "Big time."

"I can't think of anything more wonderful than raising this beautiful girl, Julia—with your help. If you'll just give me a chance—"

"Yes!" Julia pressed her hands together. "Of course! This is perfect!"

"Really?"

"*Perfect!*" Both women started to cry. "And—you won't mind if we come over to see Ellie?"

Candice smiled a crooked smile. "I won't mind if you move in with me. I have a lot to learn."

36

K enzi would have been happy to let the record speak for itself and didn't want to be accused of gloating after a major win. But her social media manager insisted that a few words were needed to keep the KenziKlan happy. With great power there must also come great responsibility...

"Hiya, KenziKlan. Here's your fearless leader again, giving you the closing summary on my big case. I know you've already read the press reports, so I won't bother with the nitty-gritty details. But I did want to give you my takeaway. You've already heard me using this case as a cautionary tale. I hope you took it to heart."

For once, she wasn't walking as she broadcast, so she swiveled around behind her desk. "I wanted to tackle a different subject today. That has to do with the subject of shame. From the very start, my opposition tried to shame my client. The press was no better. Even at trial, when the evidence seemed inadequate, the prosecution tried to compensate by subjecting my client to constant condemnation. By judging her. Shaming her. In his closing, he called her 'shameless.'"

She leaned into the phone camera, hoping they could see the fire in her eyes. "Here's what I have to say to you, KenziKlan. Be shameless. Or to put it differently, don't let men shame you. Don't let anyone shame you. Of course, that means you have to avoid doing anything truly shameful. But this old-world male-patriarchy crap where they shame women for seeking help and treatment, for having normal human desires, for doing the same exact thing men are constantly doing—that has to end. My client wanted that most elusive of goals—happiness. I will not fault her for seeking happiness and neither should you. There's no shame in it. No shame in being different. I think she's on the verge of discovering something new and wonderful about herself. I think she's starting a new chapter that will lead to a more fulfilled life. And if the bigots and haters had their way, that never would've happened."

She leaned back and smiled. "I guess in a way this is the same message I always give. Don't let other people tell you what you can and cannot do. Make your own decisions. Become the best possible you, the one who makes you proud. This case revolved around a mirror. Why? Because mirrors are magic—but also potentially harmful. When you look in the mirror, I want you to love the person you see. Whether it's about sex, gender, occupation, or lifestyle, so long as you're not hurting anyone else, you should feel free to be the person you were meant to be. So go for it, KenziKlan. Be shameless."

———

KENZI WAS NOT PARTICULARLY surprised when her father called her to his office.

He was packing.

"Are you...going somewhere?"

"I'm just taking the things I can't live without. I think my visits to this office will be...much less frequent in the immediate future."

Even though they'd already discussed this, she found herself shocked to realize it was happening. "You meant it. You're stepping down."

"In truth, if not in public. I'm going to keep my name on the letterhead another six months or so. I don't want to resign right on the heels of Candice's case and the murder and the Taylor Petrie mess. It would look like I was resigning in disgrace. But none of this is good for the firm. For now, I want you and your sister to be more involved. Later, I'll step down officially."

"Have you mentioned what we discussed before? Like, with Gabe?"

"I have. He's on his way. Emma too. But before they arrive, I wanted to thank you again for handling Candice's defense. I know how stressful that was. I had to tell the truth on the witness stand. But she wasn't guilty and I will never trust anyone as much as I trust my sweet eldest girl. What a fine lawyer you've turned out to be—and a fine person."

She pressed her hand against her blouse. "Who? Me?"

"And I'm not just talking about winning the case. I think Candice is going to be far happier now."

"I hope so."

"Any news about the...recording?"

"We'll never know for sure who tampered with it, I suspect. But it was done at Harrington's direction. The bar association has initiated an investigation. Harrington's dreams of being mayor are over. I wouldn't be surprised if he resigned as DA."

"And you cleared up the disciplinary case against me as well."

"That was a farce. You've been subjected to enough scrutiny. Once I told them you were taking a sabbatical, no one saw any need for a formal reprimand or suspension."

He gazed at his daughter. "I haven't appreciated you nearly enough. I took you for granted. I knew you could take care of yourself. As a result, I didn't give you the attention or praise you deserved. I'm very proud of the person you've become. You're everything a father could hope for in a daughter."

"*Papi.* I...don't know what to say."

"You don't have to say anything. I'm the one who keeps screwing up his life. First with your mother. Then with Candice. Then...Taylor Petrie and Venus and...one bad decision after another. I was just looking for something that worked." His eyes drifted toward the window. "But now I realize that the failure of my relationships has precious little to do with the women I chose. And everything to do with me."

"I know how you feel. I was so excited about the prospect of dating again that I missed all the telltale signs. I normally pride myself on my ability to read character. But I completely missed the boat with Alex. Sandy. For too long."

Her father sighed.

Kenzi leaned against the edge of his desk. "Is it just possible that, fine lawyers though we are...relationships are not our best thing?"

He smiled a little. She smiled a lot. He chuckled. She giggled. And a few moments later they were both practically hysterical.

"Just remotely possible," he said.

"Yeah," she replied, barely able to speak. "Just remotely possible."

When the other two Riveras arrived, they found their relatives in stitches.

Gabe frowned. "Are you two okay?"

"They look high," Emma said. "Do you smell weed?"

"I wouldn't know what it smelled like."

"Of course not."

Their father waved them in. "Grab a chair. Family powwow."

"Okaaaay." Gabe took the nearest available seat. "What's up?"

"As I told you, son, we're going to make some changes around here."

Kenzi leaned forward. "I'm sorry, Gabe. It's nothing against you. But we thought—"

"Oh, thank God," Gabe said, cutting her off. "Are we finally going to do it, Dad? What we talked about?"

"We are finally going to do it."

Kenzi was puzzled. "You're not upset?"

"Are you kidding? I hate being managing partner. You be the stupid managing partner. Let me be client development director or something. I like people. I don't like telling people what to do. And there's so much paperwork—"

"That's...not really my best thing either," Kenzi said.

"No, it isn't," her father said. "Emma is the organized one. All her ducks in a row, even when she was little. Here's what I'm thinking. Emma handles the administrative work. Gabe handles client development. And Kenzi runs the legal business. What do you think?"

The offspring looked at one another.

Kenzi was the first to speak. "Actually...that sounds pretty good."

"Works for me," Emma said. "God knows I don't want to be shaking hands down at the country club. Or playing...golf." She shuddered.

"Are you kidding?" Gabe said. "That's the best part."

Emma pulled a face. "It's all yours."

Kenzi looked at her father. "*Papi*, looks like we're in agreement."

"Good. Consider it done."

"And since I'm now running the legal business for the firm, I hereby declare that, from this day forth, we will only handle collaborative divorce cases."

Her father stiffened. "What? Wait a minute—"

"You said I'm in charge. I have witnesses. It's time for the world to move forward and we're going to lead the charge. The old-school approach, mudslinging and fighting and using children as weapons—it's toxic. So is the legal tactic of running up the bill with motions practice and endless discovery. Why does divorce have to be so ugly, mean-spirited, grueling? If people feel the need to make a change in their lives to find happiness, it shouldn't be so difficult. Every other area of the law has matured. Why is divorce law still mired in the Middle Ages?"

Her father coughed. "This sounds rather drastic..."

"From now on, we'll require clients and their spouses to sign cooperative participation agreements. We'll negotiate everything in good faith. We'll minimize stress instead of aggravating it. We'll provide mental-health specialists, financial advisors, or child-custody experts as needed. We'll emphasize mutual agreement rather than trial by combat. And that means"—she gave her father a stern look—"we will charge a flat fee. Up front. A substantial fee, mind you. But a one-time payment. No matter how long the case takes."

"Kenzi..." She could tell her father was biting back words. "Have you considered the financial ramifications of this decision?"

"There might be some at first. We can afford it. Once word gets out, I believe most divorcing couples will want to do it our way. The smart ones, anyway. We'll have more business than we know what to do with."

"Once word gets out. Maybe. But in the meantime—"

"We'll minimize the meantime." She held her phone up. "Because as it happens, I am very good at getting the word out."

Emma spoke. "I'm all for it. My divorce was the most miserable experience of my life. I think this is long overdue."

"And that's just the beginning," Kenzi said. "Soon we'll expand our approach to other areas of the law. And we'll expand our public-interest law division. And handle more pro bono work. We want to be profitable. But we can afford to give something back to the community."

Her father's eyebrows knitted. "Don't let your idealism sink the firm."

She pointed a finger. "Just so you know, these changes won't be restricted to the law firm."

"What does that mean?"

"We should also be a better family. I shouldn't learn about what my father is doing from a newspaper. I should hear it from him."

He tucked in his chin. "There are a few things no one needs to know about..."

"You're going to be bored with no wife in the house. And without your legal work. Possibly lonely. So you're going to be seeing a lot more of me and Hailee."

"And me," Emma said.

"Likewise," Gabe added.

"For starters, I propose we have Sunday dinner together whenever possible. Stay in touch. Stay close."

"Sure," Emma said. "As long as you're not cooking."

"What do you say, *Papi*?"

A slow smile crept across his face. "I think I'm the luckiest father in the world." His lips trembled. "I made a lot of mistakes. But my children are the one thing I clearly got absolutely right."

37

Crozier led Kingsley toward a small airstrip on the outskirts of Seattle. The night was dark and cold and the air was full of mist, but there was enough visibility for a plane to take off. Which was what Kingsley was counting on.

Crozier led him inside the hangar. "We can wait here till the plane is ready."

"There can be no delay. I must go."

"You've screwed around this long," Crozier said. "I don't think another ten minutes will hurt you."

"The police are everywhere. They have my picture. They have my name."

"Fake name."

"Thank God! Sandy has told them everything."

"He hasn't mentioned me. He remembers that I tried to help him. While you tried to kill him."

"I have a business to run."

"I told you he was a liability. You should have eliminated him. Instead, you used him—and me—to find a hacker. Stupid move."

Kingsley clenched his teeth. "I think you have forgotten who holds your neck in his hands. I could crush you—"

"But you won't. Because you need me."

Kingsley glared at him. But said nothing.

"Are you ready to give me the flight information?" Crozier said. "I need to know who's meeting you."

"I cannot reveal the identity of my superiors."

"I have to know where you're going."

"You don't."

"The pilot has to know where to fly and who's gonna meet him!"

"Fine." Kingsley scrawled something on a scrap of paper and shoved it into Crozier's hand. "Give the pilot this."

Crozier took the paper, glanced at it, and shoved it into his pocket.

When his hand emerged, it held a gun.

Kingsley sneered. "You wouldn't dare."

Crozier fired. Kingsley crumpled to the ground.

Crozier fired three more times. Just to be sure.

Once he was confident the man was dead, Crozier took a closer look at the paper in his pocket.

This gave him all the information he needed. Who ran the syndicate on the Canadian end and where they were located. Where he could find them. He already knew what they wanted to do. And what they needed on this end.

What they needed most, of course, was a more competent point man than Kingsley.

And now they had one.

He rolled the body into a bag and dragged it to his truck. He'd already arranged a disposal site. No one would find the corpse for months, if ever.

That was the main difference between Kingsley and him. He planned ahead. And he planned well. Years of trial work had taught him how to anticipate, rather than constantly reacting, playing catch-up.

As he slid behind the wheel, Crozier glanced at himself in the rear view mirror. And smiled.

Look out, Seattle. There's a new boss in town.

ABOUT THE AUTHOR

William Bernhardt is the author of over fifty books, including *Splitsville (#1 National Bestseller)*, the historical novels *Challengers of the Dust* and *Nemesis*, two books of poetry, and the Red Sneaker books on writing. In addition, Bernhardt founded the Red Sneaker Writers Center to mentor aspiring authors. The Center hosts an annual conference (WriterCon), small-group seminars, a newsletter, and a bi-weekly podcast.

Bernhardt has received the Southern Writers Guild's Gold Medal Award, the Royden B. Davis Distinguished Author Award (University of Pennsylvania) and the H. Louise Cobb Distinguished Author Award (Oklahoma State), which is given "in recognition of an outstanding body of work that has profoundly influenced the way in which we understand ourselves and American society at large." In 2019, he received the Arrell Gibson Lifetime Achievement Award from the Oklahoma Center for the Book.

In addition Bernhardt has written plays, a musical (book and score), humor, children stories, biography, and puzzles. He has edited two anthologies (*Legal Briefs* and *Natural Suspect*) as fundraisers for The Nature Conservancy and the Children's Legal Defense Fund. In his spare time, he has enjoyed surfing, digging for dinosaurs, trekking through the Himalayas, paragliding, scuba diving, caving, zip-lining over the canopy of the Costa Rican rain forest, and jumping out of an airplane at 10,000 feet.

In 2017, when Bernhardt delivered the keynote address at the San Francisco Writers Conference, chairman Michael Larsen noted that in addition to penning novels, Bernhardt can "write a sonnet, play a sonata, plant a garden, try a lawsuit, teach a class, cook a gourmet meal, beat you at Scrabble, and work the *New York Times* crossword in under five minutes."

ALSO BY WILLIAM BERNHARDT

The Splitsville Legal Thrillers

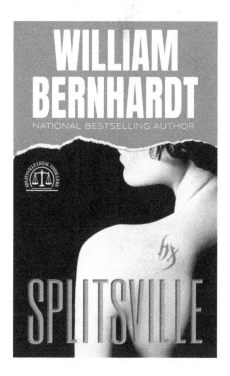

A struggling lawyer. A bitter custody battle. A deadly fire. This case could cost Kenzi her career—and her life.

When a desperate scientist begs for help getting her daughter back, Kenzi can't resist...even though this client is involved in Hexitel, a group she calls her religion but others call a cult. After her client is charged with murder, the ambitious attorney knows there is more at stake than a simple custody dispute.

Exposed (Book 2)

Shameless (Book 3)

The Daniel Pike Novels

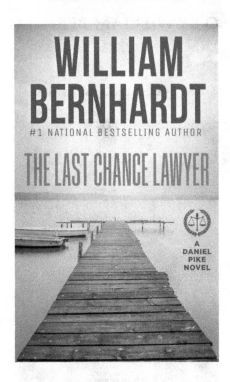

Getting his client off death row could save his career... or make him the next victim.

Daniel Pike would rather fight for justice than follow the rules. But when his courtroom career goes up in smoke, he fears his lifelong purpose is a lost cause. A mysterious job offer from a secretive boss gives him a second chance but lands him an impossible case with multiple lives at stake...

Dan uses every trick he knows in a high-stakes trial filled with unexpected revelations and breathtaking surprises.

Court of Killers (Book 2)

Trial by Blood (Book 3)

Twisted Justice (Book 4)

Judge and Jury (Book 5)

Final Verdict (Book 6)

The Ben Kincaid Novels

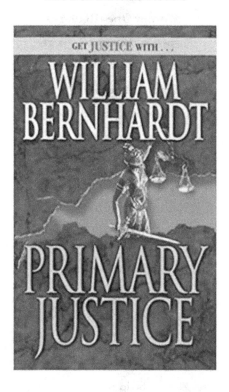

"[William] Bernhardt skillfully combines a cast of richly drawn characters, multiple plots, a damning portrait of a big law firm, and a climax that will take most readers by surprise."—*Chicago Tribune*

Ben Kincaid wants to be a lawyer because he wants to do the right thing. But once he leaves the D.A.'s office for a hotshot spot in Tulsa's most prestigious law firm, Ben discovers that doing the right thing and representing his clients' interests can be mutually exclusive.

Thinking Theme: The Heart of the Matter

What Writers Need to Know: Essential Topics

Dazzling Description: Painting the Perfect Picture

The Fundamentals of Fiction (video series)

Poetry

The White Bird

The Ocean's Edge

For Young Readers

Shine

Princess Alice and the Dreadful Dragon

Equal Justice: The Courage of Ada Sipuel

The Black Sentry

Edited by William Bernhardt

Legal Briefs: Short Stories by Today's Best Thriller Writers

Natural Suspect: A Collaborative Novel of Suspense

CPSIA information can be obtained
at www.ICGtesting.com
Printed in the USA
BVHW030923230322
632180BV00010B/234/J

9 781954 871397